T0129712

LILY LIVES
ON
MOUNT RAINIER

LILY LIVES
ON
MOUNT RAINIER

ARLEY M. FOSBURGH

LILY LIVES ON MOUNT RAINIER

Photo' credit, Arley M. Fosburgh, Blacktail deer with avalanche lily, Summerland Trail, Sunrise, Mount Rainier National Park.

Photo' credit, Arley M. Fosburgh, Mount Rainier, Reflection Lakes, Paradise, Mount Rainier National Park.

iUniverse books may be ordered through booksellers or by contacting:

iUniverse
1663 Liberty Drive
Bloomington, IN 47403
www.iuniverse.com
1-800-Authors (1-800-288-4677)

ISBN: 978-1-5320-6787-7 (sc)
ISBN: 978-1-5320-6788-4 (e)

Library of Congress Control Number: 2019901536

Print information available on the last page.

iUniverse rev. date: 07/15/2019

Contents

Acknowledgements

I've been writing and painting since I was a toddler. I'm told that when I was four, when asked what I wanted to be when I grew up, I said, "I don't have to be anything. I'm already an artist." It's interesting what we know at young age, though I also allegedly announced as a young child that I was going to have eighteen children. That didn't happen. So, who knows...?

What did happen, is years of encouragement, beginning with my mother, who as a writer, critiqued every writing assignment I was ever given, starting in grade school, "Show them. Don't tell them." She held me to adult standards, never backing down and I hid my assignments from her, just to escape, but thank you, Mom. I now appreciate your teachings.

Thank you to my publishing team, especially Gil Maley, who is patient, kind, and understanding no matter how many emails I send to her box.

Thank you to Hugo Kugiya, for being polite and friendly and open to giving me permission to use a quote from a newspaper article he wrote in 2008. I also ended up learning of his book, 58 Degrees north, read it and enjoyed it.

Thank you to Ranger Kevin Bacher, a familiar and smiling face on Mount Rainier, for allowing me to use his quote. He has been on the mountain long enough to put big messages in simple terms that are meaningful and thought provoking. Kevin is a dynamic force on the mountain, a man who gets things done.

Thank you to Ranger Maureen McLean, my soul sister and mountain mentor, for writing a forward which captures the heart of those working on Mount Rainier, encapsulating it in a succinct, yet heartfelt gift of touching remembrances.

Thank you to my son, Moses, for believing in me, researching, making dinner when I had my head in my story, reading my pages as many times as I asked and telling me "To make something good, it takes time."

Thank you to Nick Dzubinski, my longtime friend, hiking buddy and fellow Libra, who has always been there for me, no matter the terrain. He is an amazing artist and my right hand PR guy, with an eye for the unique and penchant for creating the best in everything he does.

Thank you to my daughter, Chelsey, for listening and always coming up with an "I'm proud of you Mommy."

Thank you to Nana, Carole Denkinger, for creating a loving creative environment and sharing her world.

Thank you to someone I once knew many years ago, a person who believed in me and encouraged me unconditionally. I recall one day when he decided to do some writing of his own, staring at a blank sheet of paper and coming up with one lonely line, "Work is soap for the soul." I've carried that one sentence with me all my life. Lily Lives on Mount Rainier has been soap for my soul. Thank you to Richard Keesee.

Thank you to all those who I haven't mentioned here, but have spent time with me and left their imprint.

Dedication

For my mother, Arley K, who instilled in me a deep passion and respect for literature and the great outdoors.

Foreword

What does a mountain park offer to its visitors? As a National Park Ranger in Mount Rainier National Park, I have observed many things over the years. I've seen a church under the sky with the mountain as its cross. I've witnessed weddings full of joy, and the poignant scattering of ashes. There is the family drawn together by the sheer beauty, or the shared triumph of completing a strenuous hike or climb, or for the recent widow, a hidden spot to remember joint adventures and finding peace in the loneliness of grief. There's the visitor with a life changing illness who tells me, "Here I am not my disease, rather I am human and alive." I met a ninety year old woman recalling the journeys of her youth, but my favorite is the young man who found his voice and his passion among the flower fields of the mountain.

When I'm asked, "What does a mountain park offer its visitors?" I turn to John Muir who said, "Thousands of tired, nerve-shaken, over-civilized people are beginning to find out that going to the mountains is going home, that wildness is a necessity, and that mountain parks and reservations are useful not only as fountains of timber and irrigating rivers, but as fountains of life."

Maureen McLean, Mount Rainier National Park
Interpretive Ranger

"Hiking in the rain is just what we do here."

Kevin Bacher, Mount Rainier National
Park Ranger and spokesman.

Chapter 1

A small boy sat in a large green chair by his front window. Beyond the glass he could see the blue sky, tall grass and the many yellow dandelions. He counted to three, closed his eyes, took a deep breath and with all his might, he wished he was a dandelion. Slowly, he opened his eyes and looked down at his red tee shirt and blue jeans. He was still a little boy. "Who believes in wishes anyway?" His arms dropped to his sides like heavy tree trunks as though they too had lost all hope. He slumped in his chair mumbling to himself.

Grandmother came into the room and kept her eyes to her task, drying the inside of a large mug, pushing the balled towel inside the cup and moving as though achieving a dry surface was the only thing important. "Did you say something?"

He looked up at her. "I hate wishes. Wishes are stupid. They don't come true." He didn't need a reply. More than ever, he hoped to be ignored and left to languish, disappearing into the woodwork. He saw himself more as an object than a human being and preferred to be set on a shelf with other nondescript items cast aside as decoration, giving him the ultimate freedom, freedom of thought and purpose. He did not meet her eye to eye.

She smiled. "They do if you believe. Do you want to

tell me what you wished for? Maybe I can help." She stood before him the way she always did, her simple gabardine dress an unremarkable covering, her hair usual and in no particular style. She was common with mediocre thoughts, mainstream ideas and no authentic high note to her existence though it was her patience, her serene nature that reached out to others grabbing followers, friends and strangers. She smiled an unthreatening upturning of her lips and put her hand out to him.

He sat quietly. He had no intention of telling her his problems. If he shared at all, Lily would be the one he'd trust. She knew his heart. She knew his spirit. He put his finger in his mouth and bit down on the tip, watching the woman, the female vehicle for his basics, his food, shelter and books. It was she who held the key to the front door, the car and the tool shed. She knew the precise hour lights should be out and when children should be sleeping. He thought for a moment rotating the wheels in his head and analyzing her movements. She was a robot, her behavior predictable and expressions limited. Her head turns and hand placements were not clever, or unique although repetition of body language was a comfort, both relaxing and stalling. He didn't trust her with his wishes, even as she took up a great deal of space before him making her out to be something of an expert on an environment perplexing to him and the cause of his shyness and inability to rush forth with a reply. When he'd reconstructed himself and his lips moved in the manner of spewing words, those words fell from his lips against his better judgement. "I wished I was a dandelion." He immediately regretted his outburst with disappointment showing up on his forehead as a sea of lines. He pouted, stomping his foot.

"A dandelion?"

"... So I can go outside. I hate allergies." He held his frown as a tribute to his small world and the minimal degree of power a child can attain and talked to himself, recanting what he felt deep in his core rather than giving her information.

She nodded, "Mm-hmm, you can go outside when there's not so much pollen. You don't want to go back to the hospital." She'd sided with his parents, no matter her opinion. The surest way to not see her grandson would be to follow her own lead, ignoring his mother and father. She wanted to push him out the door, tell him to have fun, be a boy. If left to her own accord, he'd be outside every day building tree bough forts, collecting rocks, studying insects, discovering animal tracks and making mud pies.

"At least there're kids to play with at the hospital." ... Not that he would play with them. Children were as alien to him as any other human specimen. He liked to observe them, mimic and choose to ignore. He kept his eyes on the important things like movement, patterns, lights and rhythm. Repetition seduced and implored him to use his instinct, his mind, his physical being to decode the world and use it to his intellectual advantage. His world was without labels and fences. He liked to watch cars move down narrow streets in straight lines and he enjoyed the green, red and yellow traffic lights and the way they ruled the streets flashing their bright colors and stopping cars and pedestrians. He liked uniforms, laws, changing of the hours and minute hands slowly circling the clock. He wanted conformity and regulations.

She took his hand. "Come on out to the kitchen. You can help me with dinner. We'll play a game. You tell me what you want more than anything in the world and I'll tell you what I want." She had no intention of telling him what she wanted... What she wanted didn't exist anymore at least not in the tangible sense and not the way she wanted it. Helping others find the path to their dreams helped her soothe the longing for what was unattainable in her own life. There, she could fade into the ether and dance to someone else's music.

He trudged along behind her. "What good will that do?" He monitored her steps, the big clunky shoes moving one then the other across the floor, up with one heel, followed by the other, up and down, up and down. He was caught there until she stopped and turned slowly clasping her hands near her chest and dropping her chin. "We can work together to make our dreams come true. ... A dream team."

In the tiny kitchen, the smell of hot tomato soup floated through the air. She set a box of saltines on the counter, taking a baking sheet from the cupboard and setting it near the box. "Open the box and put the crackers on the baking sheet. Put a slice of cheese on each cracker. There's sliced cheese in the fridge." She thought of Michael, the way he carefully spread peanut butter over bubbly soda crackers shoving them into his mouth and spitting out pieces as he chatted.

Sandy opened the box, pulled out a package of crackers and carefully removed the wrapping. One at a time, he set them on the sheet. "Now can we talk about what we want?" With great care, he placed the crackers up one side of the sheet and down the other making a design along the way. He opened the refrigerator, moved cartons of unfertilized eggs, a tub of organic strawberry yogurt and a bag of cucumbers before spotting the sliced cheddar cheese. He set the cheese on the counter while he extended his right leg as far as he was able and tried to push the refrigerator door closed, giving up, lowering his head and walking over and pushing it with his hand. Someday he would grow as tall as the trees. Someday he would be a tree.

She tied her apron around herself. "You go first."

He continued with the crackers. He did not look up from his work. "I want to live in a world with flowers growing up to the sky." He wanted a world with colors as bright as the sun, as beautiful as the moon and as full of movement as the rain. He wanted a world that sounded like the wind in the trees, thunder at night and cracks of lightening having the strength of a hurricane. He wanted life to be as fragile as a piece of glass, as brittle as an icicle and as resilient as a juniper plant. He wanted destruction and renewal in a matter of seconds.

She stirred the hot soup. Steam was rising from the pot as she turned toward Sandy. "I like flowers too."

"Then why don't you have any...?" He managed to avoid her eyes, human eyes, always a burden, spying, intruding, showing an inside view of everything he didn't want to see.

The spoon circled the pot more slowly as if her thinking process had an effect on the speed. She spoke with a noticeable drop in mood, cumbersome as though a weight had them anchored. "I guess I've given up on growing things. I suppose I lost interest after your grandfather passed away." She allowed her words to hang in the air.

Silence although golden, was at best a third person in the room. She went about stirring the soup while he meticulously positioned cheese slices atop crackers. If neither of them spoke again, it would've been okay, however, he was filled to the gills with dreams and flowers swirling in his head. He kept his eyes on the cheese and crackers while his mind wandered, "I want my very own house. My yard will be big." He stretched his hands out as far as he could, "I will grow every flower in the world and I will keep them safe." He wasn't interested in whether, or not she was listening. It was the giving of his words that made things click into place. In those few sentences a weight was lifted. He could breathe easier thinking his dreams would come true.

She set the table and cautiously poured hot soup into two ceramic bowls, and moved the small vase of artificial flowers onto the center of the table, then thinking of Sandy, back to the counter. "Do you have a favorite flower?"

He lowered his eyes and his chin fell toward his chest. He felt a lump in his throat. "I like Ava Lily." He could scarcely say her name without choking. He liked the manner in which her name ricocheted off the surfaces in his mind. He heard her name in his head, a soothing flow washing over him, blunting sounds of the outside world and highlighting his imaginary realm. It felt cold and superficial to sell her out in a voice that others could hear.

Grandmother stood tall, her thick frame being a familiar stronghold in his life. She made family, family. She pulled back her bulky shoulders and folded her arms as though she'd heard it all before. "Ava Lily, what kind of a flower is that?" She wrinkled her nose and pinched her lips.

He looked away, "She's just a flower." He focused on his shoes. "She's beautiful."

"A girl flower?"

"She's my friend."

"Well, she sounds lovely." She looked at him as though he was pinned for dissection in a Petri dish. Except for what could be read from her face, she kept her thoughts to herself, moving about the kitchen, and putting the finishing touches on the baked cheese crackers and soup.

He looked at her with squinting eyes. He didn't mind if she was present. To him, she was a solid piece, an object meant to make his life real in a manner he couldn't reach by himself. He was caught up in his own meanderings, unconsciously concealing them with superficial attention to his chores. He started to speak, but stopped. His desire to keep his secret to himself brought him quickly to his senses, but only pushed him again toward sharing and another delay. He remained quiet, uncomfortably aware that opening his mouth would allow his words to tumble forth and betray him. He pursed his lips and did not meet her eyes. He was a statue, his body tense, his muscles contracted.

She grabbed a dish cloth, soaked it under the faucet, bunched it in her hand and wiped the counter. She caught sight of Sandy and wrinkled her brow. She didn't want to engage him. Kitchen time was spent thinking of Michael and minutes were slipping away with talk of flowers. She thought of her old flower garden, gone after Michael's passing, but the memories brought fresh flower scents. She closed her eyes and inhaled the perfume of roses, jasmine, lily of the valley and carnations.

He was ready to burst. "She wears a white dress with long parts and some yellow. She looks like a star." He choked on his own breathe and rejected his exposure at the same time finding it good to release the restraints. He paused. "Her voice is soft." His own voice was so inherently soft in the telling, Grandmother could easily imagine the voice of the flower.

"She talks?"

"To me."

"No one else?"

"Just me. Lily trusts me."

"Ava Lily, or Lily?"

"Ava Lily. I call her Lily."

"Why?" She stared at Sandy. She did not blink.

"She likes it."

She held his eyes as long as he would allow, blinked, lifted her head and looked away as though answers were stored across the room. Returning to routine was best and something she did well. He was the same, always in need of routine. She set a plate of manicured celery stalks and carrot sticks on the table. "Let's sit for dinner. We'll give thanks for nature's gifts." She eyed him with a curious turn of her head. "I imagine you have a lot to be thankful for. Lily sounds like a miracle." She patted his shoulder. He rubbed it off with a palpable annoyance. She cringed, but moved on, "You say grace tonight."

He bowed his head out of comfort, more so than respect. A routine worked for him and a daily prayer said at the same time each day was a perfect fit. Catholic prayers were closure. They were consistent, easy to recite and made life simple giving the day to day less mystery.

The following morning, rays of sunshine found the modest purple house with the unkept yard and favored patch of yellow dandelions. The little boy was again sitting by the front window with his small hands tightly folded in prayer and pressed firmly against his chin. His eyes were closed and his brow was furrowed. His shoulders were tight and his gut wrenched with desire. He sat straight in his chair and slowly opened his eyes. There came a loud sigh and his lips turned down. He was still a little boy.

Grandmother hastened to the kitchen. Her melodious hum wrestling Sandy to his feet and encouraging his walk into her world, a sugary hideout with the smell of maple syrup thick in the air. It weakened his knees and his stomach gurgled. Vanilla beans plumped into a pan of hot water spread the heavenly scent of vanilla into his nose and every pore in his body. His insides ached, but his mind needed space within walls that wrapped and held him. He put his hand over his eyes, blocking the bright kitchen light and withstanding Grandmother's jubilant movement long enough to realize his bedroom was his comfort. Still, his empty stomach yearned for breakfast, anything to fill the hollow cavity. He stood in the doorway preparing his sea legs before gaining enough emotional strength to enter her domain and being innocent as he was, it was no great feat for him to believe he could exist without being seen, but sounds of digestion brought unwanted attention, prompting him to hurry about then turn back and attempt an exit before he was spotted making his break. She called to him with an inviting nod, requesting he join her. It was his choice and he hesitated, even as buttermilk pancakes, sticky and sopping with syrup nudged him in her direction. After minutes inhaling the maple scent, he broke down, washed his hands and rushed to the table, bowing his head and reciting words he knew, "Bless us dear Lord for these thy gifts..." He finished the prayer with a sign of the cross and sunk his fork into the fluffy cakes.

Grandmother brought fresh hot cakes and flopped them onto the platter. "Just can't help cooking for an army." She patted her abdomen. "Cooking them and eating them, can't stop either one and it shows. I'll be a beach ball before the year's out." She slipped into her seat across from him. "My syrup took first place at the county fair three years in a row." She poured squeezed orange juice into his glass. "It would've been four, I know it would've, but I didn't enter. I thought

I'd give someone else a chance." She looked down thinking she was owed an accolade though she'd received only a tired look from her grandson, and with that she immediately moved on tucking a rolled bite of pancake around her fork, mopping globs of syrup from her plate, quietly moaning with satisfaction and licking her fingers. "I'm going into town today."

He dropped his fork on his plate and stretched his neck, raising his chin and widening his eyes. "I want to go."

"Not this time. Cara will be here to watch you. My appointment won't be fun."

"I can sit still. Take me with you."

She carried her plate to the sink running a slow stream of water across its surface. "There'll be other trips." Her free hand rubbed away food particles, gently as if massaging out kinks and unconsciously smoothing away conversations she didn't want to have. "I can stop by the library and get a book for you." She placed the plate at the top of a stack of dirty dishes then leaned against the counter folding her arms for protection.

'I don't want a book." He mimicked her, folding his arms and leaning back in his chair.

She watched him mirror her and let her arms hang, tapping her fingertips against her thighs. "What do you want?"

He lifted himself from his chair and walked with a somber edge as though a tedious tragic walk to the guillotine. His head and shoulders hung in defeat, yet he dragged onward unaware he had a choice, promptly taking her hand and leading her to his room, flipping on the light switch and pulling open the drapes. He jumped up on his bed and stood tall, feet arched like a ballerina. On top of his makeshift mountain, he scouted like an eagle, eyes fixed on a point beyond the window. "I want to go up there."

She walked to the window looking back at him over her shoulder, a sophomoric attempt to portray power and stability. She didn't need to look at him, but she wanted him to see her looking at him, giving him a clear understanding she was ruler of the roost. Continuing her effort, she made slow steps as though taking a stroll on a pleasant Sunday morning after church where she had all the time in the world to take a look at the one thing she didn't want to see. Her fingers were crossed behind her back, backing up the lie she was about to tell herself, that she wouldn't think of Michael, and in a rush, came well run memories of Michael, her head playing tricks again. She fought back, filling her mind with ironing, dusting and scrubbing, finding solace in chores with an obvious edge of completion. Things which revolved around Sandy never seemed to end. They carried on day to day in one form or another morphing and splitting. At least she could control domestic duties and regulate when memories of Michael attacked without warning, and they did... They hunted and jumped her at all times of the day and night. It was at those times she dragged out her vacuum and numbed her mind. Of course, darkness came of its own accord, creeping from a dark crevice inside her head. She imagined bright stars shining from her soul and brought herself close to the window, fogging the pane with her breath and wiping it off with her sleeve. She forced her eyes to follow the direction of Sandy's gaze. She knew what was out there. She knew that frozen mound of rock. Her heart raced and her eye lids closed. She worked the lump in her throat, prayed her pain would cease and moved back away from the window within his reach. He poked at her as if exploring an insect. She slowly opened her eyes, recognizing the mountain in the distance. "That old snow covered thing? You'll catch your death of cold."

His brows pulled together in a scornful bunch. "It's a mountain. Can you see that?" His feet shot forward and with a plop he dropped to his back lying flat out on his bed in a pile of bitter anguish.

She watched him. An awkward, nervous smile highlighted her face. "It's thirty miles away. There's nothing up there for you." She shook her head, more an adamant, under no circumstances, aimed at herself than a negative response to her grandson. She pulled the cord and the curtain closed on the mountain like a final act.

He looked at the ceiling, eyes pasted to a white shapeless boundary between home and sky. Her voice was the sound of his dreams disappearing into an empty chasm and he declared her ignorance, peering at her as she walked from the room. Stacks of books with bookmarks sticking out the ends showed her the room was not hers. In a last minute gesture, she pointed toward the books. "Read one of these. Stay off dangerous mountains." She reached the door and glanced at him. He was where she'd left him, stretched out on his back, feet wiggling. He wore a frown and as much as she meant to walk out and slam the door on the mountain, she couldn't bring herself to leave the room and so, gave herself a minute allowing the air to clear. He lifted his head holding strong to his grumblings, took a guarded look in her direction and dropped his head back down. "I looked at the stars and considered how awful it would be for a man to turn his face up to them as he froze to death and see no help, or pity in all the glittering multitude. Charles Dickens said that." He strained his eyes to be certain they poured out his disappointment. "Great Expectations. Just like Pip, I have great expectations." His words, though not really his, hit her like the hard head of a shark, tearing into her with knife sharp teeth and spitting her out bloody in dark, salty water, yet she remained calm floating above her own gruesome memories of what it must've been like for Michael, alone in the frozen abyss.

Her eyes traveled through Sandy, allowing her to rediscover her young self, a sixteen year old girl, married, yet alone. The words he uttered triggered a helpless longing inside her, a desperate ache which she believed gave her no choice, but to hide her feelings. He couldn't possibly understand what discouragement he was sending her. She fumbled, brushing aside digestive burning and racing to retrieve her heart from her throat. She was empty, taken down by words digging deep into her soul. A humble launch of tears tickled the corners of her eyes. She cleared her throat and cleared it again. It was juvenile to think she could forget the past. "I don't think climbing mountains is the best way to spend your time." She wiped at her eyes.

He sat up on his bed and saw the back of her head as she walked from his room. He looked at the dress, the long zipper holding fabric together and seam running straight down from collar to hem, certain to pop with too many more desserts. "Lily lives on a mountain." There, he'd said it. She turned and stopped in the doorway. She folded her arms and stared at him. He felt her eyes on his face like a scratchy sweater and looked down at the floor.

"She does what?"

"She told me."

She walked to the window and opened the curtain. "That mountain?" The room was thick with thorny energy, the collision of two worlds creating a distance between she and Sandy, the same distance that sneaked in between she and Michael. The mountain would not strike again. It would not take another quiet soul into its icy grip. The thought of it slowed her, made her think. She pushed her hands into her pockets. "I will ponder this." She heard herself, "ponder this", she sounded like Michael.

He licked his lower lip, swallowed and took a breath. "Truth is often perverted by education." He lowered his eyes. "Ann Radcliffe wrote that."

She pushed back her hair and rubbed her hand across her forehead. The tears returned. She sniffled and wiped at her nose while her chest raised and lowered rapidly. She bit her lips, sucked them in and looked directly at him. "If you can tell me the name of the mountain, I'll see that you get there."

His eyes opened with a generous expansion. He blinked repeatedly. "John Muir and Edmund Hillary like mountains." The room fell silent. It was an inconvenient moment and she won. He had no chance of learning the name of the mountain. She inched closer to the window, gently pushing the curtains aside and peering out through the opening. He didn't dare move. He closed his eyes and placed his hands over his face, aware that in a flash, all of it could be undone. If he were to allow her eyes to gaze into his, to stick those intrusive eye ball life stealers on his body, he'd forever be her prisoner. Eyes, piercing into him were reapers of strength and the foretellers of his existence. He couldn't look until he had to... There was no written agreement, no handshake. He kept his eyes hidden and raised his head just enough so she would know he wanted to communicate. "If you can tell me the name of three flowers on the mountain, I'll see that you get to come with me."

Her laughter filled the space, padding cracks of disinterest with spontaneous emotion and of herself, an unbridled body shake which warmed and dampened the fabric in her arm pits. Her eyes were glossy with tears. "When did you learn about Edmund Hillary and John Muir?" She felt under her arms.

"I read dusty old books in your room." He waited for her reply.

She didn't answer right away. She thought of her books, Michael's books, setting on her shelf gathering dust, untouched, unloved. If she found Sandy's actions offensive, she didn't let on... Dusty books, old books, he had no idea of the importance, the history... Mentally, she set the books on the pile of memories haunting her. She made no attempt to iron out misconceptions, or denials. The idea of her grandson pulling dusty books from the past and bringing them to life brought pleasure and fear. In a way, he'd met his grandfather. He'd walked the path of a man he'd never known and would never meet face to face, yet somewhere in his genes the light from his genetic inheritance found a window of opportunity.

He starred at her. "I bet you don't know any flowers up there." He squinted, tightening the muscles around his eyes and pressuring himself into a headache.

She smiled. "I bet you don't know the name of the mountain."

There's a degree of grace in the ability to find comfort in spending time alone with one's self and to feel at ease in one's own essence, breathing life into only those thoughts that define you. It's a freedom not found by those dependent upon an outsider's adoration. Everyone comes to the entrance of self acceptance, but few walk through the door. The ones who do, discover an escape like no other.

With a mere four years tethered to the planet, Sandy had conquered the need to attach to people. Often he made statements about wanting children his age for playmates, but when the situation was offered, he isolated himself, preferring his own company. While other children gathered in groups, listening to music, watching movies and playing video games, he found pleasure spending time alone reading books, living in his imagination and role playing thoughts in his head. It was not out of the ordinary to hear him ask to go into town with her, however it was also not out of the ordinary for him to be pleased to have the house to himself. If the two selections were laid out before him, he would choose to be alone. Unfortunately for Sandy, he wasn't offered the opportunity to stay home alone. Today, Grandmother was going into town. He was neither invited, nor given the choice of deciding whether, or not he wanted to go... Cara, his sitter, a teen he identified as a spy, was his warden.

From the window, he watched Grandmother walk down the front sidewalk, open her car door and step inside. He heard the engine start, rev and carry on its idle hum. He watched as the car backed from the driveway, inching onto the gravel road. He saw the red tail lights disappear into the distance. He turned, walked across the front room and all was forgotten. He saved his cheeky frown for Cara. "I forgot how her face looks."

"You've already forgotten your grandma?"

"She's gone."

Cara stood at the kitchen door with hands on her hips

and head cocked to the side. She watched Sandy at the window and waited for him to come to life. He ignored her. He didn't recognize her the way he did his grandma and other people in his life. He'd memorized the constants, but Cara was not one of those. Cara didn't warrant a beep on his radar. Hers wasn't a face he would recall, being he rarely looked at her. He recognized her by her hand placement on her hips and only looked at her with curiosity and concern. He hadn't known her long enough to get down her mode of operation and that frightened him. Unpredictability in others as well as life was forever his nemesis. She took her hands from her hips and he ran to put them back into place. She eyed him disdainfully. He pasted on a face of gloom, standing guard to see to it the hands stayed put. He didn't want her to fall apart.

If he had drawn her picture, there'd be hands on hips and a face without features. He found comfort in idiosyncrasies, people proceeding in life doing the same things in the same manner. He based his memory of people on behavioral characteristics rather than facial features, hair color and the hue of their eyes. Physical attributes rarely caught his eye, or held his attention long enough to create a feeling of familiarity. Most people looked alike apart from their activities and routines and once labeled, he wouldn't, or couldn't accept them in any other fashion.

Cara tugged at a lock of her strawberry blonde hair, wrapping it behind her ear. She followed Sandy. "Do you want to do a puzzle? Remember we put that lion puzzle together?" She looked around as she chatted, "I don't remember your house being this tiny." She picked up a painted porcelain doll from a shelf, sized it up and carefully set it back in place.

"Stop that." Sandy stood outside his bedroom door. He thought of clever ways to keep her out of his room. His brows were knit closely, "Can you stop touching everything?" He hoped she wouldn't come in his direction, yet he stepped aside when she walked into his room. He slowly followed her and arranged himself as a barrier between she and his toys, books, and other personal trinkets.

She strolled, putting her hands on his books and scanning them, front and back. "You have more books than a library. Do you read all these?" She lifted a book from the top of a stack.

His eyes narrowed and his heart raced. He pulled the book from her hand and set it back into place., watching her more closely. "Don't touch anything. Just look and that's it."

She giggled. He frowned. She shook her head, "Look at all these... How many books do you have? These stacks are crazy tall. They're as tall as I am. Do you read them? Look at them! There're not even kids books." She moved in on him. He warned her, "Five hundred and eighty three. You stay back, or I'll put the police on you." He used every muscle in his face to create a menacing look, but remained innocuous giving Cara welcome ammunition.

She slapped her thigh and laughed, "Oh my God, I'm not even kidding, you're science lab nerdy."

He looked at her without registering her comment. "Don't touch my books."

"I know, I'm not touching, just looking... You have Shakespeare and Tolstoy." She read her way down one stack and up another... "You have Charles Dickens, Hemingway, H. G. Wells... Oh, I can't believe you have The Count of Monte Cristo and The Scarlet Letter." She turned to him, "The Scarlet Letter? You're too young to read that. You read

Madame Bovary? Are you kidding me? ... The Wind in the Willows, The Great Gatsby, Journey to the End of the Night? Good Lord, child! You're four years old. Didn't anybody ever tell you that?"

He folded his arms and squinted, eyes brows worked into a snarl. Cara laughed, grabbed a book, rapidly opened it and skipped through the pages, her fingers darting over fine white paper. "Let's play a game. I'll read a few lines, you know, like a quote and you tell me the name of the book."

He reached, trying to take it, but she held it above her head, "Nope, nope, nope, if you guess it right, you can have it." She pointed toward his bed, "Sit there and don't look. Okay, here you go... "I would always rather be happy than dignified." She held the book behind her back.

He scowled, pulling his arms tightly around himself. "Jane Eyre. Charlotte Bronte wrote that." He fell back into his struggle. "Now give it to me." He jumped to get the book though Cara dropped it in his hands without a struggle.

"I said I'd give it to you if you guessed it. Let's do more." She was rummaging... "This one..." She threw her head back, dramatically placing the back of her hand on her forehead as if to say, I feel faint, but she didn't, she merely spouted another line. "I can't part with it, I can't let it go... It's come to me - I've a right to keep it..." Cara smiled with the smugness of a victor. She had him where she wanted him, playing along in a foolish game, holding the book in her outstretched hand. "You can't guess this one."

"Silas Marner." His eyes were bothered slits. She enjoyed her ability to get him going, manipulating him into making his brainy statements and amusing her. He was a small dog, all yelp and no essence. He held out his hand in an emotional squeeze and when it went nowhere, he raised his voice,

"Now give it to me." He climbed up on his bed, reaching...
"Give it."

"Let me do one more, one more and I'll stop, promise."
She grabbed another book and gulped air. "There are books
of which the backs and covers are by far the best parts."

He pinched his lips and mumbled, "Oliver Twist. Charles
Dickens wrote that." He came up to her grounded and
powerful, a steam roller stopping before making contact. He
made his hands into loose fists, pressing them against either
side of her abdomen and twisting as though turning knobs
on a device. She eyed with curiosity and laughter. "What're
you doing?"

"I'm turning down your volume." Slowly, he backed
away, keeping watch from inside his head, his guardhouse,
a safer distance from the rattling.

Her levity stayed on as she handed him the book,
shooting him a skeptical glance. "Thanks, that was fun.
You're a weird kid though, you really are..." She gave him
the side eye and patted his head which he speedily wiped
away. He put his book back on the tallest stack and watched
as she walked to his window, opened the curtain and looked
out at the day, hands to her hips. "You have a nice view. I like
pine trees." He was silent with a unspoken pledge to remain
unimpressed by anything she could conjure. She looked over
her shoulder at him. "You have a great patch of forest. I bet
you see deer. Do you ever see bears?"

He shook his head, careful not to encourage her. There
was no telling where she would put her greasy girl hands.
She turned back to the window. "I love Mount Rainier."
With a graceful movement, she arched her back and threw
back her head, moving her legs like a trained dancer, gently
turning and spinning.

She bored him. A real ballerina would wear a tutu and toe shoes. She didn't meet his stereo type dancer profile, which meant she fell short. Straying from the accepted standard wasn't acceptable although she gained the advantage, pouring out the name of the mountain. "Mount Rainier? The mountain out my window?" His eyes widened.

She bounced herself down on his bed bedside him. "Are you a mountain kid, or just a weird kid? Hmmm, which is it?"

Stacks of books stood tall in the corners of his room and in every open space, books stacked like pancakes. Colorful spines laying on their sides shouting out titles and authors in large bold letters. Hard covers and paperbacks, all of them the classics, the greatest of all time, waiting for him to own up to it, to tell her he was a weird kid. He merely sat there thinking about it, biting at his lower lip and rubbing the back of his hand under his nose. "I'm a boy who has preferences."

She kicked her legs in the air falling back onto the bed. "That's it? I waited for that?" She gazed at the ceiling then closed her eyes. "I think I could just go to sleep here. This is my bed now." She giggled. "I'm a boy who has preferences. That's rich."

He yanked at her arms until she screamed an artificial release, not shaking, or deceiving him. Within time, she relented, walking to the front room and plunking herself there. "Go get the lion puzzle. "Come on, weird kid, let's do something. What are your preferences?"

He stared her down, wrapped himself in a frown running deeper than the one on his face. "Babysitting you is monotonous." He growled, bidding her to keep her distance.

She laughed under her breath, pretending she couldn't contain herself, but letting it out in a obnoxious rumble.

"Monotonous? Why do you even know that word? That's a word for stuffy old men." She patted her thigh and spit out a laughter that burned into his soul. "You crack me up. Is that one of your preferences?"

He dawdled, mumbled and kept his scowl solid on his face, but he did bring the puzzle. At least she was out of his room. The two of them spent hours indoors connecting pieces and listening to the wind outside the house spinning into a frenzy. Cara fit puzzle pieces into place and Sandy checked on the maple. The tree danced, leaves and shadows flittering across the front of the house. He held his breathe as the tree caught wind between its boughs bringing it to its knees. He stood at attention with his heart in his throat, his mind mapping out inevitable destruction. He knew the crack of raw timber and the thunder of twisted wood pounding upon the earth. He expected damage and his thoughts intrigued and ignited his imagination, but he watched in disappointment as the tree corrected its posture and regained its elegance. Instead of destruction, he watched Grandmother's car pull up in front of the house. The mountain whispered in one ear, and Cara nagged him in the other... "Sit down weird kid."

He glared at her, making his face into something producing her laughter and as she shook with the chortling he found invasive, he struggled to make himself look mean. "I will grow up to be a tree and you will climb me and fall to the ground and have blood."

She rolled on the floor clutching her stomach the way she always did, laughing uncontrollably. "Hey, do you have some kind of thing for that mountain? You were looking at it kind of weird."

"It's not an old snow covered thing."

She wrinkled her nose and crinkled her forehead. "What?"

Mount Rainier was always on his mind. He burst out the front door, bare legs and knobby knees moving nearly as fast his thoughts. He skipped across shadows of leaves taking over the porch floor, running down steps and hopping over cracks until he reached the end of the sidewalk where he stood in the center of the walkway, his hair blown straight up by a billowy gust. The wind whistled and clouds moved quickly in the sky. He was a roadblock in the middle of the cement walkway, his smile frozen on his face, holding his muscles so tight, they ached.

Grandmother walked from her car, arms filled with grocery bags and white paper sacks with ropey handles hung over her wrists like bangles. She managed the sacks and struggled to hold down the skirt of her dress from a rogue burst of air. She saw him, did a double take and looked closely. The breeze brought dust into her eyes. "Sandy?"

He pushed his hands into his pockets. "Lily lives on Mount Rainier." His eyes were lit like a street light.

She let the bag handles slip from her hands, rubbed her eyes, leaned forward, and unsuccessfully held down her skirt with her forearms, re-thought her defense, easily gave up and pulled the fullness of her skirt in around herself like a robe. "She does what?"

"Yes."

"You learned the name of the mountain?"

A warm rush of blood reddened his cheeks painting him the color of embarrassment. He pushed out words with a lilt and a squeak, "Now you have to get me there. Name three flowers." A flurry of wind brought up the back of his shirt and made her remember his mask.

She handed him a shopping bag. "Get on with you. I have a surprise." She loved the glint in his eyes reflecting back to her, her good mothering and patience. "Where's your mask?"

He took the bag from her hand, peeked inside and skipped toward the house, checking now and then to be certain she was following... She shuffled along holding the remaining bags and brushed at hair globs blown into her face. Her lavender skirt bopped up and down with the gusts. She looked up at the maple and watched it ride its own breezy flow. "I hope the tree makes it." Slowly, she shook her head, predicting it wouldn't... She stepped onto the porch and turned to give the tree another look, walking carefully over the threshold, wobbling and catching her balance. Cara was stoking the fire. Grandmother reached into her purse and placed several bills into Cara's hand. "Thank you, sweetheart. I won't need you for a couple weeks." She patted Cara's shoulder and threw in a warm hug. "You're a pro with the fire. It's toasty. The devil is in the detail in that mess of wind outside. You best be cautious driving home." She glanced around the room wondering where Sandy had gone so quickly. "Was he a good boy?"

Small talk came easily and left in the same fashion. Cara answered questions, gave specifics and was on her way. At the last minute she leaned back through the doorway, her thick orange hair falling over her shoulders. "Bye Sandy, I hope you had fun." She bugged out her eyes, looked cross-eyed and pulled a rubbery face He was in there somewhere. She knew he could hear her and hoped he could see her though he didn't appear. She fixed her face and smiled at Grandmother. "See yah next time."

Grandmother waved and spoke under her breath. "I'm too old for this lunacy. Oh, to be young again..." She wished she was young again, but just for a day. She was too tired to be young.

From the safety of his room, Sandy watched Cara close the door, waited a moment to be sure she was gone and high tailed it to the window, making sure it was a fact. He watched her drive away, rubbed his hands together and readied himself for something new. "She can never come back in this house." He started for his room, looked back at the window and quivered, disturbed by thoughts of her return. Stopping at his door, he tested the waters by briefly gawking before making an entrance. He examined toys, book stacks and notebooks on his desk. Carefully he opened one notebook and looked over his writings. If she'd read his personal writing he wouldn't be able to go on, but the pages appeared pristine and untouched by her unwashed hands. He breathed a sigh of relief and unclenched his fists. She hadn't left her mark. He jumped onto his bed and looked out at the mountain. He could hear the rapid beat of his heart and sense the tingle of excitement by the goosebumps on his arms. His world was changing, becoming a reflection of his dreams. He didn't need to be a dandelion. He was a boy. His life was perfect.

From the next room, Grandmother called to him. "Don't dawdle." The tension in her voice rang through his head as impatience and jolted him into the right direction while the idea of her surprise tangled with thoughts of Cara. He hurried to the front room, plopped himself on the over-stuffed couch, wiggled into a comfortable spot and waited for her. His head over flowed with visions of finger smudged books though instead of bolting to his room he composed himself, gathering inner strength and maturity, which he reinforced with straight and strict posture. He extended his legs and sat in an adult fashion. He was going to the mountain. He had to be an adult and the smile set deeply into his face told his story although tightness around his eyes uncovered his reluctance to sit with her in the sparsely decorated living area. He was besieged with worry that she couldn't learn the names of three mountain flowers and if she couldn't, she couldn't travel with him, meaning his dreams would plummet and fade away rendering her useless to his needs. In his eyes, she cooked, cleaned, bought books and turned off the lights in the evening, but she had a new job added to her duties, the act of taking him to Mount Rainier. She'd upped her value.

Contemplating his needs, he thought he'd carry more value if he wasn't a child. From what he'd seen, adults were more desirable. They were allowed advantages and rewards children couldn't attain. With those thoughts in mind, he was an adult and wanted to prove it by touching his feet to the floor from where he sat, however, his feet didn't reach the floor. He gave it a second run, but he was short. He stretched himself, sliding down on his seat though the floor would not rise to meet him. He realized being a adult was uncomfortable and as annoying as the tag on his underwear. He worked himself into a sitting position, loosened his rigid pose, rounded his shoulders and slouched, putting on a child's face and still, he thought of Cara. If she touched his books, or played with his toys, he'd get soap, rubber gloves, bleach and tooth paste. He watched Grandmother come into the room. Her face had relaxed into a permanent emptiness, the type of expression a person dons when the last of what they've given is the whole of what they had... He scrunched his face into a grimace, eyeing her with a daunting glare. "Tooth paste cleans off finger prints."

"What?" She walked to where he sat. "Scoot a little. Let an old woman sit."

He reached his hands behind her, just before she sat, taking her dimensions with an invisible measuring stick. She felt him back there, brushed her hands down the back of her dress and looked at him with a face full of questions.

He managed a controlling frown. "I'm seeing how much room you need for your butt." He inched his way toward the other end of the couch.

"Thank you and just how much room does my butt need?" She took her place, sinking into the cushion and feeling self conscious about the space she required.

"There isn't a day gone by that I'm not amused at your thoughts about life." She gave him the salty side eye and placed her hands in her lap, lines and pallor of her skin noticeable in the light from the window. "Are you ready for your surprise?"

He moved closer, gently running his fingers over her hands and passing carefully across elevated blue veins and arthritic bone spurs. "You have old hands. Too bad you can't get new ones, or maybe a hook."

She shook her head, sucking in her lips and laughing quietly, not certain it was funny. It didn't feel funny. It caused a break in her speech pattern and cut across her heart. Perhaps she was old and sensitive to criticism, but then again, not enough to stall her. It was the petty shudder of annoyance running through her body that caught her off guard yet she resolved it with a crisp sense of ambivalence swinging her focus back to her grandson. He was a child. "Okay, let's move on..." She leaned forward taking a large green book from her bag, self conscious of her ghastly hands and hiding them the best she could, pushing through her mind the strange idea of a hook being an ideal choice for her disfigurement, well aware it shouldn't even have been on the table. He moved closer yet. She set the book on her lap and slowly opened the cover.

He held his breath, exhaled, worked up a large amount of saliva and repeatedly swallowed before sharing his words. "Don't dawdle."

She recognized herself, shifted in her seat and received the nasty taste in her mouth as punishment. Deliberate malcontent rested in her eyes. "I don't know the names of three flowers on the mountain."

He knew it. There it was, defeat. He put his head in his hands while his world came crashing down. He barely lifted his head to speak. "Men's courses will foreshadow certain ends to which if persevered in they must lead, but if the courses be departed from, the ends will change." She stared at him. He let his head drop back into his hands, "Scrooge said that. Charles Dickens wrote it. He was right."

"And you understand that?" She turned toward him, "You memorized it?" He didn't answer. She moved around it, washing it away as though nothing was said and raised her head with a head full of confidence. "But I know the name of the prettiest flower on the mountain." She patted down her hair and raised her eyebrows, gauging his reaction. There wasn't much to see. She continued, "I'm no Charles Dickens, but I know a pretty flower when I see it."

He held his breath, fighting to contain his excitement. "Happiness is the meaning and purpose of life, the whole aim and end of human existence." He glanced at her, "Aristotle said that."

"You know who Aristotle is?"

"He's dead, but I know who he was. He was a nearly

great scientist and a pretty good philosopher which means he knows more than nothing about life. He was basically a wise man."

She folded her arms and leaned back into the couch. She didn't look at him, only smiled to herself. "She wears a white dress with long parts and some yellow." She could see the sparkle in his eyes. She adjusted her sweater and turned down the collar of her dress, "She looks like a star and when the wind blows, she floats like an angel." She turned her head to the side and batted her eyes. "Sandy Anderton said that."

He jumped up and stood before her. "Tell me." He was a lump of clay smooshed together into a face with brightness and high energy encircling him, giving him a magnetic forcefield that called and embraced her.

She thumbed through the pages... "Is this Lily?"

"That's her."

She pulled Sandy onto her lap. "See..." She pointed to the heading. It says avalanche lily. It's right here."

He looked closely. "I see it."

"How can you see it? You're looking at the wrong page. It's over here." She reached for his chin and manually turned his head, but he looked at the items in the shopping bag. "Here, here, Look where my finger is... See, it says avalanche lily." She took his finger and held it on the page near the picture.

He stared and blinked repeatedly. "She didn't tell me she's famous."

Grandmother got up and ran her hands down the front of her cotton dress. "Girls don't tell boys everything." She offered a flirty smile, remembering those innocent years. "We like to keep a bit of a mystery."

Chapter 2

There wasn't much to distinguish one day from the next, one hour to another, or one minute from those that followed... At any given time, Sandy could be found reading about flowers, thinking of flowers, or talking to a flower. When spare time presented itself, he'd hop onto his bed positioning himself near the window and stand stretched as tall as he could, tippy toes straining, monitoring the mountain.

He watched for changes, constants, cloud formations and snow melt. No nuance went unobserved. He gushed and giggled, tickled by alterations in weather and fascinated by the effects of dawn and dusk. He became absorbed with the manner in which the mountain uncovered itself in daylight and slept peacefully beneath a blanket of darkness. In the cool of night, the mountain slept and Sandy crawled between the coolness of his sheets, pulled his covers up over his shoulders and tucked himself in with his dreams. Night's hours watched him until morning smiled, toting a gift of light and an end to his dream state. With fresh eyes, he ran to the window and checked on his obsession. He examined the mountain at night with tired eyes and met the mountain each morning, the first thing of the day. Mount Rainier was on his mind.

Each day was the same. Morning swept warm golden

sunlight over his bed sheets and across his face. The mountain called to him. He lazed about, lying comfortably while on the snow covered mountain, tiny wildflowers braved the cold beneath heavy loads of snow. The fancy green babes prepared for spring with a daring, delightful splash of color, dressing the mountain in multiple fields of wildflowers spelled out in a visual recipe for spring, captivating visitors. A sensation of lupines breathed life into the meadows with long, tall strands of purple that ruled over an abundance of leafy green between striking magenta paintbrushes. Sheet white pasqueflower blossoms with petals reminiscent of cracked eggs and bits of yolk, on cue, burst to center stage. Bright pink mountain heathers, eye catching yellow broadleaf arnicas, dainty white pearly everlastings and hundreds of other wildflowers annually raced to bud, flower, fruit and seed before winter shut them down with freezing temperatures and relentless snow fall. Each spring the flowers awakened honoring the mountain with a multitude of individual brilliant hues, sweet scents, hearty nutrients and seeds, with which to feed the human senses with beauty and feed marmots, deer, birds and other native wildlife to keep them alive. Each of hundreds of plant species actively competed for soil, sunlight and water.

All of it was every bit the turning of pages in every day mountain survival in the lives of plants, trees, birds, mammals, fish, amphibians, reptiles, fungi, protists and bacteria breathing life into the beauty that is the mainstay of Mount Rainier. Wildlife on the mountain made it through long, harsh, cold and windy winters to enjoy the short, warm summer environment. Trees boxed in by hundreds of inches of seasonal snow came into their own in higher temperatures of summer months, especially in mid July and August when much of the snow melted and made its launch traveling down the mountain by waterfalls, streams and rivers. Plants did their best to grow inches while the weather encouraged them. All of it happened within the cycle that is life. All of it boomed and rode the excitement of summer while inside the little purple house at lower elevation, Sandy lived his own progression of advancement. He ate, slept, read and educated himself. In the last weeks he spent almost all of his time reading about Mount Rainier. He accepted stacks of library books on the subject, adding them to his room stacks and separating them by pieces of colored construction paper he'd torn by hand and placed within the pages.

Cara regularly dropped off print-outs from her internet findings. Neighbors who had learned of Sandy's interest brought mountain guide books, wildflower identification cards and their own experiences, offered up over a piece of Grandmother's fresh apple pie and a dollop of homemade whipped cream. Without restraint, Sandy poured himself into mountain facts, leaving his bedroom curtains open night and day, spending hours standing on his bed and gazing at Mount Rainier. Lily spent her days looking after him, explaining phenology and answering his questions. She sat near him gently brushing her petals over his arms and watching him awaken. "Are you predator, or prey?"

He wiped sleep from his eyes and his fingertips found their way into his mouth helping him think. He scratched his head and scrunched his face into a image of confusion, certain snow had disappeared from the west flank. He ran to his desk, grabbed a map and lifted it up, pushing it against the window, but even fully stretched, he couldn't reach. He pushed a chair up close, pushed the map securely to the window and made the comparison to the mountain, turning the chart in circles. He squinted, fussed and sprang to his stocking feet, jumping on his bed to see out the window. "The snow is melting." He raised his voice and pressed his feet firmly into his mattress, holding the map at eye level and struggling to find his bearings, until his hope disappeared and he'd become sullen and wrapped in gloom. He let the map drop onto the bed.. "This is a bad paper." He allowed his legs to fall from underneath himself, putting him flat on his back, where he stayed in a dramatic display of disenchantment. "I'm a predator for this stupid map." Without getting up, he kicked the map from the bed, donned angry eyebrows and pouted in a manner that didn't define him. "It's worse than a house."

Grandmother looked in on him. "What's so bad about a house?"

"A house locks me inside." He folded his arms.

Each day, breakfast came, went and lunch was barely a whisper. Dinner wasn't necessary, in fact no meals were needed. Sandy spent every second with his books. Meals devoured minutes better appropriated for anything to do with flowers. Rapidly, days passed, melding into a cascade of endless moments. He kept his face in his books, keenly aware life beyond the pages were a blur and an unbeatable facade. He sat at the dining room table immersed in his reading. That evening, he didn't see the night sky look in through the kitchen window, nor did he remember falling to sleep on an open book, his face pressed against a photograph of a Mount Rainier wild flower. He softly drifted into dreams of extraordinary flowers sharing their meadows of color. A light breeze came in through the open window bringing a blush to his cheeks, tousling his hair and offering a surrealistic effect to the thoughts in his head, yet he slept peacefully. The kitchen chair became his vehicle, his security, releasing his imagination and encouraging him to swim within the summer flood of wildflowers on the mountain. The chair, as well as other inanimate objects brought peace of mind without judgement, or change of routine. Each had its purpose and didn't stray. It was there at the kitchen table the morning sun had discovered him.

Grandmother bustled into the kitchen. Firewood, precisely cut for the stove filled her arms. She dropped wood pieces into the box in the corner, quickly reaching for a spoon to stir hot sticky strawberry jam, mad with bubbles. "This is the scent of love," she explained. "Good morning, sweetheart." She glanced at Sandy then back to the stove. "How are you? You fell asleep here last night." She pointed with a large syrupy red jam covered spoon. "I carried you to bed, but you came back. Remember?" She smiled. "You're getting too big for that. It wasn't easy."

He shrugged, consciously lifting his shoulders and holding them before making the casual drop. He'd seen the shrug, had watched it performed once, or twice and although he couldn't detect a concrete rhyme, or reason, he tried it on for himself being certain she watched his grand action. "This means someone doesn't want something." He wanted to be carried to bed at night, but he didn't want to show it. "You don't know what a person wants." If the shrug worked, he'd add it to his repertoire.

She looked at him, that's it, just looked, as if she'd find some minuscule trace of reasoning explaining the manner in which the gears turned in his head, but she'd had her moment and moved on, washing the spoon under warm water. "You must've been learning something interesting last night. What did you learn?"

He rubbed his eyes, "About wild flowers. I was reading about Lily. In the spring when she wants to get out of snow, she melts it."

She held the large spoon in place against the side of the kettle. The jam would have to fend for itself. "Melts snow?"

"She melts it."

"Melts snow?"

"She's smart."

She wrinkled her nose, a think line forming between her brows. She imagined a flower with a space heater warming up the mountain, then remembering the jam, ran the spoon in a rapid sweep across the bottom of the pot, stirring in a familiar fashion.

He yawned, resting his head on his shoulder and trying to stay awake, "There're a couple other flowers that do it, but I only care about Lily."

"You do know she isn't the only avalanche lily, don't you?"

"I know..." He was pulling at the neckline of his pajamas. "Is it too tight?"

The snugness of his shirt held no relevance. "Other flowers copy her."

She lined the counter with sterilized canning jars waiting to be brimmed with hot red jam, sealed, popped and stored. She set a clean towel on the counter moving the heavy pot onto it. "I don't know if flowers copy each other. There's a kind of natural rhythm to things they do. They have some type of instinct. It makes them come out in spring."

"Maybe." She wasn't allowed to second guess the behavior of flowers, that is, not on his watch. She should stay in her kitchen and make food. Her job entailed keeping her ever moving hands pulling, pushing, squeezing, patting, pressing and crushing things of a culinary nature. It was his job to understand flowers. He thought soulfully, bringing his best and letting her have it. "The eyes cannot know the nature of things." His eyes traced her face. He needed signs of respect. "Titus Lucretius said that."

She took her metal ladle in hand and scooped jam from the pot, tipping the ladle ever so slightly until hot jam poured into the jars. One by one they filled...

He inhaled the strawberry scent, a gift for his heart and a treat filling his senses. He was in his head, dreaming of flowers in listless fascination, but beneath the surface he was dancing with nature, turning the pages of time in another world where flowers were masters and people were cultivated for their attributes. He closed his eyes, inviting mountain flowers to dot his mind and share their beauty. They were more beautiful than bubbly hot jam.

She shook her head. She would never penetrate his world. Why try? "I'm going into town again tomorrow. I'll go to the library and get more books. The Internet hasn't made it out our way yet." She removed her apron. "I hope it never does."

He stood by the sink playing with the kitchen towel, rubbing the terry cloth over the back of his hands and face and enjoying the texture and passive abrasive effect. It awakened his brain and settled his nerves. "Don't think about it."

She tossed her apron over the counter. "I don't know how to stop thinking about things I shouldn't..." If she did, she wouldn't have spent the last forty years reliving an event that needed to be laid to rest.

He set the towel on his head and looked out from beneath it. "Think of a potato."

She looked him curiously. "Why not an elephant?"

He frowned, unable to understand how she couldn't know something so basic. "An elephant can walk away."

Chapter 3

The afternoon sun traveled up and over the property, landing at a spot behind the house. Grandmother found her way from the kitchen and into the laundry room, sorting colors, tossing garments into the machine and carrying woven baskets of clothing to the line in the side yard. Her cheeks were pink and her arms were thick with consequences of a sedentary lifestyle. She fastened shirts, shorts and socks to the line, brushed wisps of hair from her face and listened to birds calling out in sweet crisp voices. She paused, wondering what it would be like to sit in a tree and sing away the hours. She looked up at the seamless blue sky, the puffy white clouds and felt the dryness in her throat. She placed her hand on her chest, protectively holding on to the feelings of bliss. "Oh, to have a nice cup of iced tea."

Sandy was flat on the grass, elbows bent, palms holding up his head. He barely moved a muscle though now and then light laughter, a quick smile and a brief glance at his surroundings brought him to life. The ground beneath him held a coolness more like a spring mist, keeping his knees damp with bits of soil and moisture.

"Sandy, bring my basket. I have things to take inside." She pulled clothing from the line. "Be quick. We need to grab a bite and visit a friend. I want you to meet someone."

He pressed his finger on the page of his book and looked at her, his face a blank under his mask. He said nothing.

"Did you hear me?" She stopped and waited for him to catch up to her side of the conversation. She shook out the white cotton shirt she held in her hands. "Sandy?"

Her words filtered into his head, where they didn't much matter. He moved his eyes across several more sentences. "Okay." He plucked a blade of grass, carefully setting it as a bookmark and closed the book cover, putting it on top of the clothes in the basket and carried the basket to the house.

She marched ahead of him, glancing back now and then and juggling a load of clothes outside the back door. She struggled, finding support leaning against the wall of the house. "Help me open the door." He set the basket on the step and rushed to the door, placing his hand on hers and pulling her along behind him. He positioned her hand on the door knob, manipulating her hand to help her turn it. He closely watched her progress, acting as her support team. "Almost got it. Almost got it."

A ray of sunlight made its way under the porch covering and exaggerating the creases on her forehead and her clenched brows. She was alerted by the inconvenience of being stretched like a rubber band and having her hand used by someone besides herself. ... And what of the sheer absurdity of his actions? She eyed him with suspicion and a keen sense of interest though she kept her uneven tone in tow. "What in the world?" She held the screen door with her foot, jutting out her hip and holding the stress in her buttocks and down the sides of her back. "My, my, you indeed have your way..." Slowly, her body balanced itself, unfolding and taking her from the zig zag position. She shook her head, the way people do when they just don't quite get it and know they never will... She looked back at him once, then again, being sure she'd seen what she'd seen, experienced what she'd experienced, but Sandy had already moved on although he hadn't moved far and like co-joined bodies, they stepped inside the house, she, continuing to question his behavior and intriguing helpfulness, still holding contention for his odd display and method, but not so that he knew... She had no words, but words were messy. Most things were better left unsaid. The trick was not to think them at all though she thought more than what anyone might've guessed. She hung her sun hat on the hook and wiggled out of her armor, the gabardine apron, catching it on the hook next to her hat. Without losing a beat, she was on to the next, staking her claim in the laundry room folding items so fast they seemed to fold themselves.

The floors were immaculate, always free of streaks and crumbs. The carpet was clean and the beds were made. "Let me run a comb through my hair." She hung clothes, set stacks of underwear in thick heavy dresser drawers carefully lined with lavender scented paper. She placed monogrammed cotton handkerchiefs on her oak dresser next to black and white photographs in fancy frames and white frilly doilies. She called to Sandy, "Eat a wrapped sandwich. They're as fresh as a new day."

Over the rod in the bathroom she draped embroidered bath towels and ran her hand across the fold adding a much needed crease. There were never too many of those. Her house was hefty with creases in curtains, slacks, envelopes, paper and table napkins. A crease, the final blessing on a job well done and a last touch in a perfect presentation. She didn't shine until every domestic spot held a shine. She defined herself by all that was altered by a sudsy cleaning cloth. "They're in the fridge." She set a bar of soap in the tray and positioned a hand towel near the sink. "Drink a glass of milk." She pushed the rug into place with her foot. "Chips are in the cupboard." She was rattling, realized it and stopped. Too much mothering could wipe out a child's hearing. It was a scientific fact. She smiled to herself. She was a better mother this time, not side tracked with things that didn't matter. She was a grandmother, a gift bestowed upon even the most undeserving and she was taking the position seriously. There was no reason to disqualify herself based on low self esteem and she didn't though it seemed ironic she had a high amount of something so low.

She walked to the kitchen, found Sandy skulking and pointed him in the direction of the front door. If he couldn't find something to do, she would give him something to do... She gestured toward the hand basket upon the chair by the entry. "That goes along. My lemon sweet bread and rosemary vinegar." She filed in behind him, at the last minute grabbing her car keys off the nail by the door. "Go on, pick-up the basket and carry it to the car."

His shoulders drooped and his face was long. "It's a bad basket." He knew it would never outgrow its right to be carried to wherever one was headed... He lifted it with one hand, let it loose and watched it tumble to the ground. She noticed and he saw that she did which created a dramatic drop to his knees and all out flop onto his tummy. She continued to eye him. She had no idea what he was thinking and had no intention of faking it. There had been those times she understood what he spelled out in words, but anything else was a mystery. She'd had enough. "Gather yourself and get this basket to the car. She placed her fingers at the small of his back and encouraged him out the door, moving past him and reaching back to grab one of his outstretched arms. "That basket is for someone special. I think you'll like her." She maneuvered him as though manning a tiller steer and effortlessly changed the subject. "You have to do as I say. You have to focus."

He lowered the box and slowly set it on the ground. "Follies and nonsense, whims and inconsistencies do divert me." He grumbled under his breath with his eyebrows applying their own brand of angry influence. "Jane Austen wrote that."

She breathed in a fresh gulp of air and let it steam through her nostrils. "... And the book is...?"

"Pride and Prejudice."

"Of course it is..."

The car ride was five minutes, an easy road, unpaved though adequately maintained. The few pot holes were far enough apart to maneuver without drama and although Grandmother saw them before she came close and a quirk in her nature had her dropping her tires into them, not unlike a need to step into fresh cement. A life lived by the book had resulted in a hum drum existence where her only fit of disobedience consisted of chopping garlic and failing to let it rest ten minutes. Driving into pot holes was a temptation in an otherwise tedious way of life. It brought an edge to an uneventful road trip and seemed the best excitement available. She held tightly to the steering wheel and glanced at Sandy. "People do what they do."

She slowed the car nearly to a halt, pointing out forested wetland, trees, grasses, aquatic greenery, skunk cabbage and cattails, radiant in their reflection on the water. "You can eat cattails and skunk cabbage." Skunk cabbage filled the air with its off-putting odor. She turned up her nose. "You can, but you might not want to..." Her head moved side to side, more for him than for her. She'd seen it all before and taking everything in and rewrapping it for her grandson was high on the list of a grandmother's duties. "See over there, mallards. They're everyday, but I never tire of them. I love the bright green on the drakes. Can you see?" She rolled up her window and moved on... The car edged its way north, slipping by dips and chuckholes. She pointed to the cluster of green ahead on the right. "There... That's our turn. Those beautiful sugar maples, that's us."

He looked into the distance, counted leaves, lost count and arrived back at ten. "I like trees." He followed with his eyes as the car turned into the driveway.

She stepped on the brakes, bringing the car to a crawl. "I like trees too. You'll see a lot of them here. It's a piece of heaven." She made a fast turn and followed the gravel road. "Look at the blackberries. Oh, she'll have a time picking all those, come August. You and I will be here with our buckets. I'll make jam and pie."

'Is it a farm?" Sandy stretched his neck to see over the dashboard and get a look at the berries. Something that could be made into a pie had to be special. He thought about the buckets. "Every man's work pursued steadily tends to become an end in itself." He patted his tummy. "George Elliot wrote that." He wondered what a blackberry would feel like in his hand and in his mouth. Would it have stickers, or thorns? Could it poke at his tongue? "I don't like angry plants." From his window, he sighted tiny birds dancing from branch to branch, seemingly moving with the car though high above the dusty wake. "I see little birds."

She quickly turned to see, lowering her head to get a clear

Arley M. Fosburgh

view. "Black capped chickadees- They're a lively bunch. Oh, you'd just love their lovely voices."

He opened his window, struggling to get his head through the opening while tethered to his seat. "I don't hear anything," He leaned back in disappointment, his mouth turned down and arms folded before him. "Maybe they forgot the words."

She patted his leg. "It's a sweet, clear whistle. You'll know it when you hear it."

The car continued down the long gravel driveway, coming to an abrupt halt before reaching the the main house. She set the hand brake and grabbed her purse. "Hand me the basket."

He crawled into the back seat, sneaking a whiff of fragrant sweet lemon bread before handing it over. Grandmother's car door swung open. She laboriously wobbled her large round body using the steering wheel to ease herself into an upright position. Leaving the basket on the seat, she briskly smoothed out her dress and flattened down her hair. "Come on now." Rapidly, she scanned the landscape in an incomplete fashion, merely noting the familiar and taking exception to the new. "Come on, Sandy." She trotted down the country road, gritty gravel beneath her steps. Sandy tagged behind counting goats in a side yard and a border of sunflowers, the large headed yellow beasts towering over freshly painted white fence posts. She looked over her shoulder. "You get that Hepa on your face before you breathe in something that doesn't agree with you."

He'd been wearing the mask like a necklace. Carefully he lifted it over his mouth and nose, stretching the elastic around the back of his head. "I hate this thing." He slowed his pace and tried a smile. "Man is least himself when he

44

talks in his own person. Give him a mask and he will tell you the truth. Oscar Wilde said that."

She stopped in her tracks, waiting for him to catch-up. "You're The Amazing Kreskin. We'll have to get you your own show." She'd traveled back in time to a place that felt right, or at least comfortable. Too many changes made her stumble through life into unknown territory. It was not pleasing, not that her grandson wasn't pleasing, but Sandy was interesting in the way a trained seal might be of interest, if one could get past the cruelty a circus performing animal may endure. Sandy was also unknown territory though a part of her world, the part that made it worthwhile.

"Who is that?'

"Aaah- before your time."

He stopped near where she stood, looked around and anticipated her next move. Soon they got on together. She paced him and held tightly to his leisurely stride. She thought of his remarkable memory, his quotes and the manner in which he rattled them off as though it was common practice for all. "Where in the world did you get that memory? Does Lily read books?"

He rolled his eyes. "She's a flower. Flowers can't read."

She exhaled with a whoosh, tossed back her head and looked down at the ground, shaking her head in defeat. She mumbled under her breath, "Flowers can talk, but they can't read a book. Well, that's just par..." She turned her attention to the house, the yard, the long greenhouses, not unlike a row of plants in a garden. Life was in bloom no matter where she cast her eyes. She could feel, even touch it if she was so inclined... The dogs in the large enclosure became visible the closer they got to the house. She could smell them, hear them... "How many dogs are there, three, five? It's hard to tell with them bouncing around like that."

He tried to count, his finger holding his place in the air. "There're six. You probably couldn't see that little white one."

She shook her head. "Now that's a menagerie I can do without."

He followed her, enjoying the dust coming up under his footsteps and the bumpy gravel he felt pushing against the soles of his shoes. "You give me much more of your sass, I'll take and bounce a rock off your head." He was speaking to her back as she lead the way to the house.

She spun herself around, showing him a startling pale face with eyes bugged out in disbelief. "You'll do what?"

"Mark Twain wrote that."

She recovered slowly, frequently glancing back over her shoulder.

Free spirited, natural grassy areas, where plants were encouraged to stretch their branches lived amid cultivated and well maintained sections. That is not to say the natural areas were haphazardly placed and unattended, they were well kept, however, the plants within were left to budding, flowering, fruiting, seeding and releasing, without the benefit, or intrusion of human interaction. They grew of their own accord, knowing best how to put out life roots toward water sources and to turn themselves toward sunlight. As far as the eye could see, a striking array of green amid dots of flowers caused visitors to catch their breaths and sigh. Up front were brilliant splashes of color, an abundance of blossoms, bushy and elegant with breathtaking delicacy, or harsh, heavy headed varieties relying on support. Neighboring those were multiple tiny, flirty flowers spending life near the soil, creeping across ready made dirt beds. Sandy spun himself in a circle taking in what he could and pulling on Grandmothers dress. "This might be the place I like." He dropped back and stopped to count the roses.

She found herself repeatedly moving her head in all directions, her eyes zipping back and forth and her patience waning, trying to reign him in and keep a firm hold on the visit. If she was exhausted towing him along on a short walk, how would she be after watching him for another six months, or a year? "Come this way. You're dragging."

His legs worked faster, soon taking him to her side and struggling to match her stride. Together they managed steps to the sidewalk, across stepping stones, another set of stairs and onto the front porch. "It's a big farm, if it is a farm." He looked at her. "Is it a farm, a house, or a hotel?"

She rang the bell, set her basket at her feet, looked down at her dress and smoothed the front. She adjusted her collar and tugged at her hem. With the large size she'd become, it was a chore to get it to hang just right. She looked better than she thought, though not as good as she hoped... "My, but time has passed. Everything is older, thicker and heavier." She fixed her gaze on the evergreens, the magnificent towering beauties, but she could've just as well been referring to herself, the marching of time and her new creases and lumps, none of them flattering.

Edgar ran to greet her. He too had grown, the furry little pup, not a puppy anymore, but a large beast ready to bowl one over with his oversized head, that first impact and the hardened fully grown body that followed raging behind like a train engine pushing from the rear. His tongue stretched from his mouth over a fine set of menacing lower teeth. Sandy kept a cautious distance, but analyzed the dog's every move. "Looks like there're seven. This one wasn't in the pen."

Edgar licked Grandmother's hands, turned and slobbered up Sandy, leaving strings of saliva hanging from his wrists. He backed away, bringing his arms and legs in toward his body and trying to make himself smaller to avoid another close encounter. He watched closely, whispering in a helpless, covert manner as though he didn't want the dog to hear him cautioning her, suggesting she hold her basket high in the sky and run as fast as she was able to go. "He's sniffing sweet bread. Hurry..." She lifted the basket just as the front door opened.

A tall, thin woman stood in the doorway, her long blonde hair pulled back under a soft pink bandana. Her shirt sleeves were rolled and the knees of her pants were green with grass stains and brown with soil. She gave no apology for her appearance and no more than a casual greeting. She merely presented herself. The fact that she was there with a warm smile, was her hello, though upon recognition, she opened her arms. "Oh, Cheryl Anne, just look at you and the little one. You're a grand mama." She took Grandmother's hand and spun her around like a partner in a waltz. "It looks good on you.". The ladies wrapped themselves in a warm embrace. Grandmother glowed. Rebecca sized up her visitors. "It's been so long, almost a year."

Grandmother showed her disbelief. "Can't be..." She kissed Rebecca's cheek.

Rebecca laughed, "Months turn into years, my friend. I'll send you home with a rosemary plant. Your memory needs a boost." She rubbed her hand across Grandmother's shoulders. "Come inside and see what I've done to this place. It hardly resembles my childhood home." She held the door as Grandmother and Sandy stepped inside. "I can't believe I'm still here after all these years. Mom's gone. Pops gone. I had plans to move to some exotic paradise, but you don't know, what you don't know." She offered her elbow to Grandmother, not missing a step. "My heart's in the garden. This is home." She held Grandmothers eyes for a moment longer, then turned toward Sandy, carefully examining him from head to toe. He'd taken off his mask, giving her free range for comparisons. She brought in memories, but kept them tucked in her head while she looked him over and decided where he fit, who he resembled, who had his eyes, his smile, mannerisms and vibe. It was endless though her skills were well polished and her facility brisk, attracting little regard... She'd managed to size him up in a matter of seconds, smile and move on. Still she was taken, "With those looks you'll make the flowers grow." She winked at Grandmother and led the way to the kitchen, moving steadily along as though none of it was important. "Another day, another dollar."

She took a large glass pitcher of icy lemonade from the refrigerator and stirred the frosty liquid with a long handled spoon. "I was born right here, I mean literally. I was born here on the kitchen table on an bitterly cold winter night with snow so high the horses wouldn't budge. They couldn't get a doctor out here no matter the cash. Nobody of sane mind was challenging that blizzard. The snow was so thick you couldn't see your hand in front of your face." She checked her audience. "Gracie, mother's help ripped up a sheet and boiled a pot of water." Rebecca poured lemonade into drinking glasses. "It was the olden days out here. In the city, well, there were hospitals of course, cars, what ever, but here we're throw backs living off the land so to speak." She cut lemon slices and secured them on the top edge of the glasses. "It was a modern world, just not here." Grandmother and Sandy found seats at the counter. Rebecca continued, "We had no electricity. You get it? We heated water on a wood burning stove." She expected amazement, but found none.

"I still do..."

She kissed Grandmother's cheek and smiled a we've all been there, meeting of the eyes. "I know, but yeah, we had no central heating. My dad threw bricks in the fire and got them red hot. He wrapped them in a cloth and tucked them at the foot of our beds." She looked at Sandy and raised her eyebrows. "Would you sleep with a hot brick in your bed?"

He looked at her with reservations. "No, I would build a brick house like the smart pig."

Rebecca laughed, "I guess he didn't..." She eyed him carefully before continuing. "Life wasn't easy." She stopped and looked around. The room fell silent. She felt the break in her monologue like a drop of the mike. "So, I was born on a table." She handed Grandmother and Sandy each a glass of lemonade. "That's a treat, isn't it?"

Sandy was lost in the dribble. He couldn't be sure if she meant her birth, or the lemonade. Neither seemed much of a treat. The lemonade was too sweet and the story was too long. Grandmother took a sip and sighed with appreciation. "This is a delight." She looked around the kitchen, recognizing few items. "I didn't realize this land had been in your family so many years. That's quite a story though I remember the night you were born. It was just after the birth of my..." She pressed her teeth into her lower lip.

"It's okay, you can say his name. I'm fine. I got over that a long time ago." Rebecca pursed her lips and looked toward the ceiling, thinking of old times and putting away memories Grandmother brought to mind. "I'm made of the soil on this acreage." She clapped her hands twice to clear the air. "Let's get outside. I'll give you a tour."

Grandmother picked up her glass and took a large gulp. "I've barely got on with my lemonade."

Rebecca had moved toward the back door. She took a sun hat from a hook. "Take the glass with you." She handed the hat to Grandmother. "You'll need this... The sun is a scorcher."

Grandmother giggled, "Boy, oh boy, get a spec of sunlight and you're reaching for the shade hats and sunblock." She positioned the hat on her head and carried her lemonade out the door. Sandy trudged behind her, stopping to lift his mask over his face and staying a safe distance from the cheery reunion and girlish laughter while Grandmother looked for a break in the banal dragging on of nothingness, dreaming of throwing in her own subject matter. Her son could always be dropped into any conversation and with little effort she discovered a window, tossing him inside. "Do you think of Thomas?"

Rebecca didn't have words to hide her surprise, but curiosity set her chumming for an angle. "He's not around and as I remember, he gets caught up in everything I say, or don't say."

Grandmother understood, being careful not to send Rebecca running for cover. "Just wind him up and watch him go."

Rebecca made a fine effort of keeping her expression neutral to avoid an avalanche of comments and to home in on her own mood rather than what she perceived as Grandmother's intent to tie her up with her son, expecting them to reunite and demanding they make the past a blur. As far as she was concerned, the heartache was a thing of the past though beyond her consideration, feelings quietly lingered. Grandmother caught Rebecca's melancholy bent, not because she was intuitive, but because it was so far out in the air it couldn't be missed. "Don't do that. Pull on your boots and get going."

She had gotten going, that is before Grandmother brought it up. She was pulling up her boots. "You're giving me advice? You, the woman still locked up on a freezing mountain on an ancient cold rainy day?"

Grandmother followed her train of thought, but didn't accept, or appreciate it. She lowered her chin and raised her eyes, looking out under her brows. "It wasn't raining."

"It might as well have been. You've cried for forty years." She took a deep breath. "It's supposed to be forty days and forty nights." She smirked with satisfaction. "You've lost count."

Grandmother made the sign of the cross. "Is that blasphemy?"

"No, it's a faint attempt at humor. Is it funny?"

"No." She did her best to appear insulted, pulling her arms in around herself for insulation, separating her from the words she was about to say. "You should get back to church."

"In a building?"

"Where else?"

"We have oceans and mountains. We don't need a building."

"Oh honey." She crossed herself and lifted the tiny gold cross hanging loosely around her neck, kissed it and set it back into place. "I'll pray for you from inside the church, our Lord's home."

Rebecca didn't press it. There was no place to go in a

conversation about things with debatable answers. "And I'll receive your prayers on a mountain trail."

"You have your opinions and I have mine."

"Alright."

"You're so much like Thomas."

Chapter 4

In the black of night at the edge of the forest sat the small purple house with no working porch light, and no other form of lighting protecting the building, except the window in the kitchen emitting golden light as a beacon to those outside the dwelling, a signal reminiscent of a lighthouse high on a cliff above treacherous water. The omnipotent warmth glowed from inside the home unknowingly tempting nocturnal creatures and native wanderers, raccoons, mountain lions and those with beady eyes waiting out an opportunity within the darkness, an unintentional invitation to eat, if they could gain entry.

Surrounded by the deepest black bitter cold, the house was the only light within a mile, the only source of human contact within the same mileage and one of only twenty five family dwellings in what locals called South Brook. There were no retail establishments, no schools, no community center and no police, or fire stations although the wildlife and woodlands were more than a match for any greenway a large city had to offer.

Nights were brutal, unforgiving and long if observed from darkness minus shelter, a valid explanation as to why the homeless population in South Brook was zero. Neighbors were family, and sharing DNA was a genetic marker, not a definition of a relative even as a neighbor may have been several miles away, spoken to once or twice a year and absent at most social happenings. Others spoke regularly and met often. Regardless of frequency, it was the knowing, the faith that someone was there to shoulder the burden, to comfort in times of distress and to help when help was essential. South Brook residents lived off the land, or as close to living off the land as they could while spending a good percentage of their days making and growing things they needed. Most of those were families with generation after generation who had grown up in the area. Still, there were residents who used isolation as a means of solitude and silence to all things urban. They may have had a second home in the city, but they maintained their return to nature from a warm residence in the quaint forest community.

In the last hour of darkness before dawn, rain doused forest trees, drenched shrubs, native plants and grasses. It flooded gutters, flowed through tiny streams and slammed hard against Grandmother's kitchen window. A mass of loud rhythmic rain water hypnotized her there on the cozy hospitable side of the yellowing pane. From outside, she could be seen in the rectangle of toasty yellow light framed by night's black depth and surrealistically painted in the colors of comfort. She stood before the kitchen sink, washing and rinsing. In her den, she'd become invincible behind dependable walls apart from the wild.

Outside, within the black, tiny white stars told a story of a universe filled with rebirth and washed in spots of brightness. Inside, contained and free of the untamed, it was she who was the light, the brightness shining through everything tossed in her direction, or pushed onto her plate regardless of elbowing. She was the heart of her kitchen. The kitchen was the heart of her home. Inside the heart on that dark early morning, she heard the first sounds of thunder. She smiled to herself. It was a gift, nature on percussion, a forest resonance meant for meditation and reflection. She thought of Michael, his boyish excitement at the rumble of thunder, the way he casually grabbed her around the waist nudging her to the window and predicting where the lightening would sprawl across the sky. He would lean in to kiss her telling her he loved her and sharing his dreams about their future. There was a softness, a padding protecting them from the icy edge of day to day. Love and desire being their stronghold, nothing could change. Nothing could alter their bond.

She kneaded the dough, set it to rest and placed the teapot on the stove, prepared the muslin herb bag with chamomile flower tops and dropped it into her favorite cup. She sat herself at the dining room table, not actually a dining room table at all, but merely the manner in which she preferred to label it. It was an old fashioned yellow formica table top with chrome legs and four mismatched chairs, three of which were indiscriminately repaired with black tape in an unpleasant, yet functional fashion. She might have gotten rid of the chairs long ago, had Michael not done the work, delighted for her to see he could accomplish more than climbing frozen natural structures. Her mind once again was tagging her with if only and what if, pouncing on her with the poorly mended chairs, a ragtag shoot back to a special time though she ignored the reference, choosing to believe aesthetics were not her concern. "They're chairs, a place to sit." If she'd only believed that to be true.

She waited, head in hand, thoughts of Michael circling as they often did, but understanding that if she let her thoughts have their way, she would spend the day fretting, fearing, reliving failures and improbable decisions, all of which seemed good at the time. The teapot cried out, and she moved her face away from the steam, pouring hot water into her cup, plopping a tea bag into the liquid, covering the cup and setting it on the table. Five minutes were left on the resting dough.

She glanced at her watch, covered a yawn and sipped tea before it had steeped to perfection. She lifted dough from a greased bowl, punching, kneading and readying it for rolling. She stuck her hand into the flour bag, the white powder powerfully cold on her skin and easily bringing up tiny goose bumps, a secret joy in the soppy humidity of the over heated kitchen. She lifted out a handful of flour, appreciative of the silkiness in her hand and lightly dusted the counter, quickly followed by pushing and pressing the dough with a thick wooden rolling pin while the unmistakable scent of butter and yeast filled the air. Her forearms tightened with a familiar tension, forever a consequence of her unrelenting need to create creamy perfect lightly golden baked love. She rubbed the back of her hand over her face leaving a trail of flour while a feverish perspiration slid over her brows and into her eyes, amid the dividing, rolling, pinching, baking. All of it grand and inconsequential to the untrained eye, however, to her it was a piece of heaven, only accessible through labors of passion and selfless acts. Even as that, the delicate fruits of her effort had to be creatively squeezed of the finest creative juices, worn and put away before Sandy awakened and her daily routine kicked into action. If a few minutes lent themselves, she'd relax, feet up, eyes closed and at peace. A bonus, of course.

She folded and tucked portions of dough into prepared

pans, covered them with a clean kitchen towel and set them near the stove in the next room. The kitchen stove, over burdened with heavy pots and pans brimmed with thick saucy soup, bubbling pasta and breakfast sausage with raw hash browns sizzling in an over kill of vegetable oil, her culinary circus coming at her from all directions. She turned her attention to the remaining dough, rolling it into a large rectangle, rubbing butter across its surface and alternately sprinkling a fine layer of coarse brown sugar and cinnamon. The dough was carefully rolled, sliced, placed into two greased pans, covered and set to rise. She cleaned the counters, tending the stove and washing the dishes, taking a deep breath, putting her hands together and uttering a quiet prayer. The moment was dismissed without longing... "In the name of the father and of the son and of the holy ghost...."

Sandy was asleep in the hall near the bathroom. He'd gotten up in the middle of the night, accepting the spot on the rug rather than the effort it would take to get back into bed. She placed a soft warm blanket over him, carefully setting a pillow under his head and returning to kitchen detail. She wished to carry him to his room, but felt the stiffness in her back, knowing she shouldn't be lifting children. Her back was not what it used to be. She wiped sleep from her eyes, blinking repeatedly and moving back to the kitchen where time meticulously kept to another time table.

She thought of Michael, the smoothness of his skin and his haunting dark eyes. He sauntered into her kitchen, kissed butter from her lips and gently wiped specs of white flour from her face. Like a thief in the night, he'd pinched pieces of bread dough from under a warm kitchen towel and deliciously moaned, savoring sweet morsels and lifting his voice in praise. "Here's to the best of the best." His words were as smooth as his skin. Her time would've been better spent in the present, but Michael no longer had the luxury of the present, nor did the present have tranquility, happiness, or her heart. The present was a novice, a naive elf like slave to the future. It hadn't the capacity to understand her need of running losses through her mind and obsessively making promises to keep her secrets to herself. The old days saved little things, details, smiles and innocence packed neatly inside yesterday's core. Michael was with her. He was home nights. He held her, chased quiet tender glances, blundered, stumbled, recovered and recited words not meant to last a life time. His voice was a gentle hum, like a melody heard from far away. "My love, my love, I love you. You're mine."

The wood burning stove was alive with cut and split blowdowns burning hot in its belly. The fire crackled and spit, having yet to ease itself into a mild mannered simmer. Her warm fingers touched the cold metal coil handle, pried open one small lid, peeked inside at the red orange flames, set the lid back into place and closed the dampers. She mustn't leave kettles unattended until the fire slowed, granting her little choice, but to delay a nap, try to relax with one eye open, ride out her inner storm and gain a second wind.

Outside the window, gusts were much less a second wind than demanding, furious and centered attacks coming in from all angles and directing nature's symphony bringing puffs that hunted down wind chimes, wickedly swinging them, eliciting their musical cries and throwing rain drops pitter pattering on the closest landing strip. The show stopper was the boom of thunder and illuminated cracks in the sky. The storm made her spot of comfort a den of warmth and security. She flittered about the kitchen lost in her past while in her mind, Michael stood beside her, love sparkling in his eyes and passion sprinkling over his words like candy as he talked without stopping about his first love without the slightest inclination of how she might feel being his mistress. He adjusted his shoulders, smiled and glowed with every refinement, his hands in his pockets, at once hanging at his sides, moving about in the air and dashing back into his pockets. He couldn't be still when singing the praises of the mountain, carrying his enthusiasm as high as the peak itself. It was clear, he couldn't tone it down and he couldn't be stopped, but as much as she feared his ambitions, she understood his pride in his accomplishments. Three times he'd reached the summit by way of Disappointment Cleaver, Ingraham Glacier and Liberty Ridge. He planned another climb, again taking the Disappointment Cleaver route. She could see him when she closed her eyes. She could feel his strength, magnetism, his journey. "Cheryl Anne," he'd say, when he could see sadness in her eyes, "You know I love you, but this is who I am." She'd relived the words a thousand times. "I'm a mountaineer. You knew that when you met me." It was true, yet she wondered if she was to be held to the mind set and conceptions of a sixteen year old child and fastened to ideas she accepted at the time. Was broad-mindedness induced by young love something to evolve as she matured, or was it a burden wrapped around her throat and thwarting her the freedom of changing her mind?

Much like kamikaze pilots, spectacular drops of rain blew sideways slamming the window pane. Each black-hearted drop, a fine gift and startling flashback to Michael's final ascent. She could taste the last frozen snowflake nestled in his beard, the closing in on adventure, the sadness and the day hope died. Still, she retained her faith in the synchronicity of nature and the more chaotic, the better the reminder of Michael, the wildness and life circle that sucked him into its vortex. She'd banged about in her kitchen unconsciously praying for his return. When her heart slowed its rhythm and her head imagined snow and ice, he was before her. The memories of her tattered angel returned to her through details of the storm. Effortlessly, hours reconstructed with wind blown rain drops like unsettled ghosts slapping against the house. She continued her chores, the small movements that sustained and held her heart. She folded her mind around the pain of his departure and weaved the cells in her body into the threads of his passion, at the same time, measuring, adding this and that and forcing center stage, a tidy kitchen heavy on her mind. Clean counters and dishes washed and dried told a different story. Cups and saucers wiped to a shine were enough to convince her that she was good and important. She could afford to relax and through relaxation the past lost its pull. Stress felt good on a needy mind that hoped for more than the world could offer, but stress crippled her in ways she knew to keep to herself. Chores kept her mind occupied and hands busy. In those instances, Michael lost his appeal.

She'd survived. Sixty years in the forest ignited a love for the wild and an understanding of the cycles of life. Nearly the same amount of time in the kitchen gave her an appreciation for her hands, mind and the brief moments she'd let go and had forgotten everything but the mixing bowl set before her. Eggs whisked and milk plunked within those lapses of time where she thought nothing of Michael while she stirred a sauce and waited for the explosion of bubbles to remind her to start the timer. She could take the worst with the best and she had... She taken the worst of the worst while awaiting the best of the best. She'd wait however long it took to shine her flashlight into darkness before reaching the light at the end of the forest.

At a quarter to ten, she shifted her weight in the kitchen chair, her head bobbing from drop dead slumber to the rude awakening of her head jerking upright, only to experience the second fall. She was a prisoner of her own making, rising before she was ready and paying the toll. It was too late in the hour to run back to a warm bed, pulling covers up over herself and hiding from the sun. There was something brave about her choices, the way she marched on, even as her body tired... There was something courageous, not as a soldier on the battlefield, but as a woman finding her way, alone. She didn't think of herself as either though she was... There are no awards for mothers who do the things mothers do... Minding the home, or rather building a home and mapping out a small world in the midst of a larger one, a place where love really does matter and where it's given regardless of whether one believes they deserve it, or not. ... A haven where flaws are not only frequently overlooked, but accepted and where I'm sorry means more than money.

She broke away from her memories, found the stove and the pots working there. A sigh came over her as though she wore it, rather than bore it as a heavy release. The fire, not more than a scattered pile of bright orange specs spied out from under ashes giving a nice steamed touch to vegetables and spices. She added a garnish, reached for a half tablespoon and dropped Herbs de Provence into a pot. The eggs were scrambled, soft and runny. Tiny beads of oil jumped about the pan. It was clear that the dampers had earned their keep. She crossed herself, touching her forehead, chest and shoulders. "Oh, the faith, the blessings of belief..." The kitchen smelled of buttery braised broccoli, carrots swollen within spicy broth, softened cauliflower, shinny oiled mushrooms and kale sunk deep into intoxicating brine. Every member of the aquatic carnival came to the surface now and then like a water bound deadhead bouncing in the surf. There was the fennel carefully measured and added, savory, and her favorite, rosemary.... Rosemary, with its pine needle leaves and forest scent. Rosemary, that useful culinary enhancement often revered as a medicinal virtue was at that moment enhancing more than a golden brown chicken, or boiled red potatoes. She took it in with each inhalation, certain rosemary held the memories of a life time. Rosemary was the reason she had a kitchen. She had no use for a stove without it. A kitchen existed for no other reason than to provide a warm spot to apply its culinary blessings. Lavender danced across the pot's watery surface seconds before being swept into whirlpool circles, bouncing like a bobber on a fishing line and slipping beneath the surface. Torn bits of fresh basil and thyme were easier to sink, but at the end of the day, were on the sides of the pot.

Aromatic herbs healed her soul and soothed her mind, helping her find direction and purpose. She tended her culinary plants living in her kitchen and looked after native species in her yard and the forest. She knew them by sight, wildcrafted them and left endangered plants to grow. That day, like every day in her kitchen, a colorful phytonutrient feast was on the verge of presentation. She couldn't help but lean over her soup pot taking in another strong whiff of rosemary and witnessing her mind becoming calm and her heart softening, the way it did when she thought of Michael. She looked around for her next obsession. There were a myriad of things to do in a space where it was always just one more thing... An overflow of dough bubbled over its container oozing sticky goo onto the counter and calling to her for redirection. Natural order was on hand to reel her in when her mind wandered. She enjoyed being on a leash without choices boggling her perception and truth clogging her reasoning.

The oven temperature increased, luring loaves of uncooked dough to enter the magic chamber where useless shapes changed to mouth watering, toasted, butter topped bread. A buttery scent floated about the kitchen, slowly infiltrating every room, filling the air with a delicious culinary perfume of highest quality and worth, a bouquet fine enough to dance through sinuses persuading eyes to close and flooding the mouth with saliva, the tongue wild with the waiting... Time spent in anticipation of that first life changing bite was nothing short of insufferable and mind numbing. She knew her value. She was due her salt like no other moment when she cranked out loaf after sweet loaf of homemade yeast bread. Her bread was infamous in South Brook. She, more as an after-thought.

She moved about her kitchen, her weight shifting with reaching, releasing, salting and peppering. She cut yellow and orange peppers and slid comfortably into her default mode, unapologetically convinced she was nothing without her precious baking and meticulous stove stop heroics. Maybe it was true. It had always been that way. In a manner of speaking, the continuation of any silent belief made that belief a fact. She believed it and others followed her lead, holding up to her the beliefs in her core. Her misconception, what ever it was, had her boxed, labeled and moved down the belt. The fashion in which she held herself, or defined herself worked in her best interest. It was a self-fulfilling prophecy. In front of the stove, perspiration at her brow, she brought her false beliefs to life. There she stood, stirring, pouring, chopping and breathing scents of her essence. She produced baked goodies filled with love, inadvertently using baking as a tool to love herself. Truth is not always pretty.

She checked on Sandy, pulled the cover up around his shoulders, said his name and patiently waited for an answer, kissed his cheek and walked to her room, sitting before her mirror, brushing her hair and carefully applying pink lip stick. She wiped away white flour dust, stole a look at her reflection revealing herself as a young girl, teen and grandmother. Slowly, she opened the vanity drawer, lifted mascara from her make-up purse and dressed her lashes. It had been years since her face was painted and she'd pondered more than seconds regarding what she would wear.

Her chin rested on her fist while she scrutinized her shoe collection and selected a pair of black strappy sandals. She took a plain dress from her closet, held it up to herself, looked in the mirror and swayed her hips, then laid the garment across her bed in a fit of melancholy, her arms hanging like limp noodles and her shoulders drooping. She rolled her eyes, returned to her closet, selected another dress, grabbed the one on the bed and positioned one against the other. With brows furled, she made a decision based on nothing but her feelings at that particular moment. Tomorrow, either of the dresses might've made the grade, but on that day neither garnered her interest. Women can do that. They can base decisions on air and be correct in their account. She hung the dresses in her closet and closed the door. She would wear the dress she was wearing. She washed off the mascara and lip stick, pulled off the sandals, put on her slippers and was back in the kitchen as though she'd never been away.

She looked at her watch, compared it to her old fashioned kitchen timer and ignored both of them. She could smell the bread in its final cooking stage, an art to which she was entitled. She'd paid her dues. She'd baked all of her life and at the end of years of service came the moment when she could smell a cake when it was ready to leave the warmth of the oven. She could walk into a house and know whether a roast was set into the oven minutes ago, or was on its last juncture. The ability to accurately judge by scent whether potatoes were scalloped with whole milk heated into a creamy white sauce, or put together with evaporated milk is noteworthy. Regardless of her skills, she preferred potatoes au gratin with a hint of rosemary. No other method of preparation mattered to her. She was set in her ways and could have her own way accurately accessing cookie ingredients by smell alone and measuring by a batch of dough's appearance, or the way it felt between her fingers, but that day in her kitchen there were no cookies settled comfortably in a hot oven melting into shape though she could smell the browned crust and hot liquid butter running into the crispy cracks of the bread tops. Her mouth was wet with anticipation and longing, a treasured bounty from her baking experience.

She tied her apron around herself, slipped a mitt over her hand and lifted bread pans from the oven. She set the cooling rack on the counter and flipped loaves leaving golden tops standing on their heads. Something about those moist doughy bottoms up loves encouraged temptation. She hurried for a knife and cut into one allowing steam to mist her face, the heavenly scent of warm butter and yeast rendering her helpless and her knees weak. She shoved a piece into her mouth braving the hot vapor scorching the roof of her mouth and giving it the power to take her down, scalding her tongue as well, if that was the way it had to be. She couldn't wait, and there's always a price for lack of patience. Life overflows with terms of encampment presented as the first steps of negotiation. She'd escaped with minor consequence, merely the burning heat of a developing blister at the roof of her mouth. It was worth every stinging discomfort she'd endured and with hot bread delighting her taste buds, she leaned in stretching her thick, short body to gain an inch and effortlessly look out her window. She was expecting a guest.

The car engine in the driveway wasn't more than a whisper heard from where she stood, but the anticipation of family just outside her door had her straining for subtle details, a slam of a car door, foot steps on the porch, or creaking of wood under her welcome mat. She wiped a napkin over her lips, rinsed her mouth and hastened to the door, opened it and waited... Remembering her apron, she loosened the ties and tossed it over the back of the couch.

In the driveway, Thomas grabbed the bouquet of flowers from the back seat, adjusted the rear view mirror and checked his reflection. He opened his door and got out of his car, catching sight of his mother on the porch smiling with a vulnerability often reserved for a child. He cringed, reaching for his necktie and loosening the knot. He unbuttoned the jacket of his suit as he approached the porch, giving the house a quick once over and walking up the steps. Weeds cluttered the gutters, chips of house paint lay useless on the porch and the yard was over run by dandelions and tiny mushrooms.

At the top of the steps he could smell her, sweet lavender

and butter, a comfort in his childhood, along with dinners from scratch, playing cards, puzzles, hikes and fresh laundry on the line. He sauntered toward her as Michael would do, an air of masculinity trapped in the space he'd taken as his own. Peeling paint on the door frame claimed his attention and he tapped his finger there. "I'll call someone in Seattle to come out and paint the house." He nosed around the yard from where he stood on the porch. "I have a landscaper who'll get your yard into shape."

She grimaced, waving him off with her hand. "You'll do no such thing."

"I won't have you out here living like a beggar." His glossy shoes and flashy leather briefcase gave his words a complacent tone which provoked her though she left it alone. It was enough just to have him on the same sod as that beneath her swollen feet. ... No sense in sending him on the run.

She pointed at his briefcase. "I thought we'd have time together."

"Habit." He held the flowers under her nose flaunting their fragrance though no match to her own. Pricey brightly colored flowers, much like dainty princesses wrapped in floral paper always made an appearance like an apologetic blunderer seeking redemption and always running late. His intention was somewhere else, not one of redemption, or apology although guilt was conveniently packaged and stored in his head for visits to her home. Without moments of preparation, memories grabbed at him tearing his heart and pushing him to recall the minutes that he hadn't remembered in years, the bad, pleasant and worn. In those first moments on her acreage, he looked into her eyes, returning to passive explosions of passion and remorse. He was grown, secure, confident, settled though upon entering her domain, time rewound leaving his flaws exposed. He should've picked dandelions from the field. He could do better... He'd always run short. He was an attorney, respected and in demand, but his accomplishments stood no chance against life in the forest. For her, money was a necessary annoyance. There was no blasting his own horn under the canopy of trees. Still, he kept his balance, sweeping in and wrapping his arms around her, kissing her cheek and complimenting her on her dress. He placed the flowers in her hands and watched her eyes fill with tears spilling threads of joy and sadness. He could take them, or leave them. Tears were nothing more than a watery guilt trip she had no other way to put upon him, and he blocked her with indifference. She couldn't force him to feel anything he didn't want to feel. He'd spin it, forcing her to lay down her silver sword conjured of mistakes he'd made which would travel through the ether life time after life time looking for a place to take refuge. Every slight and miscalculation would stay with him as long as he looked into her eyes. Her disappointments grown on his blunders would ride with him through the forest and back to Seattle, if he let them, and he knew he would...

She looked out from behind eyes built on nostalgia and saw him as if for the first time, his dress shirt, slacks, well shined shoes, slicked back hair, the necktie, always the necktie. She remembered his childhood mop, the pile of hair she once smoothed with a mothering hand, stroking the softness of his forehead. He felt her as though he and she were sewn together by a thread, both ends knotted. Expectations ran high that they would sort their way out and find the door where real life transpired and flourished into a scenario most would recognize as success. He knew her by her movements and expressions she didn't wear. He watched and waited...

She smiled, "I haven't had flowers since.."

He put his arm around her. "Since last time I was here."

She laughed, "From you, yes--- I haven't had flowers from a man since..." She stopped herself.

"It's okay." Visits always came back to that...

She held his hand and nodded. "Well, he's gone." Time had passed. Let it go...

Thomas rolled his eyes. He knew what was coming. He tossed his hands up toward all the answers that would never be there for her. "Forty years. I'm forty four. He died when I was four years old. You haven't dated, or looked at another man in forty years." He shook his head as though she'd inflicted intentional pain. "What is that?"

Nervous laughter is a special kind of laughter reserved for discomfort, a support, like an excess of adjectives, or a sudden run on exclamation points. She could make no excuses. "I'm grieving." She gave him a quick glance.

Perhaps he meant to project his interest in aiding her on her journey, but what ever it was, the sound that came from deep in his throat was a meaty show of disapproval. If a sigh can be sarcastic, that's what it was... "Forty years?" It's easier and a pleasure to examine another's life rather than explore one's own misconceptions and misdeeds. He was calling her out, but more as a deflection than an out right unearthing of mismanagement. However he perceived it, it didn't mean much to her. To throw a life preserver to one determined to die, is a loss in action, if that's what he was doing, and it was hard to tell what he was doing, or where he thought he was headed...

"Some people go through the seven steps a little slower

than others." ... Another 'bout of nervous laughter and a shrug. The idea of she, living his reality and giving him a chance to sink his teeth in where they didn't belong set her fears a buzzing. Ultimately, the conversation sprouted legs and traveled rapidly down a path she'd decided not to follow. Personal survival was about recognizing one's core. It was about shaking off clutter and marching forward regardless of terrain. Obstacles to her were an invitation to fight, an unwanted distraction she needed to navigate herself around, but he had learned by experience that sometimes the best route is not around, but through an obstacle. She'd accumulated a modicum of confidence in the manner in which she handled her years and determined that she could not turn back the pages of time. He had bull dozed his way through life accepting collateral damage and waving his battle flag. He wasn't going anywhere, but full speed ahead. The conversation was closed before it began. He knew it and she knew it. It was just a matter of who had the nerve to be the first to move out of range. A negotiation is often between those pretending to listen, but are not even in the same room. It's a facade.

As part of the facade, they walked into the house arm in arm. Thomas glanced around and felt the familiar rush of yesterday, poured into his today. Nothing had changed... He understood it best by taking objects at face value. He harbored no protective longings, or latent affection for old furniture and nicknacks. The couch brought memories, but not tear stained remembrances and yearning for the past. The old sofa was weary and decrepit with the weight of time. He'd replace it, sending her a modern piece of furniture when he returned to Seattle. He went on with what he thought of as an involuntary pilgrimage, steadfastly unwelcome to the opening of archives and flood of recall. His stomach resisted his childhood creeping in, by stirring up another batch of gastric acid, and burning away the past.

He thought he'd slipped out of reach, but the couch caught him off-guard with lucid snapshots popping into his mind and pulling on his wistful bent, something he had no idea he possessed. He remembered the spot where his pen exploded and the night he laughed so hard he choked on a lemon drop. He hung suspended in time remembering sitting on its firm cushions and scribbling out a two hundred word essay. There was the Sunday afternoon he sat on the arm, sweated, stuttered and asked his girl to the prom. That same blue fabric, hundred years old if it was a day, covered cushions on a sofa forever at gatherings, moments of emotion and the many, "Just resting my eyes," deep, soothing naps.

Within worn cushions were pleasant family secrets and those everyday, just a little wobbly moments ear marked for years of bringing them back from the dead. The instances he was told he would laugh at one day, had yet to offer humor. He was curious of his intense feelings regarding what was actually an everyday childhood. He stood still, a cringe pulling his face into an expression he wasn't proud to wear. The ancient hours stood frozen depending on those who had escaped to return and find what they'd missed the first time. The past had its ticket stamped, granting permission to rush into his mind forever, stomping on alterations he'd made to the present. It called him out on choices, roads he'd encountered and paths he'd chosen. He was back at the starting block, skills sharpened, and ready to be released into the world.

He was an adult, most of the time. He wore a man's suit, carried an adult briefcase, argued like a mature male in court and paved his own way. He was an adult for most months, years, days, hours, minutes, that is, until he visited his mother. It was one of those things. In his childhood home, guilt grabbed him just above the elbow, pulled him inches above the floor and dragged him to a time out. He had to snap out of his reminiscing and get to the point of the visit, his mother. He felt concern and obligation, thinking of her as alone and depressed. "You can meet a man. You're young. I bought you a phone. Call someone."

She didn't need protection. She didn't need to be protected by anyone. Her life was built around long spans of time and experiences within victim trappings. She'd take care of herself. She took a vase from the cupboard, filled it with filtered tap water and unwrapped the bouquet, placing the bright pink, yellow and red roses into the vase. She snipped leaves from the white Peruvian lilies and meticulously fitted them in with the others. She smiled the way she did, with her eyes closed and her head falling to the side. "Oh, the fresh smell of roses, perfume of God's heaven. ... And the rosemary..." She drifted away with her words, her hand lightly placed on her chest. She breathed in the flowers' gift, exciting her nervous system and dousing her olfactory cells with an explosion of flowery scents. She soothed her soul and ignited her passion for every flower she'd ever seen, held, or imagined, making those before her, the fresh cut blossoms, a treat above the others. Once more, she inhaled deeply. Her memories walked up to meet her taking her down a series of remembrances of sweet roses Michael brought each time he'd come to her speaking of another expedition, extended climb, or different day with the same story. It was a gift, the sweet smell, but the fire had burned...

Thomas loathed her over reactions. He felt worthless at

those times as though she was a cup that couldn't be filled. He blew a small puff of air between his lips, sedating him and allowing him just enough to get on in the moment with a modicum of scathing.

Slowly, she drifted back into conversation. "I gave the phone away." She looked in his direction, caught his eye and the perfection of his features. Nature pulled magic from within her, creating a human being. He had a nose, two ears, hands that delivered gifts, feet that moved away from her and a heart that belonged to someone else. The beauty of her child perplexed her. How could he be flesh and blood made from her body? Profound love, again, became the material dealing her a losing hand. Circumstance had brought Thomas home, but he'd wiggled off the hook. Her apron strings reached out, wrapping him like a swaddled infant though he was a man and she knew it. How long could she address him as a child? It was true. He was suffocating. It wasn't as if she didn't know, just that she couldn't stop it. Her maternal love, once meant as concern, had become a strangle hold. He thought of her as controlling and she found him, the same. She questioned deep inside herself, within the graveyard of loneliness, why buy her a phone if he didn't want her to be at his beck and call? Inside his head, he analyzed her actions, why make an extravagant meal if she didn't want him to bow before her? Sometimes love doesn't make itself clear.

Thomas tinkered in the kitchen. He lifted the lid from the kettle of simmering soup and breathed in scents of rosemary, vegetables and sweet onions. It worked for him, giving him a hint of yesterday and the sugary promise of his own home and the possibilities. His mouth watered. He pulled off corners of yeast bread, tossed them into his mouth and braved lazy streams of steam, swallowed and cursed the burning in his chest, just as his mother would do... It wasn't the buttery taste of bread baked to perfection, it was the dive in head first plunge into the past. Homemade bread was an open door, a mood changer and act of kindness. "You gave away the phone?" He groaned and stomped his foot.

She added the last two flowers. "It's a phone." She threw her hands in the air. She wasn't waiting for an explanation. There were situations that mattered, and those that didn't...

"It's an iPhone." He closed his eyes as if he could shut down crazy. "Some people think those are important." His world consisted of more than large metal kettles on the stove and sun dried tomatoes. He desired proof of his status in the world. He wanted to own things. She needed confirmation of her existence. She wanted to make things.

She set the vase on the table, stood back, took a look, moved it to the counter, admired it and moved it to the shelf in the living room. "It's good karma. You have to think about these things. Karma remembers." There was nothing to argue about. No getting through...

His voice was low, "It's the newest iPhone. I have a contract. I'm paying for that." He didn't have to argue the point, but he was an attorney, and that was his way...

"With all your money, it's not paid off?"

"It's a contract, monthly, so you have a connection."

"Look around, do you see towers?" She motioned for him to sit and he watched her face change from a haughty, you'll never get a word in edgewise kind of beauty, to a welcoming soul sister spirituality. "Come join me. Let me serve you up soup and fresh bread."

To him she was a text book scenario of all that was wrong with mountain people and she bought the story bagging all city folks as superficial, the grass is always greener society. She had him wrapped and branded as a fallen soldier, one of her own, but a traitor. He would've donated her to the Salvation Army, if she'd only just get in the car.

"I bought it so you'd have protection when you're out driving away from this clump of trees." He'd had it and was not about to sugar coat his anger. His arms were flailing, creating a forest with his hands. "This place is the end of the world."

She shook her head, smiled and rolled her eyes. "You used to love it." She knew he did, or thought he did... She didn't intend to travel back into time when the best life had to offer was there in the present. He was in her kitchen, something she only dreamed about from day to day. Her son, back home in her kitchen... She was close to paradise, tied into her apron, waiting on family, scooping soup into a bowl, slicing homemade bread and smearing marmalade. Flowery dinnerware had made an appearance. Ceramic soup spoons decorated the table. Cloth napkins were front and center. Who even used them anymore, but there they were, folded, and oh, yes, creased. She was happy. She was created for service. She threw him a cold, yet loving piece of her mind. "And just for the record, this is a town."

"It's a bunch of people living in the forest. What're there, ten of you out here?"

She sat across the table from him. "Twenty five families. What's your point?"

He lifted a spoonful of soup to his mouth and moaned with pleasure. "I forgot how good this is..." He hurried another spoonful to his lips. "This is what you do. This is your gift." He tossed food into his mouth as though he'd missed meals, bread, then soup, soup, then bread. He didn't slow, but chaotically pushed back his chair and grabbed a metal spoon from the drawer. "Who can eat with a stone spoon? What am I, a caveman?" He sat himself back at the table, sent a smile her way and remembered the phone. "Who did you give it to?"

"It's not stone. It's ceramic and I still have my house phone. Can we change the subject?"

"Come-on, what'd you do with it?" He rolled a piece of bread, shoving it into his mouth while grabbing another, tearing it into chunks, drowning it in broth and when it surfaced, coming down hard with crushed hot pimiento. The savory flavors nipped at the inside of his mouth while salty grains tantalized his taste buds.

She watched him devour the love. Every slice of potato and kernel of corn was molded out of the inside of her soul. To deny her the opportunity to observe loved ones eating her carefully prepared food meant considerable pain lasting weeks, or more. True recovery could only be gained by her next culinary feast. Thomas was aware of her fascination and acted accordingly, overdoing his praise. She accepted it, keenly mindful that not only would flattery fill the hole in her heart, but that somewhere between the lie and the truth was the freedom to present one's own details. It was far more pleasing to settle in, gazing at Thomas and taking personally his every gesture. She enjoyed the way his tongue slipped carefully over his lips sweeping lasts bits of salt from the bread, or the manner in which he sipped her soup, spicy with garlic and freshly ground black pepper. She herself, sipped hot chamomile tea, making it last. She reached for a dollop of honey, stirred it into her cup and looked directly into his eyes. "I gave it to a young man hiking the Pacific

Crest Trail. He came down this way. He came down off the trail looking for food, or something."

"Couldn't you give him soup and a sandwich?" He wiped his mouth. "I'm canceling it. I'm not paying a dirty hippie's selfies and Youtube." He couldn't see himself supporting the bum. "I could end up paying support for acting like a father to that idiot and paying his phone bill." He leaned back in his chair and pushed his bowl away from himself.

"Life's as backward as it is foreword." She sipped her tea. "You've been here an hour and you haven't asked about your son. You drop him off and don't show up for three months, not even a phone call." Parents have a talent for squeezing in what they want heard and she did it well. She liked having her grandson in the house, bringing life into her world and giving her a reason to wake up each morning, but that day, Thomas was in the spotlight and about to receive a kick in the head for forgetting everything, but himself.

"Three months?"

"You don't know...?"

"Of course I know... I know it's been three months."

She put her finger in the tea, testing the water. "Six months... Six months, son. It's been six months." She raised her eyes brows in that way people do when they've caught someone and exposed them. Carefully, she lifted her cup to her lips, sipping the cooled water and wearing her badge with pride, delighted she'd brought light to his eyes, showing him the truth. It was her truth, her signal that she was deeply invested and watching him. She set her cup on the saucer.

He looked away, uncomfortable seeing her face and soaking up the lump of shame she was known to deliver, refusing to take it as his own. Her presence provoked him, drawing a daunting image which didn't present her pleasantly. "I'm sorry."

The apology may not have been genuine, but she could stand it up to previous lies he'd told her and make the decision to fight another day. If he was sorry about anything, it was more likely to be that she'd brought it up. "Just be here for his birthday next month. There'll be kids here." She met him eye to eye knowing her words would carry more weight if he could see into her spirit. If she could guilt him into another visit, that would work well too. "I'll put a name tag on him so you'll know which one he is..."

"Not fair."

"Life's not fair."

He rubbed his eyebrows, his forehead and picked up his utensils and dirty dishes and carried them to the sink. He held the plate under the faucet rinsing away the last hour and setting the plate aside. It was a rote process rather than purposeful following of domestic protocol, or a favor to her for the years he spent in her house as a child learning to do the right things at the right moments.

She smiled, looking out through the doting eyes of a mother ignited by the act of her child grown like a flourishing willow and bending to the domesticity she'd encouraged with endless repetition and diligence. Satisfaction wrapped itself around her and seeped into her mind implying her worth and importance. Where would he be without her love and guidance? Where would he be without her teaching and support? She knocked herself over with self pats, self appreciation and self respect though for her, it was a crutch, not a hollow congratulation meant to stroke her ego. Her ego, if she had one, was not a friend, but a tyrant disguised as an ego and ready to criticize and admonish her for seeking self esteem. She looked her son over, the shirt, shoes, hair. Everything about him were choices he'd made. She hadn't laid out his slacks on his bed, or pulled on his socks and shoes for him and tied his laces. Inside her core, he was absent. He didn't need her. She struggled to make it a blessing, but it weighed on her, a burden, pushing her forward amid a torrent of unseen steps in the opposite direction.

She sought highlights within her loss and was determined to walk with a pleasure hiding the sorrow of losing not one man, not even two, but three. Photographs of early days pressed beneath glass and settled into frames made loss easier to withstand although carefully scrutinized photo's pressed into the folds of her memory made loss a lie. In her head Thomas would always need her. "You're a great guy, but your parenting skills can use an upgrade." She carried her cup and saucer to the sink. "You even rinse off your dishes." Nothing mattered beyond a stack of rinsed dishes. There wasn't anything as important as blessing the world and soldiering on amid cleanliness. "Elizabeth's a lucky lady." She put a loving hand on his back, patted, rubbed and fell into a hug. It gave her away, all that carrying on and there she was, clinging, needing, fawning in pathetic desperation.

He kissed her cheek and thanked her for brunch. "We have help. I don't think she cares." If he meant to keep his business quiet, he was moving in the opposite direction.

She read between the lines, gathering what she needed to make her point and holding back ever so slightly, not wanting to get the best of him. To win an argument was the same as to lose it. She would hunt until she found a more concrete and sustainable platform to showcase herself. It became essential that she mattered, made sense and gained validation. He could rinse every dish on the planet. It wouldn't bring back Michael.

Thomas had his agenda, his own needs. He wasn't interested in fixing her life. It didn't matter to him whether, or not she read between lines, or had a perceptive moment and caught little things. He'd been a spotty parent. It was true, but he didn't want it pointed out, or discussed... "Elizabeth doesn't see me as an asset. She compares me to her father." He washed his hands, running warm tap water over them and drying them on a hand towel. "I don't think anyone could stand up to that scrutiny. The man could do no wrong. He was God to her."

She fell quiet and took her turn under the faucet, dripping soap into her palms, lathering up a sudsy handful and running his words through her mind. She thought of Michael, his soft voice and hardy laughter. He'd pitch in and clean the kitchen, sweep the floor, take out trash. She pictured him in his blue flannel shirt, the smell of his skin and the warmth of his breath on her face. He'd carry three year old Thomas outside to see a bee hive up in the tree behind the house, pretend to be lost and stumble upon a toy for Thomas, he'd hidden in the bushes. That's the way a father should be. That's how a father shows his love. She paused and dropped her head in shame. She'd compared Thomas to his father, just as Elizabeth compared him to her father. She wiped her hands as carefully as she washed them. "Thomas, you're a good man. Don't let her tell you differently." She threw the towel on the counter. "Elizabeth hasn't been here to see her son, ever. What kind of mother doesn't want to see her own flesh and blood?"

"She can be fun."

"She can be, but she isn't..."

He stood in the kitchen, a solemn expression covered his thoughts. She understood the silence as nothing more than silence. To sort the intangible she'd have to rattle her brain and take on a pounding headache she'd bear for days. She was not prepared to do that though it seemed worthy to guard her health with a guise and remind herself Thomas was an adult and could solve his own problems. He didn't need a mother. He needed a new way of looking at his life. She stumbled, intent on presenting evidence to support whatever she could come up with on the spur of the moment. She came up with nothing except that he was married and an attorney. He knew what needed to be done. She had to stop acting as though he was a child, something she knew was beyond her ability to see through to completion. Her greatest gift was an ability to bring others a superficial happiness, moving along and allowing it to set in and affect their mood while she scrambled to escape. She was minutes away from strutting on stage and playing out that well meaning scene. She'd bring in a measure of happiness, lift her voice and suck in the applause, cut the house lights and the show was over. She could make a meal and warm the belly, but she didn't cater to the inner spirit. That was not her expertise. She fidgeted, smoothing the pockets of her apron, adjusting the strap and patting down the hem, wanting to say something, but drawing a blank.

He waited impatiently shifting his weight from one leg to the other, checking his watch and rolling his eyes in need of acknowledgment, or at least some kind of indication that he'd been heard. She could read him about as easily as she could understand Latin, which beyond an ancient Catholic mass was virtually not at all. He was hanging on a limb and she had nothing to offer him. He shrugged, went for the door and didn't look back. The last thing he wanted was to be invited to stay on... He slipped his shoes on his feet, bent down and tied them and made his announcement, "I'm taking a walk." The door slammed. It was the end of the conversation.

Chapter 5

He held his place outside the door like a rooster managing the coop. The last few years the extent of his walks had been confined to a stroll from one law office to another and a brisk strut to the courthouse, briefcase in hand and tethered to the conventional life he'd chosen, but in the small community away from his city maze, he wasn't sure where to start in the dense wooded area. An endless sense of freedom seemed a prison of another variety. He knew South Brook, at least at one time, but at that moment with sun high in the sky and dark clouds looming, he looked out over the wilderness filled with a sense of apprehension he mistook for confidence. In the unembellished town of his childhood he was an outsider, one often looked upon with a discriminating eye and a better grip on the shotgun. He turned around, opened the door just enough to fit his head through the opening and without seeing her standing by the sink, quietly made his apology, a simple act of contrition punctuated by quietly closing the door.

Thomas walked to his car, took his sunglasses from the dash, slipped off his wristwatch and put it in the glove compartment. He felt the nippy air, rubbed his arms and grabbed a light jacket, exchanging it with the suit jacket he laid across the back seat. He looked down at his dress shoes and made a snap decision to trek as attired. It was no big deal. He'd hiked Companion trail hundreds of times. He took sight of his surroundings, stepped across the street, barely checked for traffic and took off like a expert tramping through tall lissom reeds up to the trail. Over his shoulder he could see the house, his mother in the light of the kitchen window and above her head, from the chimney, a cloud of smoke reminding him of captions in a comic book.

He'd turned in his hiking boots for a fancy pair of cap toes, a simple act, innocent and benign, but responsible for inserting a wedge between himself and locals. South Brook, once the only life he knew, seemed foreign. Even with the sun's bright and cheery face pouring a yellow glow over leaves, rocks and rich soil, he couldn't call it home. He didn't feel the comfort and warmth of familiar trees and streams. He saw himself as an outlander looked upon with reservation and distrust. He could no longer glance at the sky assessing the weather with ease, or remember clouds and their meanings. The forest, once his inspiration, was a stranger. He looked up at the white fluffy cumulus floating by and was drawn to the one dark cloud with the menacing stare. He was that one, the heavy, deadly cloud, but he was prepared to change and the hike was to be his reclamation getting him somewhere he couldn't get to in the city.

He followed the path a mile south toward the trailhead remembering the miles he once put there, the ground beneath his steps and the feel of the land. "I can do this standing on my head." It may have turned out better if he had done it standing on his head, but his mumblings were part of his habit of talking himself through situations and carrying that successful partnership of over confidence and inflated ego. He sorted his thoughts believing he was the best man. He was always the best man.

He huffed along the trail, his head filled with himself and thoughts of things he used to do and hikes he'd completed projecting a high degree of proficiency. The sun brightened his path with soft rays on otherwise shady clumps of brush and strong healthy streams of blinding sun light turning green leaves white with its touch. He'd forgotten his anger and felt his stomach relax. He held his head high looking left to right discovering tiny ponds and grassy meadows. Life could be good in the country. Sacrifices were evident, but paled in comparison to the refreshing taste of the wild. He was a man, a wanderer, a mountaineer, a frontiersman. He considered growing a beard, not a city man's beard, but a real beard, a thick woven blanket bundle of kinky hair hiding everything but his eyes and nose. The type of beard with classic strength telling everyone he's a man before they think to test him. He might exchange his law degree for fur trading and wear a beaver hat. He pondered half-heartedly through the eyes of a man jaded by life. Any change would've sounded good to him from the place he'd landed, and something in the fresh air had him believing the life he wanted wasn't behind the locked door of his gated manor, but out where he'd left it, in nature although it was still too early to see a way to return.

It was about walking back in time and finding things exactly as they were, yet when he glanced about finding the past pristinely preserved, he snubbed his nose at the lack of progress, picturing trees dropped from vertical to horizontal, making room for strip malls and theaters. That's where advancement made its mark. He felt pumped and selfish, a good satisfying comfort only matched by a full stomach though just as rapidly as he rested his head on the dollar, he was disheartened discovering those things that had changed over time. He felt the trailhead as a bitter sweet moment endlessly shifting from something he desired and something he'd regret. He was slowly discovering that nothing could please him and rattled off his complaints under his breath while the sting of his heels made him whine like a over tired toddler. He alternated beneath the two, finding annoyance in his surroundings and rethinking the reckless beard and fur hat. Choosing someone to take the blame for the blisters on his heels was a chore greater than the idea of finding a place to rest on fallen timber. Blisters, once a badge of honor, a battle scar, on that day, were nothing but pain. Eventually he became weary with his nattering and sat on a log bench. He reached down and pulled off his shoes and socks, shaking his head and wincing with what he thought was the forest's aggressive welcome, the stinging red bubbly blisters on his pampered feet. He looked up and as if speaking to the statuesque pines, divulged his sarcasm. "Thanks for this." It was easier to condemn nature than to readjust his definition of self, but life is filled with easier roads and those that handpick them, something millions of others do by default. His truth was that there was nothing he could've done to avoid the forest's wrath and it was fitting that he leave though he wasn't prepared to return to his mother's criticism. He'd shine on comfort and coddled feet, buck up and have another go at the trail. After all, he was a mountain man.

He got to his feet, surveyed his environment and made note of the weather, relying on his archived skills and mental tools in need of polish. He didn't have the ten essentials, but he had arrogance boosted by years of indulgence. Those supplies seemed more than adequate to propel him on an adventure he wasn't likely to forget. He had experience, recent experience living a life where others were willing to pander to him elevating him to a standing higher than he deserved and exactly what he desired. On the trail, he felt that sense of importance. He meant to succeed and he would... He held himself in high esteem, but even so, in measly increments. He ushered in knowledge from his past and recalled important hiking tips and the wisdom of others. He zipped his jacket, stuffed his socks into his shoes and carried them down the path making excuses for his lack of fundamentals. The forest was forgiven for the burning blisters and he hoped it would reciprocate by letting him slide on being unprepared and out of condition.

The trail started on flat terrain, a cunning approach to seduce the novice. Birds perched on tree branches, their sweet voices a beguiling come hither presenting wilderness as an everyday simplification, something as natural as a sidewalk stroll. There was no need for supplies and forethought. It would've been wise to carry a first aid kit, water, layers, flashlight, compass, map, knife, matches, extra food; all items he once thought essential though that day in his bemused state he resented the meticulous planners. He had no use for cumbersome packs loaded with extra water, rain gear, tarps and tape. He was a man, a man's man. He had his bare hands and muscle. He didn't need anyone, or anything.

He could hold himself upright and subsidize his undirected thoughts while he factored in the few times extras were needed on an adventure. The new improved Thomas was inclined to salute the spontaneous, the rebels and trail blazers out in the wilderness with only the clothes on their backs. He no longer identified with storming trails saddled with conscientiously packed bags and provisions enough to last weeks. He had two tenths of the ten point list. He had sunglasses and a light jacket. He didn't have shoes on his feet, but what he did have was determination and anger. The anger moved him forward and convinced him he had no need for concern about the things he lacked. He was on an adventure and adventures were always a cure for bored mind and tired heart.

He walked as fast as his irritability would push him and then faster, having flashed back to his mother's insinuation of his incompetence. Thoughts of her criticism quickened his pace. Annoyance rooted him on, a most unlikely training essential, but a worthy tool to move him closer to his goal. He stomped up the trail all the while living in his head unaffected by sun beams across the forest trees, plants, grasses, the hush of nature amid scattered animal chittering and deliberate screeches. The chaos of birds, insects, small animals and the color of the sky topped the list of things he didn't give a damn about. He kept his mind on personal snags and judgements, the things that really mattered... His held his head down, eyes on the soil. If he'd gone out to rid himself of his troubles and rekindle his relationship with nature, it had skipped his mind, or was shoved under a pile of grievances. He didn't notice the narrowing path, or plants that grew thicker and unrestricted with healthy branches unwinding across the trail. The bulkiness of plant growth made it impossible to walk without bending under boughs, or bulldozing through them. The sky was gray and bird sightings less frequent. He felt the distance from the house. It filled him with a sense of being alone, a sensation he thought of as a good thing. Abruptly, he stopped and held himself motionless, except for his eyes rocking like a pendulum. He maintained his place in the center of the trail.

Ahead, a black-tailed deer foraged on grasses and forbs. He set his shoes on a rock and kept his distance from the animal, watching the deer with a sense of admiration and respect, but with a rumble of annoyance. The deer invaded his space. He crossed his arms and hardened his face. He was the alpha, a mountain man. A ripple of invincibility flowed through his biceps and pride pumped through his veins. He was at the top of the food chain. The nonchalance the deer showed him, insulted him, forcing him to imagine himself as a hunter slinging a rifle over his shoulder, wriggling across the ground and hiding behind trees. He'd let the deer know who was master. He pressed his fleshy feet into the dirt, spreading his legs into a confrontational stance and wore an expression like a steel gun locker. There was nothing to take him down, not a ignorant animal, or other form of life.

While he advanced in his dreams, the deer turned and eyed him. The narrow shape of its head, large ears standing at attention and deep brown eyes, seemingly carelessly set off to the sides, shot back at Thomas, defining an animal who was alert, but unafraid. A delicate blossom dangled from its mouth. Dinner had been served and the deer returned to his meal. Thomas felt the sins of those before him, ones he hadn't known, but were forever attached to the passage of time. He averted his eyes, dancing through his discomfort by finding his pockets and resting his hands there. He shrugged as though giving up on himself, but came back to his core, addressing the deer who had already lost interest. "Who wins?" He was almost waiting for a reply though supplied his own, "Does it matter?" He thought for a moment with a superficial quality and taking his hands from his pockets. "It matters." He sat on a rock, checked his feet and rested his legs. When he looked up, the deer was gone. "Ha, I win." He felt the pleasure, the satisfaction of sucking in the knowledge that once again, he was the best. He was always the finest life had to offer, and no one dared to say no to him. With that neatly tucked into his mind, he looked around finding the trail an obstacle course of overgrown roots and jagged rocks partially buried in dirt. He lifted himself to his sore feet and continued, distracted by aches he would remember months after his journey, but still drowning in self absorption.

He moved up the elevation with the aid of a gust of wind at his back and intermittently whispering in his ears, reaching out to him with its icy touch chilling his face. He'd get up the hill, turn around and make his retreat. That was his plan. The walk to the top would be a cinch. A child could do it. Companion Trail was popular. Everyone walked it, but he was faster, more agile, a better athlete. He once flew up the trail so rapidly, he'd returned to the trailhead before fellow hikers reached the top. Showing off lit a fire in his heart and under his feet. Competition kept him alive. He would get there, sit on the boulder, put his hands together in approval and declare his victory. That was really all he needed to put the day behind him. He made another quick scan of his surroundings. A long cool breath of air trickled into his lungs. He started up the incline aware of the extra inches around his middle and the heaviness of his thighs. The hike wasn't as easy as he remembered, but he edged upward with a pledge to get there and celebrate. He demanded confidence in himself and forced his upper legs to pull him along mustering what he needed by the push of his self worth, which for him, doubled as physical strength. He drove himself, cursing constricted balls of muscles, the lumps like oversized marbles burning in his shoulders. A sting radiated through his calves reminding him to tag his thighs with the burden of tugging him toward his goal. He bent forward ignoring what he knew, or knowing he couldn't get into proper form. The pudge around his middle declared a war with his ambition and extra servings, late night dining and double shots of whiskey weren't on his side, but to see that rock, to find his name and Be Be's... Love does crazy things.

At the top, he searched for the boulder, an oversized, gray rock among many on the rock strewn path, but the one he recalled was far enough from the fold to stand out. He gazed down the path and wondered if he'd missed it, or hadn't walked far enough... He took minutes to think things through and guessed the time it took him to get where he stood. He'd come too far to go back without the prize. Win at all costs. That's all he knew. He breathed easily eying a flat and less demanding area of the trail, making the move to forge ahead a secure choice. He noticed the terrain change although the rise in elevation went unseen given the increase was discreet and deceiving, convincing him it commanded little effort and granting him a relatively relaxing search for the boulder and disregard for the subtle incline. It was he against the boulder, a contest. Nothing else was on his mind.

The trek was common, pleasant, uneventful and a triumphant journey for a city man. He held his head like a camel making its trek over desert dunes. His sense of accomplishment inflated his chest and gave a muscle man lift to the manner in which he carried his arms, as though his biceps led the way. His walk carried on as if it would drag him up the elevations whether he participated, or sat beneath a tree and with that in mind he'd agreed to cooperate, becoming attentive to areas along the path and reactively anxious as they turned to snow fields and talus slopes. Small clumps of short, deep green fir trees and mountain hemlock made an appearance, insisting he recall knowledge stockpiled from his early years, if only he could retrieve it. Mental files regarding education on survival in the wilderness were no longer available, though bits and pieces of information on forest resources came out now and then, certainly when he took on the mountain trees with his lengthly gaze and irrelevance. Dwarfed high mountain trees were old, merely appearing young due to short growing seasons and dramatic freezing temperatures. The facts popped out at him, hitting him somewhere between acceptance and contempt. He was neither an ecologist, nor a tree hugger, but he was out of his comfort zone, and little tips made him less uncomfortable. He hiked around small snow fields and had come to enjoy the solitude, but the freeze reached out feeling about his face as a student of Braille might find his place on the features of another. He zipped his jacket as high as it would go, nearly catching the skin of his neck in the metal teeth and shivering, as a slap back to the light coat, too flimsy to add warmth. He wasn't taking the blame. The coat was inadequate, simply not up to his standards. His agitation in the cold had nothing to do with the fact that he hadn't brought along a heavier jacket.

He tugged at his thin covering, pulling it around himself though it didn't do much more than engage his anger and send him chasing after someone on which to place blame. If his mother hadn't pushed him out the door, there would've been time to grab a warmer jacket. He thought of her, curling his lips toward the earth and fostering hard lines around his mouth. He despised her for the control she held over him. He kicked at the dirt and noticed he was still carrying his shoes. He criticized himself for a sorry moment, catching himself and spinning it back to her. His failures were hers. Sandy wouldn't stay with her if she didn't encourage it. He wouldn't have forgotten to visit Sandy, if Sandy wasn't at her house. Everything reverted toward something she had done, or hadn't done. He spit in the dirt, a sour taste distorting his face. Repugnance gripped him between his eyes showing him his shoes were the problem. He'd endlessly carried them on his journey when a preferable strategy might've been to set them beside the trail, reclaiming them later. He could've done a lot of things, but he didn't... He dropped his head facing what was left of his feet, the blocks of ice, thick caveman substructures he depended upon to plod along the path. If he'd made errors, there were few...

He'd missed the boulder. That was the most obvious problem and by then he'd determined he'd walked by it without noticing. He groaned, sweated and ripped open the forest air with an abundance of profanity though it didn't detain him. He rode a nature high, an affliction bestowed upon determined wilderness wanderers who made it through the struggle to get what they wanted, the reward. His brain was soaked in an over load of pleasure. He was bewitched and fierce, a warrior. The open land and fresh wind blown in from the west seduced him, blinding him to the score of unpredictable events common on ill planned trips when high winds make their presence. He was jacked on his mountain man abilities and relying on a tiny window of reality through which to recognize the reality of his situation. It was time to turn around.

He walked quickly, covering land like an expert, and

believing he was ready for anything, chest high and chin up. The down hill grade spurred him even as his priority was the boulder. It wasn't too much to ask to have a seat on the boulder and to enter the past. In fact, he was already there. The ache in his heart matched his younger self those years ago. Be Be was back on his arm, her long legs taking steps he could never quite equal. He never felt worthy of her charm. Maybe that's why he strayed, or maybe he made the errors he'd made because he could... Farther down the trail he'd come back to the area where he thought the boulder could be, but instead of the old rock, he spotted a black bear with two cubs. He watched as they moved slowly across a heather filled grassy meadow and walked lazily as though time was meaningless. Time was meaningless, and so was his life if the bears came closer. He changed his mind about marking his territory. If the bears wanted to put their names high on a tree and call it home, he'd send them a housewarming gift. No grudges.

Finally, the boulder. It was near the trail where he'd left it that summer. To maneuver into the past and have it cloak him as though his present life was nonexistent seemed a blessing. He could play house inside his mind and pretend the mistakes he'd made were inconsequential. To see the boulder with his own eyes amped his steps and forced him to believe in fairy tales. His toes were cold and his hands felt thick in the lowered temperatures, but he let go of his moanful cadence. He'd come home. Be Be's pretty face was on his mind and in his heart while he stared at the rock and directed a rush of memories through his head. He was in the middle of living the life he could've had, someone else's life... It could have been his, but missteps took what he was given, attaching it to a permanent, younger version

Arley M. Fosburgh

of himself. He had to return and take what was his and as he stood appreciating his memories, the white fluff of cloud, having been with him most of the way, was gone. He didn't notice the infiltration of low hung dark clouds, or the doom which drifted over the horizon. He was busy swooning although once he caught drift of the dark clouds, he silenced his meanderings, walked with eyes upward and scrutinized, sized and judged their heaviness. It should've meant something to him. Fast, angry clouds having come closer and moving into his space should've rung some type of bell, but he passed it off as a minor weather change, a bungle that would cost him more than a few rain drops on his head.

While it's apparent he had no interest in the appearance of the sky, he ought to have given credence to the earth below his feet. He might've considered that the dirt, that solid landing for his clammy feet was as important as the sky's attitude. Had he paid attention, one faulty placement of his foot wouldn't have caused him to trip and fall to the ground. He glanced around, seeking out the culprit and anyone, or anything to tag for blame, but the tree root extending over the trail showed no guilt and the jagged rock edge jutting from the dirt glared back at him. He slammed his fist into the earth and tightened his jaw. Plants and trees ignored him. The damage had been done. He'd been taken down by nature. Nature had reclaimed its territory. He felt the tear of his flesh and gush of warm blood under the crunchy double snap of his ankle bone. He rolled onto his back and cursed the fools who cut the trail. The sting and agony gave him no moments to ease into the situation and he immediately faced full impact psychologically, physically and topping his list, economically. He had court on Monday and he was reduced to a hobble. He'd get numbers for every trail maintenance team member and let them know who he was... They'd hear from him.

He crawled to the boulder, seated himself, caught his breath and examined the ruins. Scratches, lacerations, bruises and a bloody instep that opened in a sawtooth fashion about five inches long and a sizable width. A flap of skin hung over one end like a trap door. He closed his eyes, rationalized the pain, the hours and the foolish sense of doing things his own way. He groaned, sighed and set his fist to his lips, tapping there and blowing air into his hand. If his mother hadn't antagonized and criticized him... The pain pierced his pride sending him into default mode, the blame game. He condemned and crumbled and thought of Be Be. Love would hold him. Someone said love could change everything. He opposed the theory, but was out of options.

With haunting bygone passion hanging by a neuron, he set his suffering aside, moved closer and examined the boulder for the graffiti he remembered. A dirty white tee shirt hung on a tree branch above a healthy lay of moss on the side of the rock. He looked down at the empty cola can and candy wrappers. Be Be played in his head, "Don't pack it in if you can't pack it out." He distrusted himself for replaying her words, shook his head and left the shirt where it hung. He reached below the upper edge of the rock, pleased by the silky feel of the paint. Intrigued, he moved closer to see with his own eyes. In blue paint, the names, Be Be and Tomahawk were clearly spelled out with a tiny red heart under each name. It touched him in a manner he hadn't expected, or appreciated. Tears were not his standard. He could do better. For a few brief moments he forgot his injury and in that instant of freedom he breathed in the truth. He

Arley M. Fosburgh

held the prize. The climb, injury, cold weather... All of it was worth the time. He smiled, nodded and ran his tongue over his lower lip. He'd walked into the past, pictured her face, her long blonde locks hanging in her eyes and the way she held the paint brush more like a pencil. He'd never been more alive than when she was focused, eyes dilated and peaceful inner being radiating like a night light. She acted as his beacon and he couldn't live without her. He found her in his memory, painting their names, her face up close to the boulder in a girl without her glasses posturing.

His memories were burning through him igniting occurrences he'd forgotten, his hand wrapped around hers, the two of them melting together in secret plans and lover's vows, sitting in the last of daylight and gazing at Mount Rainier in the distance. The paint lay thick as it was the moment it was smoothed over the rock slope, it's longevity, a testimonial to what his relationship could've been, should've been. He'd made choices that came undone and heart-cross promises he couldn't keep. He rubbed his fingers over the dry paint, gliding them across the smoothness of an ancient encapsulated summer day where emotions ran high and pining lingered in the woodsy breeze. Thomas effortlessly brought the past to his senses inviting freshness to his weary mind.

Yellow arnicas with sweet petaled flowers upon tall stems protectively grew around the boulder marking its place alongside the trail, same as years ago. He imagined Be Be cross-legged in the dirt, head back, blonde hair falling behind her shoulders, exposing a smile and defrosting his heart. Her thin arms, pale and outstretched with dainty hands carefully near the flowers and fingers pinching off arnica blossoms she held to her face, breathing the scent and showing off tiny freckles bunching together on her nose. She'd wink and pat the ground beside her pulling his arm and leading him down on the earth beside her. "Arnica helps us." She'd put a flower in her hair and another in his hand. "Arnica shares its parts and life fluids." There he was years later sitting in that same spot on the exact lump of soil wondering if it had been as good as it gets, or were the two of them merely cloaked in an amorous, unaffected, nonjudgemental environment. Young love is an indestructible shield.

That evening as Thomas examined the flowers, he was in his head looking over old friends he hadn't seen for a while, observing changes in himself, nature and signs of age, concluding everyone was making their way and that what we refuse to nurture, dies. Maybe people were worth the time. Rebecca was the voice in his head. "Use arnica for sprains, bruising and trauma." He laughed, considering the agony of his baseball sized ankle and sick pain of his bright red bloody foot. Where was she now? Where was her arnica poultice and her kiss on his lips? Inconvenience always tossed him off balance.

It was Be Be, always Be Be... He thought of her, the eleven year old, a month his junior using yarrow leaves whenever his big feet lost sight of their purpose and sent him crashing to the ground. She'd turn her head to the side endlessly charming him and turning his heart to mush. His abrasions, scrapes and sprains were hers to practice upon, providing herbal remedies and singing her quiet songs, gently bandaging and whispering encouragement. He willed himself to fall from trees and tangle with blackberry thorns just to see her shake her head in her customary style, scolding and declaring disbelief in his clumsiness. "Are you blind? Can't you watch where you walk?"

He'd been accustomed to herbal compresses and field medicine, whether far from a well stocked home medicine cabinet, or at her house where traditional astringents, antiseptics and bandaids were abundant. He missed her touch, politeness, and coziness of knowing he was loved. He swooned and his memories didn't disappoint him. Nothing was as alive as his feelings and all of them were mind soothing, but far from support for his ankle, or a pressure bandage for his wound. He tried to walk, but couldn't... He remembered the shirt and pulled it from the tree branch, ripped it into strips, held his shoes bottom side toward him, on either side of his ankle area and tied the shirt strips around the shoes and around his ankle, tying each strip in a knot up and down his shin, stopping inches below his ankle. He winced and held his breath. His teeth were clenched and eyes tightly closed with each change in position. He glanced around for sweet yarrow, assuming he wouldn't recognize it, even if his life depended on it, but hoping for success just the same. The more he searched, the more every plant, shrub and tree took on the appearance of the neighboring plant, laughing and pointing out his incompetence. He found no differences between the multitude of species abundant and in proximity with their leaves proudly blended one to another. He was an outsider without a source of negotiation in the forest. He couldn't discern an Alaska yellow cedar from an Engleman spruce. The best he could do was take out his wallet.

His hands shook and his head played tricks on him telling him he was fine and giving him the go-ahead to proceed on a leg that was now, not much more than a costume store appendage. He had reason to distrust himself and the thoughts in his mind pushing him to find variation and significance in leaf shape and color, then it dawned on him, it wasn't coming. He would never find a plant that would save him. His brows pushed downward. He drew in his lips and tightened his neck muscles. How could a plant save him? Why would it want to...? It was impossible to distinguish one plant species from the next. What he once knew, he'd forgotten, and with that he settled on broad leaves from a tree near where he sat, pulling rain drenched leaves from its branches and thinking of Be Be. Herbs were crap. He needed morphine, but still, he thanked the leaves for their gift cursing Rebecca for insisting he thank nature, a ritual he didn't realize he'd internalized, and in his state of mind, it seemed all the more ludicrous.

With the weight of his injuries and complications of a past he couldn't retrieve, or ignore, he cut dangerously close to tearing out his memories with a blunt stick. To hell with thanking a stupid plant. He sat on the rock arranging leaves over his injured foot and pressing firmly despite his discomfort. He held the cold leaves in place while removing his rolled up socks from his shoes, stretching one of them up and over the leaves and poking at the area to decide whether the padding was sufficient. He pulled the second sock over the first, trying to get the top band up and under the ties of the splint, removed the shoe splint and started over. He'd given up more times than he'd admit and only moved forward because there was no road back. When he'd finished, he sat in the innocuous space between a completed task and the next on his list. He hung his head, swallowed and willed every muscle in his body to comply, to relax and give him a chance to believe in something. His mouth was dry, making the simple act of swallowing a chore. "God, if those leaves are poisonous..." He ran his sweaty hand over his forehead sinking into a rumble between anxiety and reason and hoping he hadn't chosen leaves that would end his life. "Wouldn't that be the ultimate slap?"

He got to his feet placing weight on his injury with a cautious bent, stepping slowly, earnestly testing the splint and clump of leaves stuck to the sticky blood of his wound. He grimaced, putting few ounces of weight on his broken bone and gearing up for what was coming, the full weight of a grown man. He shuddered, uncontrollably shaking and guarding his movements though carrying on folding his arms and wrapping his jacket snuggly around himself. He limped the path, keeping his cursing low and eyes peeled for a walking stick. He meant to distract himself by taking in the scent of pine, smell of rain and the magic of wildness, but olfactory overload stopped him and he no longer believed in magic. His dreams of cleaning his slate, being creative, and living mindfully were dead ended. They were lofty goals and a hard focus while immersed in physical torture. He was running on adrenalin and a significant desire to change his place in the world, but that dream was fading in exchange for the brutal reality of his situation. Still convinced he could do anything, he decided there was time to qualify himself. Dark would not fall for a few hours.

The sky became dreary, the forest, quiet. Birds stopped singing. A soft drip of water innocently landed on green leaves, beginning sheepishly like indistinct dots of water bouncing from above. He raised his chin and looked up at the sky and holding out his hand, feeling for rain drops he couldn't see, while nature with its gutsy sense of humor and a taste for an unexpected entrance, brilliantly ruptured the gray clouds above his head, sending a powerful torrent of rain water released from the heavens, drenching his hair and pooling in his ears. He twisted the fabric of his jacket wringing out rain water and bent down to empty water from his shoes. He removed his dripping glasses, set them into his pocket and rubbed rain drops from his eyes. There was no escape. Sheets of water drenched his clothes adhering them to his skin. Thunder screamed at him with a voice so deep and strong, it vibrated in his chest and pounded in his head. No one heard the sounds of his resistance.

The socks he so cleverly placed upon his foot were submerged in mud making their navy blue coloring impossible to discern. His ankle had enlarged and pushed against his shoes in a most cruel manner pressing grooves into his foot. The leaves were bunched, reared up against his injury like thorns. The cold wet leaves confused his senses throwing contradictory messages to his brain. He felt the blatant cold leaves leaning on the burning fire of torn flesh as though vultures were feeding there, cold teeth against red hot dripping blood. He massaged his forehead, moved his hand over his chin and considered wringing out his eyebrows, the wet useless guards allowing trickles of rain water to run into his eyes.

He thought of waiting out the downpour, standing under a tree, or sitting under the brambles, but haste moved him forward. He listened to the quiet, the absence of forest life. No sweet chirps of dark-eyed juncos, squeaky toy calls of steller's jays and others taking shelter, methodically loitering until clouds rained themselves dry. Squirrels ceased chasing each other up trees and across evergreen boughs. He was alone, placing one sore foot in front of the other on the sopping forest floor. Beneath his feet, the earth was alive with streams of rain water stretched out on dirt that smelled like rain. He could taste the smell of pine, but none of it mattered.

He moved unsteadily looking down at pine needles floating on rivers of rain riding the grade and mixing with dead leaves, web like mosses, clingy lichen, bark and branches, each an important piece of the forest carpet, a nutrient heavy cog in the ecosystem wheel. He remembered things he'd forgotten he'd known, little things as he walked, the purpose of leaves hastening to the ground, plant adaptations, fall colors, and climate. He was rediscovering nature, deaths and rebirths, the evolutionary dynamic and method of natural selection though it didn't inspire, or amuse him. It brought something more like anger and loathing. None of it made sense to him while his leg was deconstructed by the vary things which may have brought his musing. He thought of Bourbon and salty peanuts. Now there was a remedy... His life had taken a turn for the worst though bringing him most irritation was that Rebecca would have done it better. To her and her mangy group, his wicked forest trip would be just another adventure, and his stumble would certainly foster a laugh and a great camp fire story.

... But there it was and he had to get through it, meeting plants face to face, advancing on his bottom over dirt where the useless lived rooted to soil, not unlike himself, but still, it was not what he wanted... His ankle throbbed and stabs of pain demanded he hold his tongue rather than let loose in agony that might warrant the attention of nocturnal meat seekers. Still, he cringed with each movement as he began searching the sides of the trail for a suitable stick, carefully examining the undergrowth. He wrinkled his brow and flattened his lips, spotting a thick branch parked in the underbrush. He pulled his sleeve down over his hand

and braved the brambles, reaching into the area as though reluctantly sticking his hand into a grab bag. Blackberry thorns on long branches stuck into the sleeves of his jacket, pulling him like a marionette. He yanked the stick, slipped and fell backward landing on the seat of his pants. "Nothing is easy in nature, nothing." Nothing was easy anywhere, but the forest had a habit of showing those who dared to enter, a life size reflection of their inadequacies.

He sat on a pad of vegetation and despised his misfortune. He tried to break free from the hellish pit of self pity, trying again with the stick and easing it out with sweet words and perseverance and finally breaking off small outshoots. He wrapped his hand around an end and pressed the other into the soil, leaning into it, testing and retesting, eventually trusting it enough to make his way down the trail, but ultimately losing confidence and giving into the pain in his ankle. He scooted on his bottom creating a groove in the dirt and in his mind. It was easier to sink to the level of dirt than to white knuckle what he believed he'd lost. He knew the hours moved forward faster than he, and understood that if he could reach the trailhead, home was around the corner, but he'd been saying that for hours. He kept moving.

He felt the wind against his eyes, the sting, the push, sending a shiver into his limbs. He thought of the shirt at the boulder and the way he sat on his pedestal and chastised the world. He fell back into his dreams, remembering Be Be, her casual walk and strolling with her to church each Sunday morning. He laughed quietly, recalling her filling the pockets of her silky pink dress, with seeds for the ducks in the pond along the way. He was her date in his slacks and tie, his body stretched as tall as he could muster, becoming every bit the mature young man at only fourteen.

Life was difficult in the forest, but love was simple, real, precious and unveiled by tender hearts with open spaces unencumbered by gloss. That forest, those years ago, although the same patch of land, was drastically different from where he occupied the current moment. He saw the harsh environment he'd attracted to himself and as he discovered the errors he'd made and the impact they wedged into his daily life, he wanted what he had long ago, what he wasted... He was prepared to make wagers, give to charities, buy meals for the misfortunate, attend church and call his son. "Just get me out of here." His voice, low, serious, but more an order than a plea. He'd buy back the past.

The hours wiled away, unswayed by his need, or driven state of mind. The sun peeked from behind gloomy clouds as though never having been away, never having abandoned him, much like an inebriated man sneaking into the house, his wife asleep with one eye open, hearing his key in the lock. Thomas was saturated, cold and angry at the hour, the drop in temperature and things he hadn't gotten right. He lifted his leg high, locked at the knee to empty water from his splint shoes. He looked up at the sun and over toward the picnic tables. He was back at the trailhead without a hint to how he arrived there. His mind was as unsteady as his knees and the oncoming darkness made his perception insubstantial. It made no difference how he arrived, he was there.

He made his way to the bench, propped his foot with his jacket under his knee and leaned on his elbows. He could see the muddy mess of an appendage and felt ire rise inside his head and bequeath his eyes with a menacing glare. He laid down on the bench, his head against the hard surface, placed his hands on his chest and stared at wooden beams supporting the shelter while his mind moved in and out of consciousness, and exhaustion floated from his body. He was drifting, imagining white scorching sand near a seabird riding gentle ocean waves. His muscles were passive and his breathing slowed... He closed his eyes. Seafoul flew overhead and the slap of palm trees gave him the percussion he welcomed placing him into a soft slumber amid drifty thoughts dancing in the breeze. Trail time lunged forward without him. Lightly, like a tinkling, then a strong unearthly pounding, rain hit the shelter's roof. He sat up, pushed back his wet hair and got a feel for his prospects. The rain was harsh and unrelenting. It gathered speed and spread chaos. Thunder blasts shook the roof and lightening cracked open the sky. He watched, waited, stopped, thought and listened to the beat of his heart and the sound of his breathing, mesmerized by the rise and fall of his chest. Like a watched pot, the rain never gave him what he wanted... It didn't slow. It didn't stop. It haunted and provoked him there in the night sky. In an instant, it altered its course and brought a hard wall of rain sideways with the force of a monster. He could've wrung his clothes out in a bucket and taken a bath in it. He moved his arms like a drowning man, warding off the inevitable and once soaked and broken, he conceded, but under his breath, he told himself it was a battle, not the war. He would win the war.

"I always win." Nature was a master of manipulation, he agreed, but he was grand, more experienced and able to force the final blow. The outdoors exploited his vulnerability, broke his confidence and when he'd regained his self-esteem, it swept in and revamped its course though he would not give it the pleasure of a drop to his knees. If nature was indeed a manipulator, rain was its lackey and even after his spectacular and pompous statements, he was moving to a place washouts often mingle, a state of self pity. He placed his head in his hands and gave in to a dangerous low that could promise nothing but failure.

The heavy weight of the water pushed him back and slapped his eyes with an icy cold shock. He turned his head side to side, and his torso twisted. He shook off the shower and grumbled, spilling unpleasantness out into the night. He lifted his mangled foot, his hands on either side like a crane lifting a stack of lumber. He was soaked through his layers, clumsy, lightheaded, unsure, but steady as he got to his feet and blood rushed into his limbs and throbbed in his ankle.

He caught his breath, hand on his chest, and patted out the shakiness. His stomach lurched bringing vomit and disgust, his mouth sick with thick sticky saliva and dreadfully sour green bile. He glanced over at the dry picnic tables in the center of the shelter, thinking he could reach them, but sat himself back down into an unyielding frenzy of wind. He'd lost his walking stick. There he sat, forced to listen to the superiority of nature and trapped by the downpour. He was numb, with no plan, but the white flag remained in his pocket.

He waited in the rain, replaced his lost stick and trudged forward. His eyes darted and his heart jumped, startled by a rustling in the grass, shadows and infinite darkness. He conjured campfire stories of headless ghosts, gruesome woodland murders, the deranged, and blood stained axes. His eyes became wide, he could hear like a dog and he could smell his own fear while acute paranoia pitched in doing its part to make his journey that much more unnerving. He imagined, lied to himself, pleaded, gave up, restarted and shut down. Under the moonlight, sounds were eerie. Every twig snapped under the weight of the unknown, each screech and petrifying animal howl tweaked his senses, hastened his breath and made it difficult to think with sharpness and reason.

He shivered, his teeth clattered and he rapidly ran his tongue over his chapped lips, looking down at his bright red blood soaked socks. His mouth was dry and his teeth were filmy. He could smell his putrid breath as he felt stress release from his body. His head dropped, arms lost tension, shoulders no longer held him, abdomen relaxed, hands unclenched, his head began to spin and his knees buckled turning trees fuzzy and moving in sync with his breathing, just before he lost balance and giving in to a fall delivering him face down, sprawled in cold dirt.

He came to and grabbed his head to control the suffering. He had no phone, no flashlight and no ability to walk on his own. It was dark, cold, windy, wet and his destination was a least a mile away. He mumbled, "Failing to plan, is planing to fail". There was no one to blame. It was his and he owned it, right there where he was, off to the side of the trail sitting in mud. He moved his hips to get situated and wiggled his buttocks though they were numbed to the bone and difficult to feel. Chilled mud splashed out from beneath him, pushing up around his thighs. He shook uncontrollably, pulled in his arms and clasped his hands at his chest. He thought of Elizabeth, Sandy and his mother. He could fix his marriage. It just needed a little work. He'd make an effort to understand his son. He'd buy another phone for his mother. He thought of Be Be and wondered if she was thinking of him. He swallowed the lump in his throat, sucked in his lips and his chin slowly dropped to his chest. "Give me another chance. I'll make things right." He shook his head with self loathing and a longing for his freedom, but instead smelled the stench of failure, an odor he often caught a whiff of from across the room in the court room when he had won another case. In a moment of desperation he came to the conclusion that to take back his life meant being compelled to honesty and bonded to a pledge of candor regardless of the cost. He might've been able to pull it off if he'd fully grasped the degree of personal work attached to a life of sincerity, but with a modicum of realization in mind, into the night he loudly unloaded the words, "I love Be Be. I always will." He was beaten by circumstance, or his perception of such...

In the distance, white lights were coming toward him intermittently crossing each other at a myriad of levels and lighting the trail. Masculine voices, radio static and chatter cut through the loneliness of darkness and disconnection. He tried to get to his feet, but dropped back into the mud, looked down at his clothes and felt an influx of shame, so heavy and thick, he could smell it. He'd tottered along an unfriendly trail and the trail won, but the clock hadn't run out. It took mere minutes for his mind to turn his story into something that made sense. He was in the middle of nowhere, that was true, but he hadn't lost. The game wasn't over. He waited, heard his name and rubbed his hand across his chin. He started to answer, but emitted nothing more than a scratch into the black, and a wave to the headlamps and flashlights coming his way, a silent plea his visitor's had yet to regard. He should've had a whistle. "Maybe next time." ... But he knew there wouldn't be a next time.

The heavy footsteps came into his circle, his personal end zone and puddle of mud with lights reaching his eyes and bringing a tingle like lightly dragging finger nails across his skin, just enough to coax an abrupt shiver and recovery. His hands were cold and damp with sweat. "I'm here, injured." He fought the cracking in his voice in an effort to sound brave and in charge, but the weakness in his ability to lay out his words betrayed him. He looked up into faces of strangers and began his charade, that of a man on the side of the trail by choice, not of harrowing circumstance. His chest puffed with self importance and his face revealed that of a hiker taking a casual break on the side of the trail though pain bit down on him crushing his facade. It was clear, even to him that the elephants had rolled into town and the circus had begun. It was a joke to even try... His ankle was the size of a grapefruit and the laceration had widened, becoming a chasm he could see through the stretching of his socks. He was spent and he knew it. He had to surrender.

Shouts of celebration penetrated the darkness, prickling his arms with bumps of unreadiness and intrusion, a welcome entry into his worn out condition, but a state of trespassing, just the same. Someone spoke into a two way... "He's here. We got him. ... Companion Trail." A man introduced himself, "Martin, Search and Rescue. Try to relax. We'll get you out of here." He wrapped a blanket around Thomas, asked questions and relayed answers. Black dressed the trail in an affecting void, a striking contrast to the lighted area where Thomas found himself. He shielded his eyes with his hand and shivered under the blanket. A second group of lights moved down the trail making him more an animal in headlights than an overwhelmed, irritated, injured man, flooded with questions. A second rescuer introduced himself, "Thomas, I'm Paully Norman. How are you doing? I'm going to put a pressure bandage on the laceration, get a splint on your ankle and wrap everything up real good. Is that okay with you?"

Thomas nodded. He recognized the name and was hoping Paully didn't remember him. He held his breath as Paully knelt down near his foot and announced his every move. "Thomas, I'm going to remove this splint and get a new one on here. Do I have your permission?" He looked back at Thomas gauging his state of mind. "You did a fine job with the shoe thing you've got going here. ... Highly original. It's surprising you thought to take your shoes off in this weather." He cut the ties and carefully removed them. "Thomas, I'm going to cut your socks away from the wound. Is that okay with you?" He continued, his hands moving quickly, nearly always using Thomas' name and getting permission. Thomas thought it annoying at first, but soon was hypnotized by the pattern, heavily relying on it for reassurance. It was the repetition that sedated him. He thought of Sandy, the way he repeated lines from books and needed everything in his life to be the same from day to day. Remorse slipped into his consciousness reliving the times he'd forced his son to alter his essential routines though he just as easily excused himself and pushed it from his mind. "Thomas, I'm going to move your foot. It may hurt. Do I have your permission to reposition your foot?" He worked through the process and put Thomas together in a temporary fashion. Someone placed a needle in his arm and started an IV.

Paully's bright and searing headlamp was a mean invasion and spotted Paully's movements. Thomas pulled the wool blanket over his head and from beneath his shell, he waited out the minutes. He cringed on cue and grimaced when necessary. It was a night of disappointment dressed in technical chatter and a bubble of energy, the likes of which he didn't want, but required to get on with his life. He was already rethinking his promises. He'd bought girl scout cookies. Certainly that's charity. He paid his taxes on time. A portion had to go to feeding the homeless. He didn't see the point of calling his son when Sandy, no doubt, didn't know what day it was anyway. He pushed the blanket from over his eyes.

A middle aged woman leaned down next to Paully, "The basket's here. ... Ready to transport?"

Paully stood up. "Thomas, I have a splint in place and pressure bandage on your foot." He patted Thomas' shoulder. "You ready...? We're going to put you in the basket and move you down the trail to the transport vehicle." He signaled to the others... Thomas was lifted into the basket. "The road is out there beyond those trees." He was pointing out the area and making a circle with his arm, attempting to bring everything into perspective and expecting Thomas to stay calm and think in a positive manner. "It runs with the trail about a mile, so it wasn't bad getting gear up here." He put his hand on Thomas' arm. "You can do this, buddy. You're going to be fine."

Martin wrapped a blood pressure cuff around Thomas' arm while several team members positioned themselves around the basket, the one at the head calling out orders, "Okay, one, two, three, lift." Thomas was packed, cinched and on his way down the trail ready to lock himself away, block out the present and once out of the damp forest he'd forget the past. He closed his eyes and imagined he was at home in bed, but the uneven bounce of the ride brought his eyes open and he stared up into unwanted views of his rescuers. He saw three quarter views and the back of helmeted heads unless they turned, one to another, but mostly they walked in silence. Head lamps and other beacons guided the way making a friend of the dark path.

Thomas squirmed under the blanket struggling with his insides, the emotional pain too heavy to quiet and the outside pain, the one commanding he shout out in agony. He didn't... His heart beat rapidly and sweat beaded on his forehead, under his arms and the back of his thighs. He shivered with hands as cold as ice as the basket bounced along with the gait of the rescuers churning the contents of his stomach. His head was full, blood vessels throbbing and sharp knife stabbing pain shooting into his temples. He felt he deserved what he'd gotten, but it's not unrealistic to consider that he didn't want to accept what he deserved.

He lowered his eyes, disengaging from things he knew he'd set into action, but observing the scene, just the same. He was the horror movie watched with hands over one's eyes. Maybe it was denial, the way he wouldn't allow himself a look in the direction of his injury, or it could've been self preservation, his tunnel focus on the men carrying him and the glory he saw in the men's intonation. It was an aspect he hadn't found within himself though it may have been present, only overlooked... The rescuers were bigger than the moment and larger than the things they'd accomplished. He looked down at the lump of blanket at the end of the basket. He should of planned... He looked up at the men, certain they would've planned... They'd have first aid kits, pocket knives, extra water, food, maps, compasses, all the essentials he, himself carried on his hikes long ago. He blinked away drops of rain, aware he should've turned back before daylight slipped away. They would've turned back. He'd disrupted lives and placed strangers in peril. "Paully..."

"I'm here, Thomas. What do you need?"

"Thank you." Thomas closed his eyes.

Paully nodded, "You'd do the same..."

Chapter 6

Grandmother pressed her hands against the door frame, ample curves filling the entry. She was neatly wrapped in a full skirt and cotton blouse with a tiny white cotton bow. She stood there in a contrived state of bliss, kissed and washed out by sun rays in a halo of white, a goddess like vision, backlit by heavy golden streams of sunlight granting her immunity from the harshness of her son's troubles. It couldn't have been further from the truth. She smiled at Rebecca, making a gesture toward her own expanding middle. "Remember when there were a few inches leeway on each side of me. Another year and you'll have to push me through..."

Rebecca returned her smile, but with reservation. A wave of stress marred her features. She reached out to her.. "Come here."

"It's okay, honey. There›s a lot going on. Things will get better." She was an expert at deflection and open to opportunities built to display its usefulness. "Do you know England and France used to hate each other?"

Rebecca stopped and starred at her. Her chin dropped. A wrinkle of bewilderment lodged between her brows. "What?'

"I'm just trying to help." She lightened her mood with

upturned lips and warm eyes. "I think I've been around Sandy too long. I'm starting to sound like him."

Rebecca sighed, dropping her shoulders and melting into a place where she could once again feel her her fingers and toes. Thomas' accident had given her a numb feeling in her mind and had recently extended its grip to her hands and feet. She was made of wood and moving through a void since hearing the news and more than anything she wanted to avoid a hug. Too much tranquility would throw her into a flood of tears. Human touch had to be rationed and kept at bay in situations where emotions were impossible to contain. Grandmother's caring arms wrapped around her were a risk, but they came for her and in that instant, the damage was evident. Bits of composure she had retained, bolted, leaving her with tears and a chest, tight and hollow. Her thoughts weren't hers. She'd given them away, listening to Grandmother and relying on the words she whispered, believing them to be law. Everything moved quickly, an urgency squeezing in and rendering chaos. Thomas didn't rule the moon glistening on a cool night, but in her sadness, he did... The world would stop until he had time to heal, then there would be an opening for pause and she could return to the hustle. Sandy tugged at Rebecca's shirt tail. "Which is my room?" He didn't wait for an answer, but hurried down the hall to the first open door and began to bring in his prize possessions from the car.

The conversation in the kitchen moved forward without him, neither woman noticing Sandy's scampering in and out with his tall piles of literature, or realizing the length of their chat until Sandy eased back in between them expecting them to take notice. He pulled harshly on the belt loops of Rebecca's jeans. "Laws die. Books never." He covered his face with hands, speaking in muffled words, "Edward Bulwer Lytton wrote that"

Rebecca bit at her knuckle, cocking her head to the side and giving a slight nod in Sandy's direction. "Does he know?" Grandmother shook her head with a cautionary finger to her lips. A look of concern swallowed her forbidding she speak.

Rebecca brushed her hand through Sandy's hair. A myriad of concerns dogging her and showing up on her face. She wiped tears from her eyes and gathered herself. He was a child. No one was to blame. Grandmother rubbed her hands over Rebecca's back easing away the tension. "Oh, honey, it breaks my heart to see you like this." She watched Sandy flapping his hands and blinking rapidly. "Everything's left to chance. We just never know."

Rebecca lifted her head and shook out her shoulders, turning to face her. "Is he okay?" Mascara watered by her tears blackened the space under her eyes giving her a macabre undercurrent.

Grandmother took a deep breath. "Oh yes, he always blinks and flaps in times of stress. He doesn't know what's going on, but he feels it. Oh my, yes, he feels something."

"I mean, Thomas. Is he, is he fine?" Rebecca patted Sandy's shoulders and pulled him close to her.

"He's got two pins in his ankle and a stitched up foot." She pasted a smile on her face warding off a dramatic scenario though it only served to make her ghoulish, emitting tragic details with an awkward grin, and there was the awkward chuckle rising up beneath the surface.

Rebecca regarded her cautiously, pressing in her lips and narrowing her eyes. She took her chance and exhaled. "I'm glad it wasn't more..."

Since she'd taken that well, Grandmother felt she could

give her the remainder of the story. "He's got some scrapes and a dislocated shoulder." She based the words she used on Rebecca's expressions. "He broke his little finger and he has a black eye." She paused for a moment. "I don't know about the black eye. Maybe a branch hit him in the face." Rebecca could barely see through her tears, the symptoms of emotion which held Grandmother captive, forcing her to face a reality she wasn't prepared to accept. She shrugged. "He fell a few times. Who knows...?" She discovered her own sadness in Rebecca's eyes, but progressed as though she was stone. "He used two walking sticks. One slipped from under his grip, something like that..." She looked around... "Paully said he asked Thomas if his shoulder hurt. He said it didn't, but Paully said it didn't look right. He just let it wait 'til the hospital." She rubbed her nose. "I guess he put in an IV."

Rebecca sniffled, turned and looked down at Sandy. His hand was held tightly to her sleeve. "Sorry sweetheart. Put your things in the room straight down the hall."

Grandmother winced, tucked her head and lurched forward with her torso leading... "He doesn't know." She took Sandy's hand. "Come on kiddo. I'll show you your room."

He bounced behind her. "It's my room all to myself. I knew it. I already put my books in it." He looked up at her, mostly viewing the roundness of the underside of her chin. "There's room to fit more books."

"It's yours." She showed him to the room, taking sight of the book stacks, but a shrug was about all she gave to the scene. It was Rebecca's turn to bug out her her eyes and shake her head a little Sandy and his antics. Grandmother was soon to be on her way out of town. She walked back out to Rebecca with Sandy at her tail. She bent down, hugged

Sandy and smiled at Rebecca, including her in what felt like a colonizing move securing a united front. "Have fun and thank you for doing this."

Rebecca kissed her cheek. "My pleasure."

"I know..."

"Call me when you get to Seattle."

"I will... I'll check into my hotel and get right over to the hospital. It's a three minute walk." She went out to the porch. Rebecca followed, "Which hospital?"

"Seattle General." Grandmother walked the steps and glanced over her shoulder. "It's a good place." She headed to her car, thought better of it and walked back to Rebecca and placing her hands on Rebecca's shoulders. "Honey, you're the daughter I've always wanted. You're family." She promised herself tears wouldn't come. "I love you." She cleared her throat. "You know he loves you too." Her head fell to the side as though she'd held the heavy thing far too long. There weren't enough hours in the world for the horrendous amount of time it would take to heal what had been broken. "I know he loves you." ... But no one knows a thing like that. She knew it and Rebecca knew it. She could have lived her life to completion without having seen the sadness in Rebecca's eyes and as a mother, a friend, a human being with a heart, she handed it to her one more time. "He loves you." It was a gift. Grandmother would accept nothing in return.

"Don't say that." Rebecca crumbled, falling apart as the past traipsed back into her life, grabbing her by her dreams and drowning her, yet the smile she managed was convincing, still, tears welled in her eyes.

Grandmother regrouped, sighting her car and marching off like a soldier, light hearted and with a sense that things would be as they were to be... She'd saved another disoriented soul. She'd gone beyond everyday, witnessed suffering and acted to make a difference. She scooted behind the wheel and sat tall in the seat, adjusting mirrors and checking her reflection. It wasn't her face, it was her eyes tormenting her. Behind them, was lost innocence. The face she owned wasn't hers. In a look, it sold her secrets. She spent an instant in meditation and moved on looking toward the end of the driveway, a place where pain was certain to make its departure. For her, despair permeated South Brook. Seattle would bring comfort. She forced herself into the person she wanted to be, massaging her psyche with silly lines of encouragement she'd heard and thrown out, but on that day, were ushered in, and she didn't feel dirty using them to break her fall. "Fake it, 'til you make it." Emptiness swallowed her, creeping inside, thwarting and consuming her. She sobbed. She'd failed. She was weak.

Rebecca was in her own form of survival. She inched toward Sandy, meeting him on his level. She didn't know what he knew of his father's accident, or how to explain things to a child and in the instant she crouched before him, she was speechless. She cleared her throat and stared at him. He ran to his room. She watched his legs kick up behind him moving him forward in a direct path to security. A breath of relief came from between her lips as the back of her wrist rubbed across her forehead. She doubted her skill in caring for a child at the same time accepting that she was once a child, and by that alone, she should've been able to understand a child though perhaps it was best to let him dissolve in the privacy of his room. They would have two weeks together to find common ground. It would give her time to grow up. They'd been granted two weeks to make a difference in each other's lives.

She took in a fresh breath filling her lungs with courage. She felt the wood floor beneath her thin flats while taking that all of a sudden long walk to his room. Sandy sat in the rocker near his bed, his feet barely making it onto the foot stool. He held a book close to his face and devoured the written words, from time to time putting on a sneer, or shady grin, both of which animated his face. He laughed out loud and as often groaned, tightening his fists and shaking out his hands. If the room had blown up around him, he would've overlooked the destruction, enraptured by the written word and reading within the cinders.

She stopped outside his door, peering inside before lifting her hand and ineffectively sounding her knuckles against the hard wood. He was content inside a world of his own, merged with the images he could conjure through mentally playing with the ideas conveyed in his books. For that reason, when she knocked he didn't look up. He was living between the pages of his book, locked in an imaginary setting, wading and loyally weighing every wordy morsel. It was just as well, Rebecca craved silence and was inspired in the midst of isolation. She took moments to make business calls and talk with employees outside the house near her front window, close enough to dash inside and see if he was okay. It was a first, living for another human being, a child who depended on her for security and support. She'd lived her days mindfully connected to her nursery and interacting with employees and business associates, but that day, her head was elsewhere as she poured over invoices and inventories, reading them a second time to get what she'd read. Sandy touched her soul, inspiring something in her and lifted her above the day to day, providing her a look into another universe, one of creativity and an outstretched hand peddling the rush of freedom. She left him to himself.

Outside the inner workings of her home, the sun climbed to the top of the sky. Birds were again foraging, chirping and singing their high pitch serenades and invoking little attention from workers going about their duties. Rebecca's greenhouses and outside flower beds were alive with color. She walked the rows and made marks on a notebook she held under her arm. Watering cans waited under faucets. Hoses moved from one section to another sliding across soil like green snakes and were firmly gripped by large hands protected in heavy gloves. Rubber boots came down solidly on the metal end of shovels, their pointed tips pushed into the ground. Busy hands pulled weeds and fingers carefully aerated the soil. Rebecca pulled a garden glove from her hand and pressed her finger into the soil. The dry dirt moved easily under her nail. "Gerald, not this row."

He was new and learning his way. He put his hand on the pot and turned it, moving the large rounded leaves to eye the soil. "It looks dry."

"Two inches down its wet."

"Yes, Ma'am."

Sunbeams settled on her hat and shielded her eyes hiding the excitement showing up on her face. Summer was a heart beat of colors on dainty chamomile flowers warblers, bees, bugs and workers with over tanned necks and forearms. Roses hid in a side yard though their intoxicating fragrance forever rode air currents holding the area to an overwhelming elegance. Marigolds sat with pride, full and glorious, while white snowball Chrysanthemums didn't seem to fit any where except an icy cold snow sledding hill. Their beauty astonished admirers provoking thoughts of life beyond consumerism and dissension. Snowy white blossoms held them frozen. Plants, wholesome and electrified by growth lifted expanding leaves, raising their abundance in height and dashing colors. At their best they were loaded onto trucks transporting to retail outlets to be purchased, tamped into pots, garden beds, stirring appreciation and wonder in the hearts of those creating a better world.

Everywhere, cultivated sprouts peeked from nutrient rich soil gaining a first look at a world meant to raise and protect them. Each flower bed held promise. Under the soil, germination made preparations, cracking seeds and progressing to another stage. Quiet mounds harbored life ready to make its entrance. Roots wiggled under the surface, willing to carry the burden of becoming a life line for fabulous above the ground beauty and reverence. The nursery bustled with an energy packed into nature and the employees spending their hours laboring in the haven surrounding them, the only retail and wholesale business in South Brook.

Notebook in hand, Rebecca stepped over garden hoses and jotted ideas. She walked through her gardens greeting workers, mingling and making suggestions. Sounds and scents of nature reached her senses and validated her choices and the difference she hoped to make protecting and preserving from a green point of view. Up the driveway, a car closed in, dust trailing. The deep sound of the engine cut a hole in the songs of nature. The smell of dust erased scents of pine and roses. Rebecca turned from her notes. She watched as the car came to a halt. The sweetness of recognition warmed and flowed through her veins rushing into her cheeks and making her hands sweat. She knew his face, a pleasant face, masculine, but soft as though his life had been easy.

His walk was his signature as much as his blonde curls were his trademark. He had a rough gait, like a plow horse, but a gentle eyes and a big grin. He'd learned to walk on those big puppy feet, horribly unmatched to his frame and used them to get closer to her and to hand over his bouquet. A smile turned the sides of her lips upward in a glow that held every secret in the world. He didn't ask... He knew she'd never tell... She was the girl who acts surprised, but knew all along.

She grinned, "Thank you, you big silly. What're they supposed be?" She laughed, watching him and being careful not to miss his lovable smirk and dimples. They were there for her pleasure entitling her to shelter from abandonment, a buffer from the unbalancing effect of change.

"It's celery. You already have flowers." He pointed out the surroundings. "What do you need with dead ones?"

She didn't listen with her heart, having been cornered by his attractive smirk and dimples coming at her full strength. She couldn't be blamed... He was her friend with the innocence of a little one, hand in a cookie jar. "Ah, why do I adore you?"

"I tied the red ribbon around them. I thought you could wear it in your hair." His dumpling face, a boy face with a little chub that wouldn't leave that meant she'd buy anything he wanted to sell. "I mean later when you're brushing your one hundred strokes."

She giggled, falling into a thousand years back to days when they stomped mud puddles and were soaked and tired. "You're a clown. That's why I love you." She hugged him with a sloppy haphazard baby bear grip, in a this doesn't mean a thing frame of mind, even as his biceps caught her attention. They weren't like that ages ago when he pulled her hair, or chased her with a bloated toad. Perfect muscles meant strength and protection. Mentally she added up his attributes. He didn't lie and didn't steal, but she had no intention of getting in over her head. "You know what? I have things to do around here, so I have to go, but come inside and get herbs for your momma." Her expression turned serious. "How is she doing?" She started toward the house, turned to him and held the celery up like a torch. "I grow vegetables too, you know." She shook her head, stretched up on her toes and kissed his cheek. "You're such a boy, but I love you. Now come-on, get that stuff for your precious momma."

"I love you too, Beck." He hugged her as though it was his only chance. "How's your guy doing?"

She clasped her hands behind her back and leaned forward. "He's not my guy." Satisfaction, much like a grin crept about her features making her a challenge, but accessible. She side eyed him, carrying the hint of a smile while her long thin legs moved in a summer stride. In his eyes, the sun hovered about her splashing sparkling diamond rays of light, brightening her pale complexion and turning her hair to spun gold. She was his princess, his fantasy.

She looked away, "He's married." She rested her elbow on her right arm folded across her middle. She had her fingers in her mouth. "His son is here. I'm babysitting for two weeks. Grandma's in Seattle." She shrugged, "Well, she's well on her way by now."

He pulled at her arm, taking her hands in his teasing, clumsy way of gaining ground. "Come on, Beck. You're stronger than this. Show me the girl I know." He rubbed her hands, brought them to his lips and kissed them. He hoped she'd fall into his arms and love him forever, but that was his thoughts on a basic level. On that day, he meant it to mean no personal gain, but that's not all it was... "The Beck I know would be out saving the world. There must be an orphaned little critter out in the woods for you to rescue."

She knew life didn't happen when one was looking. It wasn't only created by conscious effort, yet she should move forward rather than prod the coals of misery. "You make me feel better." She knew how to make herself feel better, though she also knew when to accept another's words as her own. Life can become messy and challenges unsurmountable tipping the strongest of the bunch over the edge. Not having one to hold at night may have been the break in her chain of perseverance, but it didn't have to be... She hid her tears. "Thank you for picking up the herbs. You saved me a trip."

"You're my friend." He kissed her forehead and pulled her close. He wrapped his arms around her and held her. "I need to get the stuff for my mom." He tilted his head and displayed his dimples. "You, a babysitter? That's something."

"He's a wonderful kid and nerdy, like me." She grinned, "... And you." She reached up and put her hand on his shoulder. "... But, yeah, I've got herbs for your momma. I also made a tincture. How is she doing?"

"The cancer is making her cranky, but she's hanging in there." They walked up the porch steps. "I appreciate what you're doing for her. The herbs have helped with all that chemo."

She stopped at the door. "We should've started earlier." She stepped inside the house and grabbed the brown sack from the counter. "This is the tincture and other herbs with recommended dosages. There're extra herb bags for infusions and I put in turkey tail mushrooms. Boil them and have her drink the water while it's warm, or use it for vegetable soup broth." Paully's eyes glazed over. She playfully hit his shoulder. "Or, I can make the soup for her." She rolled her eyes with a sweetness, a smile slowly brightening her face. She pretended to be put out, but enjoying being needed... "Come back in a couple days and pick it up." She shook her head. "You're like an annoying little brother getting me to do everything for you."

He took the sack, held it under his nose and inhaled. "Every time I smell fragrant herbs, I think of you. I'm at your mercy, my queen." He bowed, one hand behind his back.

She pushed him out the door. "Go on, get out of here." She smiled and kissed his cheek. Go on, get..."

She pulled the ribbon from the celery, smiled to herself and tied it in her hair. She set the celery in the refrigerator drawer and leaned over the kitchen sink, peeking out the window from behind the curtains. An emptiness consumed her. Paully was gone, it ripped at her soul, but at the same time a tinge of melancholy ran through her like a razor though the last thing she wanted to do was place her heart on the line. She heard Thomas in her head spewing forth his tarnished words of wisdom, "Caring creates a whole lot of trouble." She went in to check on Sandy, knocking on the bedroom door and expecting a no show.. She was not invited, yet proceeded to open the door anyway, maybe just a smidgen to see if he was okay. He looked up with a puzzled expression. Rebecca smiled, "Everything alright?"

Sandy nodded. "Everything alright." He continued reading as though she wasn't there.

She poked her head through the door opening. "There's

a lot of books in here." She hadn't seen him bring them in...
"How many?"

"Three hundred and forty eight." He kept to his book and answered giving her the least amount of his time. His eyes darted back and forth across the page. "A room without books is like a body without a soul." He saved his place on the page with his finger. "Marcus Tullius Cicero said that."

"I understand." She wondered how he carried the many books inside without her noticing him. It had to have been while she was talking to Grandma. She'd look after him more carefully, maintaining his safety and as a step in that direction, she kept her place at the door watching him run through the pages of his book. His eyes smiled and his fingers wiggled. Some of the words slipped from his mouth with an explosive volume and voracious thirst for knowledge. For the first time, she felt him more as an equal than a four year old child. He had an edge she didn't yet grasp as though he lived in a realm apart from the boundaries of human influence. He was an adult in a pint size body. That part was simple to comprehend, but there was something more...

Her hand rested upon her chest, trapping outside hurt inside where it belonged. Thomas was walking into her mind and taking things over like he was known to do, but his son was suddenly crawling in and removing Thomas with an unusual slight of hand She was caught appreciating, empathizing and thinking her way through things she didn't understand, comprehending that those things would bring her suffering in the end if she didn't learn to navigate the open road. There were mixed feelings and old agonizing trespasses, but whatever was pent up inside her, she dismissed, turning her thoughts to the little boy in her spare room. The youngster with books, bookmarks and life markers enough for a world of time travelers. ... A kid who tuned out the world and bit down hard on what he needed for himself. She was conscious of her breathing and fragility of her sighs. "I'll go out in the yard and be about my business." He ignored her, didn't notice, or didn't care. She was insignificant and no match for words on the pages that held him, but she persisted, "You can come along, if you'd like... I'll show you around, introduce you... We can meet flowers." She pressed her lips together in a last ploy for some kind of recognition, or reply.

"Flowers?" He looked up. "Can I call you, mom?"

She remained still, unsure and unprepared for what was coming down on her shoulders. "You have a mother."

He set his book in his lap. "She doesn't like me."

Rebecca lost her smile, becoming nothing more than a mirror, a reflection of his feelings. "How do you know that?"

"She told me." He tugged at the collar of his shirt and pulled up his socks. "She said she loves me, but she doesn't like me."

Rebecca pushed her mind to match what her ears were collecting. She heard his words diluted by her experiences and what she thought of as her own pile of wisdom. Goosebumps made her tingle as if reinforcements were finally on the way, but nothing rushed forward to rescue her. She was forced to find appropriate words, those clinical, unemotional cop-outs. "How do you feel about that?"

He rubbed his arms and readjusted his socks. "I feel fine. Lots of people don't like things." He looked across the room, directing his eyes away from her. "For example, I don't like peanut butter. There's a boy named Joey. He doesn't like pickles."

Her eyes were forced slits as she worked her way through

what she believed were his thought patterns. "Are you comparing yourself to a jar of peanut butter and a pickle?

"My mom doesn't like a kind of boy like me, but she likes peanut butter and pickles." He sat up and placed the bookmark inside his book. "I'll time you one minute then you tell me if I can call you, mom." He pulled a timer from his pocket. "Start thinking." He pushed the button and tapped his fingers on the arm of the chair. "This is how you do it when you wait." He tapped one finger at a time.

"I can't decide that quickly. There's a lot to consider." He'd saddled her with a project she could never complete. She wrinkled her brow and licked at her lips, wiping off the wetness with her hand.

He looked at the timer. "Your time's almost gone."

"I'll think about it tonight after work. We'll talk then..."

He folded his arms and tapped his fingers, scowling with a nasty pout appearing fairly decent on a child, almost comical if the subject matter had been less serious and demanding. He stared at her. "When I go to bed, you have to come in my room and put my blanket on me." He put the timer back in his pocket. "Then you kiss my head, up here." He touched his forehead. "That's what moms do."

"I can do that."

"Then you say sweet dreams."

She nodded with a measure of regret. "I'll do what I can." She'd do whatever he wanted done because that's what it would come down to and she knew it.

A house guest can be an invader in the daily life of the host. The invasive species crashes another's sanctuary and brings change, or variation in routine. It's not far fetched from that of visiting human mongrels and their immersion into taking one up on an invitation although how it drags from the initial hello is mostly about personalities and length of the stay. Suffering through the intrusion when the end is visible in the distance takes patience, but disgust and burden many times hurry to the table if the visit is unending. Solo moments may become lost and apologies worthless until the time of the visitors departure and the host suddenly becomes gracious and receptive. It was different with Rebecca and Sandy.

She enjoyed living as a hermit, or so it seemed, but she did love people. She liked to be solo more than finding pleasure with others though she went about her professional duties and personal relationships with a light step and social awareness attracting admirers. In her core, where truth prevailed, she sought time alone with her thoughts. She knew this about herself and nourished her solitary times, well aware she'd be expected to give up pieces of her seclusion though with Sandy in her house, soon after he arrived it proved quite the opposite. She came after him. She wanted conversation. He was interesting although void of a need to cultivate a relationship with others. In some ways his skills were rudimentary, but she quickly noticed that his other isolated superior characteristics accentuated similar qualities in herself. What she found as character flaws within her introverted nature, began to appear acceptable and seeing a quiet, deep and gentle swirl upon the dark water that was Sandy's mind introduced her to her own soul and the hauntings she'd seen there. He was a ghostly placebo satisfying things that first bothered then became her. He was acquiescent, unresponsive and remote, yet warm, loving and kind in ways no other human had been. The more she understood him, the more she understood herself. He was a child, but a child with a gift, or substantial imperfection that fascinated her.

Their hours were filled with unfolding truths rationed into day to day occurrences. It was nothing unusual though Sandy's perspective made them exceptional. She extended her time with him, choosing him over sleeping and alone time with maternal love always at the forefront and dressing everything she was prepared to give in cozy unconditional passion. If she recognized her attributes, it was a convert admission which ended in a sweep of understanding another person's constitution and psyche, a conscious melding of old and new resulting in a novel point of view which she felt compelled to explore. The sadness in his eyes made it easy to dissolve feelings of guilt and allow him to call her, mom. Still, it didn't seem right, but it didn't seem wrong. It was temporary, not the real thing. That's what she told herself to keep a balance, and a balance would come in handy if Thomas learned she was watching his son.

Unfortunately, or fortunately depending on who was doing the pondering, it was beginning to take hold as more of a permanent thing. She asked him to call her Mom Rebecca, if the word mom was to be there at all, but Sandy declined. He wanted all, or nothing and she felt the guilt that covertly drifted her way when ever he called out to her accentuating the "mom" modifier. Slowly her name was dropped all together. She couldn't help but wonder what would happen if he told his dad she was his new mom. She steered clear of those thoughts. They only existed to upset her.

As each day blended into another, he learned more about the lives of plants. He understood germination and the importance of watering. He knew about the first root and the emerging shoot. He was able to discuss photosynthesis and he was excited by the effect of the light spectrum on plants. For seven days he wore his red tee shirt hoping to give the plants needed colors to help the nursery plants to flower. On the Fourth of July, he wore a red, white and blue shirt, not to be patriotic, but to offer plants around the yard a full spectrum of colors to enrich their lives and help them build strength. He spent a great deal of time with his friend, Lily, who had recently accepted Rebecca as a trustworthy companion. Lily rode on his shoulder keeping him company and answering his questions. "I live with many wildflowers, just like me. We help soil become healthy and strong. Without us, mountain soil would slide away with melting snow, or be blown away by fierce mountain winds."

"What else can you do?"

"We're there for bees and we're food for wild animals who live on the mountain. They help us by spreading our seeds."

"Do you want them to eat you?"

"It's part of life. Without flowers, the mountain wouldn't attract as many visitors. The animals would find new homes in other areas. Birds would fly off making new friends in places where foraging is easier and more productive. They have to feed themselves and their families. All life would suffer. When small animals leave, large animals leave. Everyone of them is looking for food. If their food walks away, they go too."

"Do you like trees?"

"Trees have always been kind to me. They provide shade and oxygen. We all do, except at night when were sleeping and growing." She moved to find comfort on his shoulder. "Trees understand a flower's life is a short one."

"I don't want your life to be a short one."

"But it is..."

"The wicked man and the persecutor has no bonds in his death; he may flourish for a season as a green bay tree..." Sandy checked to see if Lily was still there. "John William Polidori wrote that." He monitored the steps he was taking, looking down at his shoes and watching them press on the wood floor beneath them. "The Vampyre and Other Tales of the Macabre." He didn't smile, or engage her though she knew his words were meant for her. He caught himself reacting and reigned himself in... "It doesn't have to be..."

Lily stretched out her stem, relaxing and enjoying the ride. "It has to be..."

The three of them, Rebecca, Sandy and Lily checked on the employees, did a variety of chores inside and outside the house, allowing each other moments of togetherness which required no conversation, or other means of communication. Sandy jumped to reach his coat from the coat hook by the door, and turned toward Rebecca, "Are you going to wear your mask?"

"As long as you have to wear yours, I'll wear mine."

He knew she'd answer that way. She responded every day with the same words as though he hadn't asked the day before. He was testing her, even if he didn't realize it. He enjoyed seeing her slip her disposable mask over her face and become just like him. Finally, he felt included, accepted, normal. He went from detesting his own bulky mask to feeling special and wanted, many times asking to wear his mask just to watch her put one on as well bringing the two of them closer. He designed a world in his head where everyone wore a mask, where everyone accepted one another. He adjusted the strap around the back of his head and looked up at Rebecca with questioning eyes. "Everyone should wear a mask."

"In manner of speaking, they do." She didn't want to be heavy and a burden, but the truth is always a lip slip away.

He put his hand on his shoulder feeling for Lily. "I thought you were gone."

"I'll be here as long as you need me."

As night dropped in, bringing lower temperatures and a settling over the land, she prepared dinner, insisting Sandy help in the kitchen and he made sure Lily performed her portion of the duties as well, causing everyone to pitch in and work together in a blissful harmony which penetrated every corner of the house. All house meals included fresh vegetables and hearty grains, herbs from her garden and organic homemade ice cream, muffins, or other nutritious desserts sweetened with stevia leaves fresh from outside her front door. It's was the same that evening. The meal was put together and she sat at the table across from Sandy and Lily, twirling a spiralized zucchini around her fork. "So, why don't you like peanut butter? I thought all kids liked peanut butter and jelly sandwiches."

He looked up from his dinner plate. "I don't eat brown food."

She pushed the bite into her mouth and began twirling another... "You don't like brown food?"

"Nope."

She chewed the vegetable and swallowed as though swallowing his words. "I was thinking of having brown rice tomorrow. Is that a no?"

"Is it brown?"

"Brown rice is brown. I guess we can have white." She hid her disappointment. "It's bleached, you know..."

"I eat white food."

"Sounds racist," she smiled, expecting him to do the same, but he froze.

He sat looking at her and without warning became animated, sticking his fork through a piece of zucchini and pulling the prongs across the glass creating a disturbing screech. "Don't you believe that the Lord made them of one blood with us?" He lifted his fork and watched the vegetable fall off onto his plate. "Harriet Beecher Stowe wrote that."

"Is that...?"

"Yup, Uncle Tom's Cabin."

"That's mature reading."

"A classic is a book which people praise and don't read." He looked at her with the same narrowed eyes and furled brow. "Mark Twain said that."

"Alright, I concede. You're something." She warmed her words with a smile. I'm not sure what to do with you." She shook her head and sipped her tea, allowing her last remark to hang in the air. She said it and she meant it. He was something fantastic. She'd have to manage their time together in a more serious fashion, not pull something out of the side of her head on the spur of the moment. There would have to be a plan. "Do you want to hike Companion trail?" She threw it out as though it merrily fell from her tongue and she hadn't thought about since the day she knew she'd be watching him. "We can go around eleven and hike to Mission Pond. It's short. You'll be able to do it. We'll wear our masks." She smiled, "We'll pack a lunch."

"Is it on Mount Rainier?" His eyes brightened.

"No, it's across the street from where you turn into my driveway."

"Our driveway, Mom."

"Alright, well, the trail goes in both directions, but we'll get on across the street and hike a short distance to the pond." She didn't consider it was the other direction on the same trail that Sandy's dad got into trouble. Thomas might take it as a vicious slap if he knew, but of course he wouldn't..

His enthusiasm dwindled. He squirmed, closed his eyes and slinked down in his chair. His large vocabulary was reduced to groans and sighs, accentuated by a monotone droll of chatter. "Some people are slow to do what they promise. You are slow to promise what you have already done." He evil eyed her and crossed his arms. "Suetonius wrote that." His frown became more pronounced. "The Twelve Caesars."

"You don't stop, do you?"

"When can I go to Mount Rainier?" He pointed to a spot near him on the table. "Lily wants to know."

"Lily's right there?"

"She's waiting to go to the mountain. I will meet her family and see her home."

He had little feeling in his expression and presentation, but she knew he was nearly begging. He had his own customary approach and she sensed the urgency he was unable to project, mostly a scrap she'd been tossed since she had nothing else to go on, but if It was important to him, it was important to her. "Why does she want you to go?"

"To make me happy."

There it was, the last ingredient, guilt, a mortal wound sprinkled at the appropriate moment to bring her to her knees. She argued with herself, questioning whether he had the ability to apply guilt so effortlessly and with the skill his actions had shown, but he had her. A little boy disliked by his mother, deserted by his parents, allergic to the world and only a flower could save him. She'd been taken down by her empathy. She rubbed her hand across the back of her neck and wore the expression of one admitting defeat. "Talk to your Grandma."

"If you can tell me the name of the mountain, I'll see that you get there." He placed both hands on his chest. "Grandma Anderton said that."... He looked up from under his brows. "It's Mount Rainier and I'm a boy not on a mountain." He was a crumbled cookie with nothing left of him, but tiny pieces. There was nothing superb about the moment although there was something alerting... She just couldn't put her finger on it. He had her heart though and she wanted to be the one who wouldn't let it go... Ideas came into her head rapidly, pushing her to free them, but she said nothing. She silenced herself by touching her finger to her lips and narrowing her eyes then attempted to explain the situation. "Grandma has reasons. She doesn't think of Mount Rainier the way you do." She covered her mouth with her hand and let her head fall upon her wrist. "Oh dear God, why?" Her words were spoken quietly, well under the radar as they should've been. They were meant for herself, not Sandy. The deep sigh was hers as well... "I'll take you there." She heard her own words and sat with an expression of disbelief. She felt at ease and yet uncomfortable. "Sandy," She slipped her hand under his chin and looked into his face. "Grandma is good and kind. She's afraid of the mountain. That's all it is, fear."

He wiggled from her grip. "Life is better life, past fearing death than that which lives to fear." He scratched his head and watched her closely. "William Shakespeare wrote that."

She had nothing to tell him. She found herself pathetic in the manner in which she sold repetition. He gave her energy, honesty and a rush toward knowledge. What could she bring besides the mountain, and why not the mountain? It was in the palm of her hand, a geological landmark, but to him it was magical particles she could softly blow into his personal space. "I don't know how I'll make it happen, but I know why I'll make it happen." The why was magic, and the how would take work. "Trust."

Trust... He didn't know how to do that. He operated from a literal platform and a show me, don't tell me system. He respected her commonplace meanderings and her quiet demeanor, but believing in something he couldn't see didn't fit into the comfort of his maze. It helped that she made no movements he didn't know were coming and kept her facial expressions to a minimum though telling him about the future was lost on his self protective need for living in the moment. She knew he could not easily read expressions and that those small things she did to help him, such as keeping her facial expressions to a minimum, erased, or at least lowered his stress. It gave him less to process and brought his anxiety to a level he could function within without turning to repetitive movements for stability. Lily whispered and offered advice. He listened, laughed and looked toward Rebecca. "You're nice."

"You think I'm nice?" It was the boost she needed and the best thing she heard in weeks, possibly months. "Thank you." The energy sweltered around her. She was beaming.

"No, Lily thinks you're nice."

Clarification isn't always what's needed and in her case it made the compliment droop, but she took what she could get. She thought it through, determined to stick to the positive and let all else slide. A flower told a little boy she was "nice". It could've been worse. Accept it and move on. "Tomorrow we trek Companion Trail. It's a preparation for Mount Rainier." She watched him approve and ignore. "Tonight we're going to the city to get hiking boots for you."

"You mean, town."

"When people around here talk about town, they mean Eatonville. City means Puyallup. We're going to the city." She thought about the life he must of lived in Seattle though it was a door she couldn't open. "I have something for you. Hold out your hand and close your eyes." She dropped fifteen small seeds into his hand. "Open your eyes."

He looked at the tiny dots in his hand. "Are these life?"

"They're avalanche lily seeds. I'll help you plant them." She studied his face. "Have you planted seeds?"

"A plum seed tried to choke me."

"I'm glad your fine."

"You won. Nothing can keep an Anderton down." He rubbed his throat and pulled at the skin of his neck. "Thomas Anderton said that."

"You call your dad, Thomas?'

"He prefers it. Thomas is his name." He moved the seeds around in his hand. "Small seeds. They're a pin dot."

"They are small, but listen, we'll play a little game. We'll call it cold stratification. We'll put the seeds in the freezer and pretend its winter and they're cozy under the snow. In a month we'll take them out and put them under the grow lights. They'll think it's spring."

"I want to go under the snow."

"No."

"I can go in the freezer and it will be snow."

"No."

"What can I do?"

"You can get them ready for their winter vacation. You

have to get them a wet paper towel and let them get inside, then fold it over to keep them cozy. Then you wrap them and we'll get them into a little container, a little house and we'll put them in their winter wonderland."

"I want to go."

"Do you want to take a bath? We'll add lavender."

"Yes."

The dogs barked in the first signs of daylight, running in circles and digging holes in the ground. Edgar was up on his hind legs trying to see in the side window and whining for Rebecca to take him for his daily walk. She hurried past the kitchen counter with a cup of bergamot tea pressed to her lips. She sipped and pulled open the second drawer lifting leashes from beneath dog chews and breath mints. She'd thrown a light shawl over her shoulders which had shifted and caused her to trip. She thought of Thomas and his fall on the trail. She would teach Sandy to be careful and prepared for anything.

She stepped out into the morning air and quickly walked to the gate, opening the pen and readying her dogs for their stroll while behind her back the screen door slammed shut turning out an awkward little puppy of another breed who had scrambled up behind her, hair wild and legs flying. He reached her, head hanging and his breathing harsh and loud, coping with the extra air gulped into his lungs. He managed a frown. "You forgot me." He was panting, mouth wide. "Abandonment is serious."

She secured the pet collars and followed the dogs as they rushed out the gate, dutifully waiting near Sandy. "How could I forget you?" She pushed back his sleepy head of hair. "Look at you. Aren't you the cutest little thing."

"I'm not a thing. I'm a human."

She loosened her grip on the leashes, followed the dogs with a watchful eye and glanced at Sandy. "I thought you were still sleeping. I'm only walking them around the yard. You can come along..."

"The dog is a gentleman. I hope to go to his heaven, not man's."

"You believe in heaven?"

"Mark Twain said that." He licked his lips. "I believe in Mark Twain."

Rebecca's backpack leaned against the wall by the kitchen door. It held essentials and not so essentials. She put final touches on last minute items and called Sandy to get himself where she could look him over. He twirled like a leaf caught in a nature made dust devil. The next minute he rolled on the floor as a tumble weed rotating across a dusty field. The house was alive with electricity and excitement. "I like my pack and boots." He danced, waved, skipped, jumped and spun his body until he fell on the floor spread out like a Christmas snow angel. He looked up at Paully, who had just showed up outside the front door, and was looking through the screen. He stepped inside and met Sandy, who placed himself front and center. Sandy puffed his chest accentuating his new hiking shirt and marched in place to show off his new hiking shorts. Paully heralded the old thumbs up and nodded, "Nice hiking threads. Let's see your pack." Sandy slid out of the straps allowing the pack drop to the floor. He stared at it, picked it up and spun it in circles making sure Paully could take it all in...

Rebecca stuffed things in her own pack. She glanced at Paully and pointed in Sandy's direction. "He slept in them."

"The clothes?"

"Yes, those too, but I meant his new boots."

He laughed, shaking his head and smiling. "That's how it's done. First day of school stuff." He glanced around the room. "This will be fun."

Chapter 7

The sun climbed toward high noon and the three of them moved down the trail taking in what their personal experiences and agendas led them to observe. Sandy got down on his knees and smelled every flower. Paully was caught up in Rebecca's face and the scent of her skin while she was noticeably besotted and melting with passion over the beauty of plants, blue sky and the fragrance of yarrow hanging in the air. They were floating along in different worlds.

Sandy kicked pebbles, aimlessly bouncing along on the balls of his feet and calling out names of flowers he recognized at the sides of the trail. "I spy trillium. I smell skunk cabbage."

Behind him, Rebecca and Paully walked at a leisurely pace keeping him in sight, but allowing his independence and his right to call the shots. If they ended up short of Mission Pond, or passed the pond without him noticing, it was all the same. It was a day to explore and sense a connection with the wild. She pushed back her hair, "I didn't know he'd never been shopping." She looked up at Paully. "He's never been in a grocery store." She tapped his shoulder.

"I heard you. I was just taking in the scenery. It's amazing here." He glanced at the trees and listened to the quiet.

"You mean no clothes, or shoe shopping, no picking out his favorite chips?"

"Yes, that's what I mean. Apparently his parents think he is too sick to go anywhere. I guess he was... He was having allergic reactions everyday and asthma emergencies. I don't know what else..." She pursed her lips and stuck her hands in her pockets. "... But yeah, he doesn't seem to know about stores. He calls them big houses. He's like an alien. He couldn't believe all the stuff out there."

Paully grinned, touched a lock of her hair and moved closer, winking and reaching for her hand. "I can't believe there's all that stuff out there either. Give me a couple choices and get me out the door." He glanced around at the foliage making an exaggerated effort to inhale the scents of nature. "There's about 40 kinds of bread. Have you been down the bread aisle?"

"I know, clutter, but you know what I'm saying... Poor little lamb." She watched Sandy run after butterflies and try to second guess squirrels. The funny little moppet in his usual bouncing style running like a dog chasing its tail. "I just can't believe he didn't know where all those clothes he wears come from, or where his parents get the food they put on the table."

"He has a nanny."

"He had a nanny and yes, I know..." She was thinking too hard, trying to cure the world in a day. "It's okay. Forget I mentioned it." Though he better not forget, judging by the passion in her eyes. He'd gain more points remembering it for the entire span of his life including holidays and hours of leisure. He wanted a lazy, fun hike. She wanted to fix everything. Fortunately, the hike was a little of both, but he'd better straighten his shoulders and come to attention. He could do that.

She felt Sandy's soul while Paully's soul was flailing right next to her. She sensed Sandy's pain, even if Paully didn't... Moments stacked on top of each other, each one filled with verbal notes on how to help the boy, or minding her own business, going her own way and leaving him alone. She mentally strolled the virtual terrain and came to the conclusion that she should go with intuition, dig deeper and push through full steam ahead, and with that she focused her eyes on Sandy, who was right where she'd left him, a few steps in front and moving up the trail with sun glistening on his face and bliss radiating from his pores. She watched him, taking in his extra movements, flappy hands and persistent chattering. "He's a ray of sunshine bopping along like a push me-pull me toy." She laughed, "He isn't missing a thing."

It was true, he was up, down, up, down, turning side to side and catching views of the sky, soil, trees, insects and spiders. His hands hung loosely, swinging in time with the rocking of his head side to side and now and then flapping like bird wings. He walked as though hinged at the joints, bobbing like a bouncing ball, or puppet on strings though despite the inconvenience, he made good use of his wobbly ankles, parading flat footed, suddenly rising to the balls of his feet and just as rapidly going into a spring step, alternating one to the other as his needs arose. She smiled after him. He was her star pupil. Still, she walked along next to Paully relying on him as comfort, a comrade and barrier between things created to upend her, or stall her life's journey. "My life was going in a different direction, that's for sure." She spoke to him softly, holding herself to the unspoken order of nature, but throwing out questions until she sounded more like a rattle than a person merely making inquiries. Her watchful eyes pressed hard into the back of Sandy's head like circles of fire. She shook her head, fascinated by his awkward gait which was surprisingly smooth, but inside her head, she told herself it was also nonjudgemental. She rubbed the back of her neck. "How can someone's walk be nonjudgemental?" She bit at her finger nail. "A walk doesn't have a brain. It can't judge." ... But she stuck to her guns. "It is nonjudgemental though not like a psychological thing. I think it's more, this is the way I get around and it works, so leave it."

Paully stretched his shoulders, leaning back into his pack. "This is my day off. I'm not supposed to have to think today." He took her hand in his. "Take a day off."

"... But he doesn't judge anyone, you know? He just flops on down the road and melts into the world around him." She pushed back her hair. "I just feel like not even his walk, judges. He accepts it and that's it."

"I don't know, Beck. You're getting me in over my head. I can feel my brain matter falling out."

"He reminds me of a yo yo doll." A drawn out sigh lifted her shoulders and raised her chest. "The way he's like a jumble of joints rotating all at once." She looked up at Paully. "Do you remember yo yo dolls?" She nudged him. "I had one. ... That blue clown with the plastic face."

He knew the doll, remembering the fresh cotton bed sheet smell and hodgepodge of colors. He brought his hand to his face pretending he had to work to recall it, but he didn't have to launch a fleet of soldiers to ensnare the memory from his files. It was stashed at the top of the pile. It hadn't even made it to the archives of his brain. He could picture Rebecca's soft hand and her scrappy pink nail polish, cracked and peeling. He recalled the manner in which she washed that plastic doll face and posed those circles of cloth legs and arms. "You carried it everywhere."

"You threw him in the puddle." She squinted, playful, dormant anger fighting to surface, but defeated by their friendship.

"I didn't do that." Of course he did and of course he knew it, but years tell altered tales and that which can be shoved forward, or thrown at the wall and sticks, is just as good as the truth. Truth is conjured in the mind of the story teller. He knew that, but he didn't want it to be his undoing.

She set her blaming eyes on him. "To see if he could swim." She pushed her elbow into his side.

"Yeah, maybe." He shrugged, "I'm sorry."

"Too late." She locked her arm in his with a square dance informality. It wasn't a serious moment until it became serious. "If I could put Sandy in a shoe box and protect him from the world... He's too innocent for what's out here."

He felt his pores shrink as though his body was on the same wave length as the brain matter hurriedly fleeing from his head and running without looking over its shoulder to stay clear of a deeper conversation. Goosebumps held camp at the nap of his neck, at the roundness of his shoulders and across his forearms. "You make me shiver. You always do that to me." He wasn't a fan of the disclosure he knew was coming, once again causing his body to react, tightening his muscles and pressing him to become alert. He was painfully aware he'd be required to make some profound statement expected to float into the ether salvaging the disaster smoldering in her mind. He wasn't a day saver, but straight from a mundane over-stocked barrel from which most men came forth and he wasn't certain whether to respond, or let her talk. Both avenues had advantages, but to remain quiet which turned out to be his choice, brought a jab in the ribs, a kick start that worked well forcing him to break his silence. "He's an amazing kid, but for a kid like him, he'll have to learn to box."

She covered her ears. "Don't say that." She fixed her sight on the ground as she walked. "That's not how it'll be." She looked at him. "Do you know he wants to be a flower?" She waited patiently. "Probably to get out of his life."

"What kind of flower?"

"Stop it."

He reached deeper... "What do you want to do with your life?" He anticipated the points he would gain, questioning her on the future and showing interest in her goals.

"I want to celebrate women, women and children." Her face relaxed and her eyes turned soulful. "Men will celebrate themselves." She looked out at the side of the trail. "Oh, I love St. John's Wort. People think of it only as a cure for depression, but it's an antiviral too. It's good for wounds."

"Heals inside and out." He expected applause, but settled for not getting reeled in to comment on her free all women chatter. He took a closer look at the yellow flowers of the herb, nodded appropriately and gazed ahead at Sandy sitting in the dirt farther up the path. The closer they got, the more pathetic he appeared, dropping his arms, closing his eyes and hanging his head in gloom. His last drops of enthusiasm had left long ago and he melted in the bright sun and humidity. "How far now, Mom?"

Paully rolled his eyes, but knew it had to happen. "Come-on, get on my shoulders."

Sandy was up on Paully's shoulders hooting like an owl, arms waving and eyes filled with glee, presenting more as gloating. His new mode of transportation made the last stretch easier for everyone. It was worth the extra poundage on Paully's shoulders and saved time. In minutes they were standing together scanning the pond for familiar plants, ducks and frogs. The sun heated the tops of their hats and Sandy breathed heavily through his mask. He wiggled from Paully's shoulders, plopped down on his bottom and pulled off his shoes and socks. Rebecca helped him take off his pack and watched him put it back on. "Okay, wear it." She patted his head and put her pack on one of the picnic tables. She glanced at Paully. "Which one?"

"Which one, what?"

"Which is our table?"

Sandy planted his pasty feet in the mud, sinking and recovering, making his way to the edge of the pond and with one brave step then another, he dipped his toes into the cold water.

Paully glanced at Sandy, then Rebecca, "Never been to a pond either?" He opened his pack whipping out a checkered tablecloth and waving it out like a flag before bringing it down across the table in one even sweep. "The best is yet to come." He grinned, setting his backpack on the bench.

She was more impressed than she let on, but she covered it well while watching him unload his bag. "Everything but the rabbit."

He lowered his front teeth over his lower lip mimicking a rabbit and proceeding to lift items out, announcing each as they arrived. "Hot dogs, hot dog buns, marshmallows, catsup, mustard, relish." He rubbed his hands together in satisfaction. "See, look at that."

"Sorry, but no..."

He held to his post, exaggerating his movements and holding up the package of hot dogs. "I'm a step ahead."

He pointed to the package. "Soy, meatless, gluten-free, no preservatives, non-GMO." Placing a hand over each item, he ran through his spiel. "Organic sugar, no corn syrup, real tomatoes, raw honey, no artificial colors, nothing at all." He smiled, resting his case. "They're made of air."

She felt a rush of warmth across her cheeks and nodded. It was the best she had to offer a man who she knew caught all the little somethings. He was working his way inside her heart in a way he hadn't before and she felt it with a stern caution and yet certain abandonment. He comprehended the scope of that one thing above and beyond individual pieces of a puzzle, detail, often misunderstood as a burden. He knew small things were the big things and better, he met her all the way, looking into her eyes without hiding himself. It was imperative that she didn't wipe out the insignificant and lose what was important. She kissed his cheek and looked away, depending on the rest of the day to be better, more productive and enlightening, though the remainder of the day turned out to be a noisy brew of grown-up chatter, quacking waterfowl and uprooting of flocks of ducks surprised by a small, thin, gangly four year old's sudden arrival near the pond. Sandy jumped in ankle deep, splashing cold wetland water up his pale legs. He watched frogs and counted pebbles. Canada geese glided in and out of the pond while a Great blue heron posed in the safety of brambles near the backside. Paully built a campfire and poked sticks into hotdogs they held over the heat, turning, and checking to see the brown bubbly markings of a well done piece of soy. Sandy learned to roast marshmallows and taste the sinfully sweet gooey blobs without gumming up his mask. The day was productive. It was enlightening. It was also at a close.

The sun neared the end of its evening rotation, coming

down toward its last spot in the sky. Sandy too, was winding down and losing his gumption. Rebecca tapped Paully's shoulder, pointing out hot coals, a reminder to douse and give a swift clean up. They stood together looking about their picnic site, thinking and memorizing. However the day had begun, a shift had taken place. Tiny movements, awkward silences, a gaze, sparkle, a touch, clogged the routine sending them packing and heading back down the trail with intrigue and curiosity. Flowers bowed their sleepy heads. The curtain fell.

She helped Sandy with his shoes and slid into the straps of her pack, her mask sweaty on her face. It couldn't be any better for sleepy Sandy holding on by a thread and a load of adrenaline. Twitchy, nervous and exhausted, he presented as cranky with no patience. She put her hand on his shoulder. "Next time we go out, we won't wear masks." She crouched and meeting him eye to eye. "I have an herbal blend, just for you." She poked under his chin and he put his hand there, rubbing out her touch. She kept her eyes on his and as he looked away, she turned his face back toward her. "You can drink it like tea. It'll help you breathe better." She watched his face for a reaction and looked up at Paully. "Help me, please. He's had it. He's falling to sleep standing up. He's falling over like timber."

Paully bent down while she put Sandy on his shoulders. He moved himself, finding comfort. "Dead weight." He straightened. "Okay, ready." He began the walk to the house with Rebecca matching his stride while Sandy lifted his cumbersome head. "Think you're escaping and run into yourself. Longest way 'round is the shortest way home." He dropped his head, wrapping his tiny arms around Paully's neck. "James Joyce said that."

Paully grinned, "He's out like a light."

Chapter 8

Alone in her car with both hands on the wheel and her face too close to the dash, Grandmother eyed the road. The world was coming at her fast like a hardball. She absorbed the abundance of trees on the sides of the road and made little effort to force out distractions. Her sight was on the horizon out of reach, but calling her name. She thought of Michael and his mountain. It called him by name inviting him closer and offering its power, all the while letting him think he could possess it, then turning the tables and possessing him. The enchantment of its beauty replaced any doubt and caution she hoped he'd had, setting a sense of entitlement and importance before him. How could he resist, or why didn't he resist? She didn't blame him. She blamed the mountain. Was she beginning to understand his obsession, his relentless need to be up on that icy death bed? She wouldn't let that happen. She wouldn't give him that... She couldn't... Humans, with their faulty perspectives were no match for a beguiling volcano, perfect, with sun glistening blue glaciers and whipped cream like frozen snow ready without notice to thunder a descent faster than those in its path. The adrenaline rush, beating chest and hyper alive sensation was always worth the struggle of an ascent, but the calm after the storm, letdown, broken hearts... No one talked about that.

She rolled down her window bringing in the scents and sounds of the forest, moving her car through the opening between the trees and rolling along the road she traveled on into the light. Trees bowed and swayed encouraging her, but no matter the car's speed, or Grandmother's motivation, the horizon kept its distance. She had time to think and her thoughts flowed as freely as the fresh forest breeze. She imagined birds making their southern pitch in an endless sky, flying high over the canopy of trees and green fields. They knew their way enjoying the safety of numbers and familiar milestones. She sighed and quickly shook her head scratching at her temples and mumbling, "Even birds have navigation landmarks. I have trees." ... But she didn't need more than trees, and in her own way she acknowledged it realizing that looking for more than she needed would amount to wasting what she'd been given. She had no intention of going down that road, although the road she was traveling didn't promise to provide her with what she needed either. She set her fingers into the small glass bowl of holy water neatly tucked into her cup holder, and placed her wet fingers on her forehead, chest, left, then right shoulder, making the sign of the cross and beginning to pray, "Our Father, who art in heaven, hallowed be thy name..." All the while gravel crunched beneath her tires spitting pebbles past road boundaries and creating a bumpy imbalance, a kind of amusement park ride without screaming teens. Her meaty arms jiggled and her throttle foot was unsteady on the pedal. She wiped her hand across her forehead, a habit consistent with the farther she moved from her home. She thought of Sandy and Rebecca, slowed the car and considered going back, stopped and gave herself seconds to think, cranked the wheel as far as it would go, and began the maneuver. Dust flowed up from behind appearing smaller and less a dirty mess as she left it in the distance. She'd come to the spot where gravel met solid road. She should've expected it, but she didn't... She was too far up in her thoughts to think of what the gravel road was doing, or whether it would end, or carry on... It renewed her faith though and inspired her. She corrected, rolling her wheels onto the pavement.

Being the only car on the roadway, she could stop for a moment and check her mental compass. She did just that biting on her thumb and chewing her nail, an act primal, yet reassuring like a kitten suckling at momma's teat. She looked around at the outside environment. "Welcome to the toxic world." She wasn't fond of asphalt, but there it was waiting and approving her admittance. To her gravel roads were fuzzy stocking feet stuffed into warm slippers, but all that was in her rear view mirror.

Cars began to appear, one then another strapping her to her lot, a place in line. The steering wheel was something to cling to... It wasn't going anywhere and before she knew it, land marks showed up and she waved goodbye to the mountain, or thought she was saying goodbye, but when she checked her rear view mirror, she saw it differently. She hunched forward, on full alert and eyes inches from the mirror, she squinted with anxiety lines forming on her face. "Darn it. That dang icy mountain followed me to Seattle." There was no escape. She stared it down attaching a hostile personality to the large mound of rock. The best thing was not to look at it. "I won't give it the satisfaction." ...But she did look at it, time and again as if being stalked and frightened with no way to escape.

She made her way along the Interstate and followed navigation on the new phone from Thomas. The hours passed slowly though she reached her destination, finally gazing up the great wall of one of Seattle's largest medical centers, a building surrounded by cars, sidewalks and people. She'd almost forgotten the mountain, but another mountain was before her, one of groups of people and busy streets, tying her up in anxiety and paranoia. She was dizzy with anticipation and mumbled to herself, "Is everyone in Seattle going to the hospital? Is everyone in this city sick?" She looked for a parking space traveling slower than the flow.. "If they're not sick, they should be... Pollution, drugs, chemicals, stress, germs, guns, knives, homeless, loneliness..." Her mind rushed through societies maladies and she worried, winding herself up and giving herself no way to assimilate what she believed was a rabid environment. If she could only turn around and go home... But she couldn't... She managed to find her hotel, the front desk, her room, the loneliness beyond it and eventually came to a stand still at the entry of the medical center, an oversized opening of glass and posture. Come one, come all, she imagined the slogan, "We have nothing to hide". The rain began with a drizzle, an apology for what was about to follow, what in her forest would've been a virtue, but in the big city, she saw the down pour as hideous, ordering those caught to run inside. Still, she glanced around to see what others were doing, noting the street signs, painted crosswalks, pigeons tearing into french fries dropped on the walkway and the people, always the people. She tried to take it in stride. The only thing missing were bread crumbs assuring her way out at the end of the day. She smeared a smile across her face. "Useless bread crumbs. The pigeons would eat them."

She wasn't a beaming light and though she may have thought she was just another two legged being on the street, she was impeding the flow. Steady in her spot, she'd become an annoyance to hasty patrons making an encumbering two step in an effort to move around her to gain entrance. Groans, heavy sighs and unkind words, pushed her forward through the doors out of step with pace. The walls closed in around her. Her heart raced and dots of sweat were shiny on her forehead. She entered the flurry of activity where everything was fast, impatient and important. Elevator buttons, rolling chairs, faces, pens, papers, laughing strangers, carpeting, paintings, potted trees and plants. It was a carnival, an illusion. Her son was some where in the aesthetics lying on a hospital bed, his body broken. She didn't need soft carpet and paintings. What she did need was a place to hang her grief.

She thought of Michael. What were his last hours? He didn't make it to a hospital. He didn't take that ride. He didn't hear rescuers calling his name. He didn't know that somewhere in the invisible strands of time someone encouraged him to hold on. There were no life saving IVs and stabilizing splints. He was frozen like a block of ice in a cooler. Her eyes filled with tears. She wiped them away as though it was nothing. Maybe it was... It wasn't tangible. She couldn't flick it away with a quick twist of the wrist. The truth jumped out at her while battle worn memories wrapped in emotion forever circled, as threads of long ago tied her into knots.

Somehow, she arrived at Thomas' room, stopping outside the door, taking in a deep breath of confidence and centering herself. She tapped on the door with a weakness more appropriate of a field mouse checking a clearing before making its run. The door opened inward startling her and causing her to catch her breath as though the movement suctioned out the contents of her chest. She imagined he was in there somewhere. She blinked out the light change and there he was displayed like a holiday ham. Across the room, Elizabeth tossed back her head and flipped her hair with her hand, a propitious move meant to mark her territory. She kept her painted eyes on Grandmother and turned on a smile from under heavy red lipstick.

Grandmother reached to wrap her arms around her, to let her know she was family, but Elizabeth stepped back retracting her claws, then to Grandmother's disappointment, extended her hand and in a bone crushing grip held Grandmother's hand in hers followed by a quick retreat and a return to her cell phone, where she held court in the corner of the room giving off an over powering scent of perfume and the unmistakable smack of avoidance.

Grandmother brushed herself off and pulled her purse strap up over her shoulder, unabashedly noticing the wrinkles in her dress, worn areas in the fabric and the expression on her daughter-in-laws face and revulsion in her eyes. She understood she was unwanted in the hospital room, and perhaps she was feeble and unloved, but she got up with a smile, walked to Thomas and took the seat near his bed. Her hands shook just a little, wondering if indeed she did need a hook for a hand, but stealing a look at Elizabeth told her a hook wouldn't change things for the better. She was old and unworthy while Elizabeth was an extraordinary woman, attractive and intelligent. Why was she expected to compete with her? Those days of being put up against a female rival were over, weren't they, or was this something else?

Elizabeth was thin, not an emaciated starving third world

country scrawniness, but wealthy socialite thin where fat takes a look at the pocketbook and knows it doesn't stand a chance. It turns and running in the other direction and pushing its roots into some irrelevant, unsuspecting stooge eating junk food and living from pay check to pay check. Whatever blessings life bestowed upon her piled up abundantly on her physical attributes, but missed her personality. She was most likely even smug in her sleep, giving credence to the fact that her over the top self approving overtone was her defining characteristic. Grandmother didn't understand what Thomas saw in her. She brought her lips close to his ear, "She's a horror, an absolute fright." She gently took his forearm massaging it lightly, a bleak attempt at throwing him off her scent, but she couldn't help herself and pointed out the shoes pretty on Elizabeth's feet. "If she falls off those she'll be maimed for life."

He held his finger to his lips. "Thank you for coming." He squeezed her arm. "Is there anything I can do for you? Is there anything you need?"

She raised her hand to stop him. "No, no, I've got everything I need right here in my bag." She opened her purse lifting out her bible. "This." She tapped it twice, carefully slipping it back into her bag and setting the bag on the floor by her chair but as she leaned forward, extending her arm and coming closer to the space beneath her feet, she noticed the thick plush carpet and questioned its existence in a hospital room, while feeling the comfort of rubbing her hand over the soft fibers. "Red carpet? Are all the rooms like this?"

He knew what was coming, but squinted away the inevitable, hesitated and with a toss of his head supposed it didn't matter. She'd guess it herself. "Elizabeth brought it in." He rolled his eyes and shrugged.

She sat up in her chair. "Well, it won't show the blood. That's a plus."

He knew it wouldn't end there. He ran his hand over the back of his neck and glanced at his wife. She was busy on her phone.

Grandmother couldn't help but scan the room for other surprises. "And the silk curtains, expensive bedspread and Tiffany lamps. This place is a king's castle." She leaned forward sliding her hand over the fabric. "Lavish." She pulled her eyeglasses from her purse and slowly, almost lovingly moved her hand across the bedspread. "Every stitch, perfect. These tiny threads are spun gold." She lifted her glasses from her face. "The life of Midas."

Elizabeth whisked herself out the door without as much as a nod, and Grandmother kept her eyes on her as she moved past her with the bouncy steps of a confident young woman. She didn't want to be young, but when she spent any time in a room with Elizabeth, she didn't want to be old. Something about the encounters made her check her own inventory and measure herself to the high bar she imagined Elizabeth set. She felt her age at those moments and seemed to have a secret key to the awkward passage of time. She'd been in the same room with Elizabeth on several occasions, but she'd never met her. She rubbed her hands together and self-consciously noticed her paper thin pasty skin and the river of lumpy blue veins with arthritic bumps gracing her finger joints. She looked toward her son. "Elizabeth is a beautiful woman. You hit the jackpot." She was being sarcastic, but that was the joy of not being well liked. She could say what she wanted. It didn't matter how she handled herself, or the blathering which occasionally fell from her lips. It wouldn't make much difference if Elizabeth would've talked to her, but if she did, Grandmother's disparagement was all in fun, but since Elizabeth didn't speak to her, every word Grandmother uttered was a stab, making her feel a tiny bit better about herself, even as sometime later she would loathe her indiscretions.

He closed his eyes. "You wanted to meet her. You met her."

"I met her make-up."

"Don't be catty."

"Is that what I'm being?"

"Just stop."

"Okay." She understood her place. She didn't always stay in her place, but she knew where it was located. "I can be here for dinner." She wondered if he and she could wrap up their differences and have a quiet meal although she knew she might make an unacceptable remark and that would be it. She was riding on adrenalin at that point, and there was a strong possibility she would toss in her hat and call it a day, but he was her son, she had to try... They hadn't said much so far. She sighed and felt pathetic. It was grueling to want and not get... Was it too much to ask to go back to being that mommy with a young child filled with wonder? She'd declared an end to all of that the last time she saw him at her house, but now it was coming back without abandon. Her past was swallowing her whole. For a moment, could she just see her two year old running into her kitchen with a caterpillar in the palm of his hand? Could she please relive that moment until she settled into a box below the earth's surface? Would that be too much to ask? Might she have an instant feeling the shiver on her arms with the flurry of winter coming in from an open door, and the pleasure on her face catching a joyful frozen child looking up at her with rosy red cheeks and snow on his clothes, handing her a snow ball? There's no shame in reliving the past until it catches up and tramples those that can't forget it. That's the risk.

Here we go, he thought. It will never end. "Elizabeth is having dinner brought in for us."

"Tomorrow, breakfast?"

"Elizabeth has breakfast ordered from a five star…"

She interrupted, "Lunch---?

"Same."

"Dinner, tomorrow night?"

He lowered his eyes. "Do you want to eat with us?"

"I was thinking, the two of us."

"You can join Elizabeth and I."

She readjusted herself in the chair, pulling the hem of her dress down over her shins and brushing at her sleeves as though removing lint. "It's fine. I'll sit here and be with you now." She patted his hand. "I love you. I'm sorry you hurt yourself up on the trail, but you look good."

"Elizabeth will be back in a half hour for dinner. He avoided her eyes. "In a couple minutes one of my slaves is coming with my injection."

She rubbed his arm. "Honey, do you hear yourself?"

He scoffed, throwing his arms out as if embracing the room. "I'm paying this god forsaken place to keep me out of pain. This is private pay. You think they're not milking me?" He shook his head, gauging her reaction, but not caring what it was… "They're keeping me here two weeks. If insurance was paying, I'd be out in a day."

"I'm relieved to hear you speak of God."

"Are you hearing me at all?"

"Honey, it's not the nurse's..."

"Don't defend this place."

"I'm just saying..."

"You think she'd be here if she wasn't getting paid? Everything is about money."

"Not everything."

"Name something that isn't. If you want to live indoors, it's about money."

She watched the nurse walk into the room and medicine being pushed into the I.V. She did her job quickly and the smell of Heparin lingered in the air. Thomas closed his eyes while Grandmother pulled the covers over his shoulders, lightly kissing his forehead and speaking to him, well aware he'd already slipped into slumber. "I did bad. I'm sorry." She had nothing to be sorry about, yet from where she stood there was nothing she could do to undress her carelessness, but to start again. She understood she didn't always think things through and in a moment of haste, she was irresponsible. Things that matter the most, always come undone.

She walked toward the door, looking back and memorizing his face. A wisp of hair had broken free from its regimented style and had fallen over his forehead giving him a more spontaneous appearance as though he'd combed his hair with his hand and merely dusted off the knees of his jeans in preparation for her visit. The truth was far less dreamy and validated by the fact that he was laid up in a hospital bed after an accident that he surely could've avoided by appropriate planning, but those were her thoughts, thoughts which would not make it into words.

Moving through the door and out into the hallway, she made a rapid intake of her surroundings, getting her bearings and deciding her direction. The hall was quiet with few people going here to there, most of them in hospital attire, tunnel vision propelled... She walked toward the cafeteria navigating by the scent of processed food though intermittently thrown off by plates of sandwiches, salads, meat and cookies, moving through the hall in the hands of those with little time to consume them. She was lost, not in a geographical sense, but emotionally. What was real, she made real, the rest was decoration.

The cafeteria was large, every table cluttered with meals and beverages, elbows and baggage, both mental and carry-ons. As expected, every chair was occupied. She bought an oversized piece of chocolate cake and on a whim, macaroni and cheese, paid for her selection and mentally licked the frosting off the top a thousand times before reaching her table. She didn't have a table. It was a chore to scan the area for a chair while pretending not to care. Desperation is never a precious projection. Don't ever let them see you sweat. She'd taken that to heart, yet beads of sweat wet her brow. She held her cake allowing last bits of hope that she'd find a seat, move her toward the exit, but as fate would have it, a man stood, stepped behind an empty seat and slowly pulled the chair out for her. "Be my guest."

She had no plans to be anybody's guest though with the shortage of available seating, she examined his table space as though she had a choice and was missing out on better seating. It was neither rude, or protective, but merely a ploy to keep what little self esteem she possessed and to hold judgmental eyes at bay, far from her aging hands, flighty hair and thread worn coverings. The gentleman making the offer seemed too clean and well kept to share his table with what she felt she'd become reduced to, but she had no other plan. She accepted the seat though slighted him on common courtesy, more a self esteem issue than an act of impoliteness. She'd never see him again. Why would it matter?

He smiled, waving her near, "Come-on, I don't bite."

She didn't want conversation. Her mind was on chocolate cake and it was all she could do to keep from biting through the plastic wrap. She was ready to become frosting face with crumbs smeared around her mouth. "Thank you." She saw his eyes go to her slice of cake, she had no intention of sharing. She thwarted what she thought might be an advance with cafeteria talk. "Chocolate fudge, I think. Not as good as mine, but it will have to do. There's two left." In other words, get your own. There's one fork and it's mine.

"I'll have to get one of those." He didn't budge, but asked to take her coat and when she agreed, he slipped it over the back of the chair as if he was dressing a mannequin. She raised a little and he pushed the chair toward the table and sat across from her. "This place is a zoo." She nodded. He watched her open the cake. "Eating dessert first? Somebody's got a sweet tooth."

If she could've stopped his chattering, she would've... She was there to enjoy her cake and feed her "sweet tooth", not form attachments. She had all the friends she needed, or wanted, however, there was that sense of obligation. Most of her generation suffered from it. He had offered her a chair, but did she have to offer him her life? "Chocolate cake is my favorite."

He wasn't surprised. Chocolate had its reputation to uphold. "Name one person who doesn't like chocolate."

"Can't..."

He laughed. "What're you doing here? Me, I've got a friend, long-time friend fighting C."

"C?"

"Cancer."

"Oh."

"No, don't... He's uh, going down for the count, I would guess, but there must still be a chance, or he wouldn't be here."

"I'm visiting my son." She dug into her pasta. "I don't know if I'm wanted, but I'm here." She could feel her eyes warm with tears and gave herself a mental scolding, not now, no, this isn't the time, think of something else. ... A joke, think of a joke. She smiled awkwardly. "Tell me something funny. Hurry."

Her eyes were red, but his politeness left it alone. "One of those days...?" He put a hand to his chin as though possessing the wisdom of the ages and at any minute, he would spill it. "Knock, knock."

"Who's there?"

"Banana."

"Banana who?"

"Knock, knock."

"Who's there?"

"Banana."

"Banana who?"

"Knock, knock."

"Who's there?"

"Banana."

"Banana who?"

"Knock, Knock."

"Who's there?"

"Orange."

"Orange who?"

"Orange you glad I didn't say banana."

Of course it was silly, but effective. "Thank you."

"Heard it before?"

"Everyone has…"

"Did it work?" He looked into her eyes, moving in to get a good look. Most of the red had become pink. "It did."

She blushed, moving uncomfortably. "I'm fine now." She didn't want him rummaging around her eyes and finding something in there she didn't want exposed.

He pushed his plate away from himself. "Where are you from?"

"I'm not from Seattle."

"I can see that."

She cringed inviting the old familiar feeling of being the odd one out, the fifth corner of a square. She'd always been lonely in a crowd. "How do you know?"

He laughed. "You're a fish out of water." He smiled, laughed again and looked at her kindly. "Why don't you let me show you the sights?" He grabbed a French fry from his untidy plate just beneath the crumbled napkin. "… The Water front, Pike Place, Space Needle." He grabbed another fry, soaking it in blood red catsup. "Back in my day it was Pike Street Market, but I'm old." He grinned.

She looked at the table while he tapped with impatient fingers provoking her, she thought, like a prompt from the wings. "Yes?"

She looked up at him. He waited. "If you're thinking serial killer, I'll show you my license." He reached for his wallet. "Law abiding citizen, right here."

She took the card in her hand and felt the smooth surface. It felt like Michael's license. She often took it from his wallet, just to see his face as he slept near her. "Nice picture."

She stared at the card, turning it over in her hand. "You're seventy one?"

He laughed, seemed to laugh a lot. "That's why I need an answer, soon." He looked at his watch, mentioning people don't wear them anymore. "Proof I'm ancient and don't have much time left." He'd made her laugh.

"Yes," she smiled. "Yes, okay."

People connect, blocking out each other's flaws and seeking hidden gems in each other's personalities and movements. It's a masquerade where nefarious points of character are tucked from view. Grandmother had no hideous secrets though she did press herself into a definition she'd developed and in doing so, became inaccurately pegged and labeled. Long ago, she'd placed her heart and breath into the love of an adventurous man whom she believed had taken those things with him when he passed. Their history ravaged her, ripping last bits of meat from her broken heart. Still, she took the gentleman up on his offer, which meant there she was at Seattle's waterfront where he was pointing out seagulls fighting over dropped fish sticks and tubs of tartar sauce. "That's what they do... One of them will get it all."

She watched them. "We don't have seagulls where I live."

He looked out at the water with its passive swells and lack of enthusiasm. "It seems like they don't have anything where you live. No internet, no crosswalks, streetlights... Why are you secretive about your residence? You could live in a dumpster for all I care. I'd still want to spend time with you." He expressed his confusion with a long loud exhale. "I want to know something about you. You know all about me, at least everything I know about me. I don't even know your name."

"I told you my name."

"Grandma isn't a name."

"It's what everyone calls me."

"Everyone calls me "old man", but that's not my name."

"I've been Grandma for forty years, long before I was one."

He smiled, hesitated, "So what's your name, your birth name?" She looked out at Puget Sound, listening to the gulls, and the water slapping at the sea port wall. She disregarded the traffic, tourists, cell phones. He took her hand. "Come-on, let's watch them throw fish." She looked up at him, a curiosity exaggerating her features. He got it and reassured her. "It's a fish place. You'll see."

It was a fish place. The market was a lot of things. It was a mixture of street musicians, tourists, screeching gulls, car horns and smells matched to each merchant's open door. The scent of chicken burritos, calazone, gyros, cheese burgers, vanilla bean sorbet, Limburger cheese, old newspapers and vehicle exhaust, those were the scents of the open market, the life of an old area painted with yesterday's flair and the new day's promise. There were spices, vegetables, herbs, perfumes, incense, board games, tee shirts, pedestrians and flowers. Slow moving cars gnarled cobbled streets. She wanted to pull in her feelers and ignore the visual chaos, even as she'd miss out on Seattle car noise, one way signs, seagull droppings, pigeons and graffiti. She didn't see an upside.

He, on the other hand, didn't see a downside. He found history in every crack in the walls of buildings, pillars, book stores, gift shop, curios and clocks. She found abundance unnecessary, ungodly and gluttonous, intended for the fallen, those lacking in natural environmental rhythm. He pointed out artisan shops, handmade crafts, authentic food from around the world, fresh rosy apples, crisp green lettuce, colorful flowers and musicians singing out with open guitar cases, or other containers to be filled with coins and bills. She pointed out trees trapped in unhealthy spaces and birds with no other options, but to scarf down greasy fries and cotton candy. He looked at the architectural masterpieces, raving at the artistic excellence. She pointed to the homeless, dirty and without hope.

He saw nostalgia and historical meaning. She saw long rows of shops squeezed into spaces not much larger than an outhouse. She leaned her head back as far as she could, and raised her eyes to open pipe ceilings above never-ending dismal halls littered with streams of faceless human cattle in dark fall colors, moving at a mind draining pace. She wrinkled her nose and inhaled the scents of incense, herbs, perfumes and an old buildings covered in fresh paint. She walked through a living collage of over-stocked shiny keepsakes that no one, anywhere, needed.

Creaky wooden stairs took them from the lower level to the main floor where street noise melded with bright primary colors and a myriad of conversations in many languages, all of the words hitting her ears like a hurricane of useless clatter. An urgency manned by her sense of time had crawled inside her head like the constant banging of a loud ticking clock, bringing on the pain of a hammer hitting into the side of her brain. Everyone bustled on their way to where? To somewhere else.. Individuals nudged and pushed around her. She was certain she was old and a bother. Rebecca, Sandy, her house, birds in the forest, her forest, all came to her mind, to free her. He leaned in, his face near her ear. "Let's get out of here and get you home."

She looked up at his face, a bewildered expression falling upon her. He read her, seeing the questions in her blank face and brought himself closer, "I mean back to your hotel. I'm taking you to dinner tonight."

She thought about it and put her hand on her abdomen. She felt the pressure of showing up, putting up and keeping up a charade. "Will you drop me off at the hospital? I want to see my son tonight. Can we go to dinner tomorrow? Is that okay?" There wasn't a dinner date the next night, or the few days after... She finagled a way out of each invitation keeping close to Thomas and trying to build a friendship with Elizabeth, but she couldn't see a natural progression toward something better, no matter her attention to warm social protocol and thinking time would change things, or bring miracles. It didn't, yet she went about her visits and endured, collapsing into a place of despondency and seeking out minuscule amounts of anything to stop the pain and loneliness. She spent her evenings in her room with her bible though one evening after a hospital visit, she looked out through the windows of the hospital while walking through the glass enclosed overpass and met face to face with the black of night crawling into the city streets below and adding a haunting temperament to what she'd already perceived as daunting and unfriendly. The night was coming without the grandeur of her beloved nights in her forest community. She was headed back to her hotel, but chocolate cake had come to rescue her, settling into her thoughts as an escape, and with that, she entered the cafeteria expecting the late hour to assure her an empty space to rest her mind and lay aside her suffering. Jaimie smiled. He wasn't supposed to be there. He wasn't supposed to be a warm blanket and welcoming harbor, yet there he was calling to her. She could've sat anywhere though there she was at his table, and at the end of the hour, she had a date, a real boyfriend-girlfriend kind of thing. She was neither happy, nor sad.

On the night of their date, she stopped to see her son at the hospital, slowing her steps and approaching cautiously toward his open door. She tapped lightly hoping to rouse Thomas, but leave his lovely wife in her corner on her phone, and held unaware... It didn't surprise her Elizabeth actually was in the corner on her phone, her lacy heels thrown off and her high fashion hosiery covered feet propped over a silk pillow on a flawlessly vintage floral upholstered ottoman. She sat posed as though upon a parliamentary throne, smug, overdressed and over-done. Thomas looked up. "You didn't visit me yesterday."

"I'm sorry."

"Did you see Seattle?"

"The market."

He saw the look on her face. "Not impressed?"

"Not."

"I have you paid up at the hotel until tomorrow. Not sure what time's check-out."

"Noon.."

"A young man in scrubs stuck his head through the doorway. "X-ray. Ready to take you over..." Thomas looked at Grandmother. "Kind of a bad time. I have X-ray, then dinner." He looked at Elizabeth. "Give Mom the Black card." He looked back at his mother. "Take it. Get what you want. You have one night. Do it up big."

She shook her head, lowering her eyes, aware Elizabeth was peeking at her, eyes beady and hungry for a misstep. Grandmother's stomach sold her out with its rumbling and bubbling, prompting her to say words she couldn't get out, then a painful quiet, she filled with her feelings. "I can't take the money." She rubbed at her eyes, covering her mouth and tasting the salt of humility.

Elizabeth tossed the card on the bed, slipped into her heels and stepped across the room making the most of her time on display. She whipped back her hair and blew Thomas a kiss showing her mother-in-law her flawless complexion and old fashioned seam in the back hosiery before going out through the open door. He strained to reach the card and handed it to his mother. She accepted it, feeling the cold plastic and pain of taking money from her son. From there, under the covering of a woman seemingly content and in control of her emotions, everything began running through her head, the accident, Elizabeth, Sandy, Rebecca and Michael. She sat prim and properly, feet together and hands in her lap unconsciously pretending to be an everyday housewife gripped in a life changing decision as what to make for dinner. As strange as the situation appeared in her mind, it felt ordinary. The wicked had become normal. She scooted her chair near the bed and took Thomas' hand. "I love you, son."

"Love you too." He laid his head on his pillow. "Don't worry about her. She can be difficult."

"I don't know."

"She doesn't care about money. She's got more than she can spend in a hundred life times."

"I know she comes from old money, but I feel..."

"Don't, old money, my money... Be glad I can do this. I didn't grow-up rich."

She kissed his forehead. "Don't I know it." She kissed him again, turned and turned back. "X-ray is at the door."

"I know. Are you leaving?"

"I'll see you tomorrow."

That evening, Jaimie knocked on Grandmother's door, bringing a colorful bouquet of roses, complimenting her on her dress and reciting perfect words of passion he'd practiced before a mirror. She stood before him, hair piled high, polished, perfumed and rosy pink in a classic gown. On her freshly washed feet was hand lotion, stockings and dressy shoes. She looked at his slacks and cardigan and groaned with embarrassment. "Oh, I'm over dressed."

He smiled, "No, ma'am. You shine like a new copper penny." She did. She glowed like bright sun on a lake, or full moon on freshly fallen snow. "These are for you."

She took the flowers, held them under her nose and inhaled... "They're beautiful."

"You're beautiful." He waited for her to respond, but there was nothing. "I could stand here all night gazing at you with stars in my eyes." He stopped and stared at her. "You're darn pretty, woman." Again, he stopped without warning, then looked a his watch and threw his hands in the air. "Darn it, we're on a time clock. We have reservations at the waterfront." He looked her up and down as respectively as he could muster. "I want to show you off."

She walked with him. She could be his charm, if that's what he wanted from her. It didn't seem wrong. She felt things she didn't expect to feel and she was doing things she hadn't expected to do... Her dress didn't give her room to move the way she wanted to move and she was shackled to a superficial manner of holding herself in a brutal posturing where a bend too far forward allowed things to fall out the front and moves too far to the sides or backward threatened the ripping of seams and unknown horrors she could only imagine. She was wearing shoes she'd never wear and the way she saw it, she was walking out into some other woman's world, painted and sprayed with goop as thick as armor. She was out of sorts, conscious of her movements, exaggerated and distant watching herself from outside her skin. She was too far from home.

He held the door as she stepped into the cab. She gathered her dress from behind, smoothing the fabric to drape beneath her, and immediately taken aback by the odor of cigarettes and pizza. She was in Seattle, the great city known for something... something she couldn't recall, but no matter, it was Jaimie's show. She was a lamp post. He was the director calling out directives. He patted her knee. "This place is five star. It has a waterfront view and we have window seats. We're no where near the kitchen." ... But It was kitchen sounds that brought her to life. She took pleasure in the clatter of pots and pans clanging in mischievous disharmony, a utensils losing its balance and taking a fall, or a dropped platter slipping out of one's hands and glass breaking into shards around her. It was a dopamine rush, the familiar, the noise of a busy kitchen filled with garlic and rosemary, smelly cheese and twenty four hour yeast buns. It was home, a chance to dream. She closed her eyes and there she was bustling in her own paradise making pasta and ham, brown rice and curry chicken from recipes in her head and around the world, or she, wrapped in an apron prattling amongst the best chefs, tending award winning sauces and coveted main dishes. Her dreams were her own, incomparable to another's, and a life style away from his.

He was well settled in another world. He knew what he was doing, placing folded bills in willing hands. The evening, the mood, the weather... He'd planned well, avoiding the downfall of insignificant moves and the expertise of knowing the answer before asking the question. Everything was too close to perfection to be considered hit and miss. White caps danced on the water and waves slammed hard against the breakwater. He ordered all of it and added the details. He looked at the waiter as though a friend, asking for the finest on the menu. Poached lobster, oysters on the half shell, jumbo prawns, teriyaki tenderloin and grilled king salmon, shared the table with a top notch salad, colorful with Napa cabbage, arugula, avocado, roasted tomatoes, candied hazelnuts and 30 year old balsamic vinegar. It wasn't her ordinary day, but she was there, taking it in and wondering why... Jaimie pointed out landmarks, "Alki Point is over there, and here, we have the beautiful Seattle waterfront. That big mass of water is Puget Sound."

"Yes" She stared at the water, capriciously detecting the beat of its heart and the power of its influence. The beauty of a large unspoiled body of water moving in and out and defined by ebbs and flows, waves building and their glorious crashing upon man made dead ends charmed her, filling her with a spotty understanding of her minuscule part in the universe. Puget Sound churned and thundered giving her a taste of what wasn't hers, but a tale she knew too well. The dreamy dark water was merely another method for those lured by adventure to lose their lives. Tiny cracks in earth's surface invariably served as portals enticing explorers and guaranteeing their disappearance. She knew the portentous Seattle bay was cut from the same cloth. She put her hand on her chest working to balance her breathing and cease the overwhelming urge to run from the restaurant, leaving Jaimie in the dust. He was nice man. He seemed too old and tired to grab an ice axe and slam it into a frozen waterfall, inching up where he didn't belong. She watched him from her side of the table and decided to stay a while, observing him a little longer and making some kind of decision about something that has slipped her mind. Without pause, she fell into her default, her familiar kitchen trance, still eyeing him, then trying to see him as a stranger, one just passing through her life without meaning, or substance. How did he look to others? How did the two appear as a couple? Some couples fit, others were misfits leaving onlookers to wonder about the disaster, or desperation adhering them, one to another. She couldn't help but wonder if she and Jamie were a matched set? She thought of candied hazelnuts and preparation... White sugar, or brown? Eggs? Vanilla extract, vanilla bean, cinnamon? What of the tomatoes, Roma, plum, beefsteak, Campari? No blanching, no steaming. Caramelization, yes. It was awkward sitting and waiting for food instead of marinating, stirring and chopping with imagination, motivation. She could see herself behind the scenes, a part of the preparation, a team member working within the stubborn wills of well versed culinary masters competing and employing excellence to plate creations they would serve to hungry patrons. She looked around thinking there must be something she could do to end the need to move and be a part of life. The floors were swept and tables wiped though to grab a white hat and stand before a shiny cooking surface preparing extraordinary food art for the masses was a page torn from her book of dreams and no matter how she hard she tried she kept going back to it.

He read the expression on her face, sensing her discomfort. "No need to fret. The fish are safely under there." He motioned toward the bay. "Not flying around." She grinned and he knew he had her.

She shook her head in dismay. "Hopefully, with their heads not cut off."

He reached across the table and placed his hand on hers. "That would be a fright."

She disregarded the direction of the conversation, mostly because she had little to say in response and she was doing what she could to avoid being discovered for the common woman she believed lived in her skin. Still, she was curious. "Why do they throw fish?"

He threw his arms in the air with a breezy flair. "It's a show, a performance. People like it. They remember it. They remember Seattle. They tell others. They come back and spend more money."

She shuddered. "It's awful."

He shrugged. "What about you? You said you hunt."

She positioned her hands under her chin, getting a good look at his face, his features, the lines. "I said, my dad taught me to hunt. I didn't say I killed animals."

"Then what did you do out there?"

"He taught me to aim. I moved the barrel a little off target and shot."

"Missed every time?"

"Every time."

"Why?'

"So I wouldn't shoot them."

"Why go? What was the point of the hunt?"

She looked down at the table and lowered her voice. "Being with my dad." She closed her eyes, just for an instant then looked at him. "Spending time with him. He had a warm plaid flannel jacket." She paused, throwing the night into silence. She wanted the silence to carry on with a mind of its own ignoring the words she heard herself uttering and to stop playing the passive aggressive, a quiet brimmed with unheard words. The thoughts in her head and the painful memories were rising to the surface. "I used to love the smell." She smiled. "It smelled like him, like the woods, campfires, tents and eating pork and beans out of a can. I'd put on his jacket and wrap up like it was a blanket." She looked out the window taking in a rush of air through the tiny opening and emitting a sigh. "I wanted to spend time with him, that's all."

"Couldn't just go to a movie?"

She shook her head.

"Didn't he know?"

She smoothed her hair, feeling the harsh firm strands. "That last hunting trip, when we got back to the truck, he asked me why I fudged my aim. He said it like I was lying and depriving him of something that was his. I asked him how he knew…" She laughed. "He said, "No one has that bad of an aim." She wanted Jaimie to live with her in her story and enjoy her dad's humor. It was important that he knew her father was good and strong man. He should laugh and understand her passion for someone she could never replace, but most of all, he had to know her dad loved her. Someone loved her. Someone loved her more than anything in the world. There really were people who cared about her and would miss her if she was gone.

He gave it a minute while he wrestled with his feelings. He'd become tangled in her underlying plea and neediness, but it didn't worry him. He got it. He knew he had to show appreciation. She was opening her soul and expecting a reward. To give less would put them back where they started and he'd worked diligently to get to where they were, making him a willing participant to walk into her past, sweeping away the debris, but how deep was enough? To pretend to care would be a rue though too much would be an obstacle. He did care, but she was flighty bird and he knew it. He didn't want to send her flying... "Does he still hunt?"

"He's gone." An awkward smile, turning up as discomfort came over her face pointing the spotlight on a grieving soul wandering aimlessly over a loved one's passing. "I guess somehow I knew I had to spend time with him. He died three days later. Just never came home." She didn't give herself freedom to wear sadness on her face. She wanted to see Jaimie's face, his expression and whether, or not he was emotionally stirred by her sorrow. Was his face a blank? Did lines appear across his forehead? Did his eyes show compassion? Who was the man sharing her space? Would he take her hunting and pretend not to notice her pathetic aim? Would he climb an unfriendly mountain and make her a widow?

"What happened?"

"Logging accident."

"Dangerous profession." He fell silent. "I'm sorry." Another well-spaced silence. "How old were you?"

"Thirteen."

"That's a shame."

"It is a shame."

Her eyes were puddles, pools of tears yet to fall...

He saw his reflection in her eyes. He could see his failings and vulnerability causing him to concede. He wasn't her teacher, nor was she his, but maybe they found each other at a time when each needed someone to hold and take away emptiness falling deeply in the cracks developed by all the other times in their lives. Maybe they were joined to teach one another and learn about themselves through friendship and perhaps love. They had come together to heal and survive. With little prompt, he vowed to keep her with him, for as long as she would stay. He knew what he had to do... Tears started in her eyes. He smiled. "Knock, knock."

"Who's there?"

"Knock, knock."

"Who's there?"

The cafeteria was rife with eaters, butterers, dippers and crunchers. Grandmother moved effortlessly in the neighborly environment, indiscreetly waving and showing other gestures of recognition and appreciation to familiar faces. She sat a table across from Jaimie, barely seating herself before beginning to talk. "I don't think highly of myself. Everything I know I got from someone else." She observed him, searching for a subtle reaction, glazed over eyes, sudden interest in something beyond their table, a tick, anything offering an indication of where his head was at the moment, not that it mattered... She was willing to share everything she'd kept bottled for what seemed like forever. "My mother taught me to clean and cook. My father taught me to chop wood and hunt animals." She looked Jaimie over once more. "My husband taught me to love another so completely that I lost myself. My son showed me how to argue without anger. I don't think there's a piece of me that's not owned by someone else."

"Oh, come-on, we all learn from our parents and the people we meet." He didn't mean to call her out, but felt inclined, still he was intrigued. The woman had come out of her shell and was spilling herself all over the table. He wanted to encourage, not discourage, but give a little heat too, in the form of adversary responses and minor bumps to give her a need to work harder in getting it all out there. He didn't mind taking the plunge and seeing if she'd jump in with him and show how far she could swim.

She leaned forward and looked head side to side as though bestowing a dark secret. "Birds taught me to sing." She sat back against her chair. In an instant, she was empty, a hollow shell thinking she dumped her insides out and now there wasn't a speck left for her. She'd said too much causing herself to become haunted and bewildered. She'd shared more than she expected and wanted her words returned to her, every word, every experience. If she could've reached inside his head and retrieved them, she would've done it. Her blabber was an incredible violation to her emotional balance and she was ashamed. A large lump arranged itself in her throat bringing her to take heavy breaths to remove the sick feeling and promote her stomach to ease up a bit on the nausea. Goose-bumps marked her skin adding another source of embarrassment. Couldn't she please, just disappear?

He had no idea what was going on inside her head. What had happened since he last saw her? Before him was someone he cared about, sharing her life. "Why, look at that, a bird taught you to sing. That's unique and beautiful."

"It's not. It's poverty. My parents couldn't afford lessons."

"You had a gift."

She pursed her lips, turning her head to the side, a slight smile coming over her face. She whispered, "I'd sit in the yard and listen to the birds and try to copy their voices."

"How'd it work out? Can you sing?"

She cleared her throat and pushed her chair from the table. She parted her lips, closed her eyes and tossed her head back delivering achingly harmonious falsetto notes that compared in beauty and depth to anything nature could offer.

His mouth hung open and his eyebrows raised. "My God, woman." He glanced about the cafeteria. "What you have there is a gift. Everyone hears it. They're all looking at you."

She shrugged and rolled her eyes. "It's not the gift. They're staring at the crazy. If you do something out of the norm, you'll always get a stare." She stretched her neck and shoulders. "I can crack every vertebrae into place after that. That's about the best use I have for it."

"You have to let people hear you. You have talent." His head stormed with ideas, stuff coming in from everything he'd ever known, experienced, or heard, but he recognized the hour was a bit late for a career. He wanted to encourage her, but focused on her other issues. "I think I have a pen." He felt around checking his pockets and came up with nothing.

"I'm not eighteen. Do you really think a record company is going to give me an opportunity?" She took a pen from her purse.

He bit at his lower lip, unfolding a clean napkin and setting it in front of her on the table. "Draw a line down the middle." He waited for her to proceed. "Now write the words, bad, on one side and good on the other side." He pointed to a spot on the napkin. "No, right there at the top."

She looked at him. He smiled reassuringly. "Just bear with me on this." He waited. "Now underline them."

She underlined the words, awkwardly handling the pen and not a bit curious about what was to follow. She felt like a child. He guided her with his soothing manner and warm smile. She felt swaddled and secure. He felt like a man, a protector. "Write everything good in your life in the good column and the bad in the bad column." He turned his chair toward the other side of the room facing the windows. "I'm not going to watch you." He looked off into the distance. "Take your time and write what ever you want."

The pen was poison in her hand. She turned it between her fingers and disliked it for becoming a blathering tool. Still, she worked it, and as emotionally bedraggled as she found herself, she made the effort.

He kept his eyes on the windows. "What do you have?"

"Nothing."

"Come-on…" He waited for substance. Certainly, she'd come up with something useful. He walked to the fountain and brought back two cups of ice water in time to hear the sound of the pen dropping onto the table, the clatter of accomplishment. "You finished?"

"I have it."

He brought his chair back around facing her. "Now what you do with that list is up to you, but it can tell you something about yourself and how you're living your life." He sipped from his water glass and handed the other to her. "It can tell you what you want and what you don't want. It's up to you to take it from there."

She held the napkin close to her eyes, reading the words she'd written. "Good list, One, Sandy."

He nodded, "Nice."

"Two, Rebecca."

"Your friend, good."

"Three, Thomas."

"Of course, your son."

She lowered the napkin, bringing it just below her peering eyes. She looked into his… "Four, Jaimie."

His eyes widened, and the beaming smile couldn't slip from his face. "How many Jaimie's do you know?"

Her cheeks reddened, the gushing painting her face in crimson. "Just you."

"Me?" It was everything, but soon would be nothing if he made it out to be everything. He nodded appreciatively and moved on... "What about the bad list?"

She looked down at the napkin. "One, Elizabeth."

His laugh was contagious and robust gathering strangers into his private circle while her contribution came off as reserved and self-conscious eking out a faint giggle and making the two, one within a mysterious bond coming on faster than societal norm, but for that divine minute they were united by light bitterness and a side step to sarcasm. She breathed louder than she expected, surprised she could be a part of something larger than herself, something that didn't include Michael. It was an accomplishment that would've tasted better in the coziness of her kitchen, yet she settled nicely leaning back in her chair and folding her arms. "It's strange. I wrote her name on the list and she disappeared from my thoughts." She leaned forward, closer to him. "This is the first time I've been free of her since I've been in Seattle."

"No one else on the list?"

"She makes my life a living hell."

He nodded. Nothing else needed saying.

She dressed herself in gloom, setting her elbows on the table and resting her head in her hands. "She's back in my head now. I spoke too soon."

"Ignore her."

She sighed, dropping her head back. "Ignore her while she's ignoring me?" She rolled her eyes, gathering her thoughts. "I've been here over a week and I haven't had a moment with my son without her hovering like a vulture up on a wire. She's in his room like an elephant." She paused, narrowing her eyes. "Make that a big elephant with twenty pounds of make-up."

He understood her frustration. He hadn't lived seventy one years without coming across women battling and tying each other into knots. "I like elephants."

"I like elephants too, but she's right there, glaring, ridiculing and ignoring me and no one talks about it. It's like she's not there, but she is."

"Talk to her."

She shook her head, looking down at the napkin. "Before this, I'd never met her. How can she hate me when she doesn't know me?" She paused then picked up momentum. "I saw her in the hall Thursday. I could tell she'd ignore me, but there were people around, so I kept calling her name anyway." Grandmother took a deep breath. Anxiety and anger had her in their grip. "I asked her nicely if we could have a cup of tea together." She threw her hands in the air. "And nothing... She didn't say anything. I asked her why she didn't like me and she said, "Are you finished?" I said yes, and she clomped off with those... Who wears stilettos to a hospital?"

"She does." He pulled his cap over his head. "You'd be surprised how cold my head gets now that I don't have much hair." He chuckled. "Why don't we get out of here and get you where you're not thinking about zoo animals."

She crumbled the napkin and picked up her purse. He held her coat for her while she slowly slipped inside, then quickly removed the covering, placing it back on her chair. "I'm not used to being pampered."

He adjusted the cap on his head. "Pampering is what I do. I'm an old man with no children, no grandchildren, so no one to indulge. I'm a pamperer." He gazed at her, noticing she wasn't getting ready to leave. He laid her jacket back over the back of the chair, lowered his eyes and sat back down. His smile was difficult to read. He just looked at her as though he was prepared to throw in the towel. "It's been two weeks." He folded his hands pressing his thoughts together in one cohesive lump. "This is the end of our time together. You're going home tomorrow." He peered into her eyes searching for a morsel telling him he was on the right track, but her skill at hiding didn't give him much ground. He didn't question. "I can't think of anything more devastating than to not see you again."

Her eyes watered. She felt a stab in her chest and a lump in her throat. She prayed she wouldn't have to comment while sitting wrapped in herself with her troubles spilling out onto the floor. She was shaking inside and praying her nervousness wasn't visible.

He passed over all of it. "I don't want this to end, but I know it will..." There wasn't a place for him to slip easily into her life. She had nooks and crannies locked. There were too many spaces brimmed with every misfortune and sour thought she'd come across in her travels.

She placed her hands on the table, hoping he'd know what to do with them. "Say something funny."

He saw his opening... "Knock, knock."

"Who's there?"

"Knock, knock."

"Who's there?" She started to cry.

He put his hands on hers. "I care about you."

She nodded and didn't ask for more. She gave what she

could give. He sensed she felt the same though he cursed the past for hoarding her feelings. He knew everything about her, yet nothing though with all that he lacked he was able to find the energy to soldier on, that burst bringing him to his feet. He stood, eyes bright and for a second time, lifted her jacket from the back of her chair and held it out for her. This time, she slipped inside and stayed inside. He melted, but displayed none of it. "Come-on, I want to show you the most beautiful church in the world."

"Catholic?"

"Of course, the cathedral."

From the cafeteria, they walked into the hall immersed in their own universe until Elizabeth saw Grandmother at the same moment Grandmother spotted her. Grandmother readied herself for the cold and brutal disregard. Her body tightened. Jaimie felt the change and held her near. "Are you okay?"

She was an amateur ventriloquist, barely moving her lips. "That's Elizabeth." It was hard for her to breathe.

He turned his head, catching sight of her. "Ah, good ole' queen bee..." He moved his tongue across his front teeth. "She's got her sparkles and bangles. She's a spiced up show pony ready to circle the ring." He shook his head with little satisfaction. "Oh, she's a dandy."

Grandmother wrapped her arms around herself, rubbing her skin raw. "Do you like her?"

He laughed, "As much as I like gum stuck to the bottom of my shoe." He pulled her in like she was the love of his life. They were two lovers on a boardwalk. "May I put my arm around you?" With a protective arm wrapped over her shoulders, he called out... "Good afternoon, Ms. Elizabeth---And a fine day it is."

Grandmother tucked her face into his side. "She's staring."

"She's on the bad list. No one cares."

Grandmother giggled like a child. She was safe and secure for the first time in for as long as she could remember. He was a seat belt, a lock keeping out the darkness, but he was more... He knew the combination. He could unlock passion living inside herself, passion that long ago she's placed in a strangle hold. He was a warm shield, someone finally, to lean on and to love. Her eyes hadn't been open since Michael made his departure. "Should I see if she's watching?"

"No, don't look back. Keep walking." He kissed her cheek.

"She'll tell my son."

"Good. Keep walking. Know your audience."

"She'll know the truth."

He put his hand on her face, gently lifting her chin. "What is the truth?"

"The truth is I have to stop here at the little girl's room." She broke from him and went for the door." I'll be right back."

"I'll be right here, my good lady."

She went inside, checking herself in the mirror, putting her hands on her face and screaming into them. With an honest sense of compassion, she spoke to the woman in the reflection. "How did this happen? How, how did this happen?" She walked back out into the hall, saw Jaimie and walked in the opposite direction as though she was alone. She took a deep breath and called over her shoulder, "CherylAnne."

He followed her. "Pardon?"

She turned around and walked backword still a few feet

ahead of him. "It's CherylAnne. My name is CherylAnne." She turned and kept walking, leaving him behind.

"Oh, boy..." He shook his head, sparks of happiness slapping at him. He walked faster, catching up and standing before her. "I knew it."

"How could you know?"

"I knew your name would be as beautiful as you are." He bowed and extended his hand. "May I have this dance, Ms. CherylAnne?" He took her hand, twirling her across the ballroom floor, the hospital floor to those gawking. She stepped on his toes, tripping over her own feet, but managing to hang on to him. She knew from that moment she would always hang on to him. He made it easy. He didn't draw attention to her stumbling. "Just follow me. You're doing fine." When those around them applauded, He ended the dance. "Now, as you were saying... The truth is..."

"That I don't like her."

"That you don't like Elizabeth?"

"Yes."

His body shook with laughter. "The truth shall set you free."

Chapter 9

Barefoot and up on his toes, Sandy set the jar on the counter. He hopped onto a stool and took a single serving of strawberries from the freezer. "These?"

Rebecca was across the kitchen preparing astragalus root and slicing reishi for an herbal blend. "Let's use the berries we harvested today." She watched him set the package back into the freezer, carefully moving it into the spot where he found it. She couldn't help, but smile. There wasn't a better roommate. "Good job."

He was moving about the kitchen like a tiny butterfly fluttering over summer blossoms. "I want to use our dried marshmallow leaves, Mom."

"Argue your case."

He thought a moment. "Because they're soft and squishy. They feel nice, Mom."

"And the chamomile?"

"I want to use the dried because it's more sweet." He shook his head, erasing his words. "I mean sweeter. It's sweeter." He didn't think she was convinced. "It's too late to harvest fresh chamomile today. Chamomile should be harvested in the morning when volatile oils are in the flower heads."

She beamed with joy, rushed to him and kissed

his forehead. "You're a treasure. Now what about the elderberries?"

"Whole dried."

"Fine." Between her fingers were red clover blossoms and calendula in a medium glass bowl where striking red flowers and bright yellow calendula petals were as beautiful as a summer rain. Without turning, she continued… "Grandma called this morning."

His heart sunk to the pit of his stomach, dropping him to the floor in a heap of disappointment, an extraordinary body droop, starting at the head and moving down through his shoulders and culminating in a dramatic torso slump, then a fall to his knees in the flat out, face down, stiff as a board spectacle.

She went on with her tasks. "Listen to me."

His arms were flying and his legs were in rapid motion with his feet pounding the floor in an uninterrupted exhibition of loss of control.

"Tell me when you're ready to talk." She stepped over him to get measuring cups. "When you feel calm, let me know."

He dragged himself across the floor on his tummy grabbing onto her leg and pulling himself up in desperation. She walked awkwardly mixing ingredients and tending to her harvest. He wanted to be rescued. She hummed quietly. When the time was right, he gathered himself, got to his feet and affixed himself to her shirt tail. "I don't want to leave you, Mom." Tears ran down his cheeks.

She wiped a tear from her eye, then another… "Grandma is staying in Seattle another couple weeks." She lifted him onto her hip. "That's fourteen days." Sandy slid off her hip and jumped up and down until she touched his shoulder and stopped him. "I get it. You don't want to stay here." She smiled.

"I want to stay here, Mom."

"I know." She knew he wanted to stay, but she wanted to hear him say it. She held him, wrapping her arms around him with more love than she knew she was capable of giving though his arms hung to his sides giving her a taste of emptiness, something on the lines of telling someone you love them and meeting vacant eyes. An uncomfortable hollow haunting resided in her chest. She could've grabbed his arms and placed them around her, but that would've been like writing her own love letter and passing it off as a note from the one who had her heart. She rubbed his back, thinking of ways to explain herself. "You don't know it, but hugging without being hugged in return is like sleeping with the lights on. It saps energy." He looked at her with empty eyes as though whatever lived there had abandoned him. It didn't matter. How could anything matter anymore? So much was going on around her. "Your grandpa used to say that new paths appear when old paths falter. What do you think of that?"

I think he's old and dead. Did he write a book?"

"I don't think he wrote a book."

"Do you want my honest opinion?"

"Yes."

"He should've written a book." He pushed a chair up to the stove, turned on the burner and set an empty pot on the element. "It's like this." He positioned it the way he wanted it. "I know how to do it."

She pointed to the faucet. "Water in first." She looked after him to be sure he complied and to enjoy the way he moved, his eager foot placements and determined little hands seeking out what he'd seen her do many times. He was intent on getting everything right and accepting her approval, showing his need in the way he carefully took a pitcher from the refrigerator and poured water into the pan. "Now honey and strawberries. I want to put in blueberries." He turned his eyes toward her, knowing she was the key to his success, that she owned his future. The things she did, like coaching him through what he was able to do painted a crosswalk he could pass over to teach someone else tomorrow.

"In the freezer. Do you know why we aren't using fresh blueberries?" She pointed out the chair. "Move it. Unsafe."

"Yup." He pushed the chair. "Blueberries aren't ready to harvest." He did know… "I think a blueberry is blue because it's not a fish." He settled the chair in its place.

She was curious, but challenged him by keeping her thoughts to herself and casually moving forward. "I think it's a good day."

He tended his means, waiting for the water to boil. "A good day is when a plant grows." His toes curled, uncurled and his fingers moved endlessly. "Avalanche lilies are white."

"There're yellow avalanche lilies."

"What about mine? I only want white because Lily is white."

"The flowers you planted will be white. You'll see… You can't plant carrots and get potatoes."

"Huckleberries are red, or blue."

"Yes."

"Blueberries are blue so they won't get called salmon berries."

"You've lost me."

He ran to his room and laid on the floor near his small

flower pot. "They're coming up green. It's the first leaf. I'm a father. I'm a single dad."

Evening was the same most nights, dinner and a walk about the grounds after employees had gone for the day. There were rose petal and lavender baths and on most evenings Rebecca rubbed Sandy's shoulders with rosemary and chamomile essential oils and tucked him in for the night. A forehead kiss and a special pattern of words in a calming manner with her dutiful gentle hand bringing his blankets to his chin were a given. Lily had to be snuggled, identically. What appeared lengthly was nothing in the context of a child's lifetime. She wanted to teach him everything she knew about plants. It wasn't clear as to how long he would stay with her, but by then, she knew he was a gift and she would do whatever would take to provide him with a positive home base. Their routine felt natural, real and after all was said and done, an aspect of his world that would stay with him forever.

He absorbed her kindness, enjoyed the kiss to his forehead, closed his eyes, waited until she moved on, sat up, checked out his window for the light of the moon and read a book. She knew it, but it soothed her. It brought a charming familiarity, wrapping both of them, in a richness, a synchronicity, illuminated in the power of written words. She was in her room, lying in bed, reading by lamp light. He was in his room reading by the light of the moon. As though together, but not... Two lamps, two windows, cozy in a way she couldn't describe. She shared his passion. He knew about hers. The best is done in stolen moments, and to read into the dark of night, willing the eyes to go one more chapter, or until they sting and close, is what gives life its crust.

Every moment was crisp and pure with Sandy on board lending mornings and evenings a harmonious rhythm and subtle whisper of new beginnings. It wasn't unreasonable to think that, that pleasant sequence would forever be part of life at the nursery. The days were rewarding, with Rebecca, jubilant and always up first, checking in employees and making certain business was running smoothly. She went over notes she'd penned the night before, called workers into groups and delivered her thoughts. She received opinions, suggestions and welcomed new ideas.

He awakened on his own. He was free to gauge his sleeping hours by the set of his inner clock. She expected him to get into bed by eight in the evening, but she didn't dictate the workings of his mind. Reading and writing, important and soulful needs were best experienced with a clear head and minus daily struggle. Midnight oil was to be used. That and an empty stomach were the means to creativity.

Wednesday, the day of the week known to have gotten sea legs and thus moving by momentum, was the day she'd chosen to have Paully eat dinner at her house. She rejected Monday, whom required levitation to bring it into action and there was no hope for Friday. Yes, Wednesday, Paully's day off at the hospital was the best plan. She would let Sandy know soon after he'd gotten out of bed. It was sensible to wait until the last moment, to let him know of coming events. He couldn't stand anticipation. He'd become anxious, irritated and unable to eat, or sleep. She'd make it easy on him and easy on herself.

He wobbled to the kitchen and rubbed sleep form his eyes. She smiled. "Good morning, sunshine."

"My name is Sandy."

She picked him up. "You're a big boy, but not so big I

can't hold you. I better do a lot of this before you grow so tall you touch the ceiling."

"I want rice with blueberries and honey." He swallowed with great enthusiasm, much like the yawn of baby lion and in a flamboyant manner began stretching himself to life. "I don't want fish berries."

"What kind of honey?

"Raw, local honey."

"Okay, honey it is."

With each passing day, he gained and retained an increasing knowledge of plants and flowers. He devoured books on flowers and trees, as well as picked Rebecca's brain matter for the wisdom of her experience. He sat at the table, legs crossed at his ankles and a hint of a smile turning up the corners of his mouth. "I'm going to grow a Boswellia sacra tree."

She swallowed a mouthful of rice. "I'd like to see it." She took another bite, but kept her attention on him. "You know our climate is cooler than their native environment."

"I'm taking that into consideration." He balanced his chin on his clenched fist.

"Have you thought about weather?"

"It's hot."

"Over there it is…"

"Lily said it will grow in the greenhouse." He was barely tending his breakfast, merely picking at the food on his plate. "They're almost gone." He let his head fall and closed his eyes. "I like the smell. It's happy." He picked-up a blueberry and put it in his mouth. "Extinction is bad."

She fell silent, appreciating his enthusiasm and concern for the struggle of living things dependent on the intelligent and sustainable use of humans. "Let's look into it, but understand it's July. Seeds won't be available before September. "There's a season to everything, you know." She knew it was an up hill battle. "We have more avalanche lily seeds in the freezer. You can plant those soon."

He whispered to Lily, offering spoonfuls of rice and intermittently looking at Rebecca. His expressions were stereotypes he'd adopted as his own, products of observations he'd made while watching others suffer through complications and harmonious occasions, then seamlessly applying them to his own life, mimicking with cartoon like performances and amusing those around him.

Rebecca and Sandy carried their conversation well into the dinner hour. They talked of daily routines, though frankincense commanded the attention. "Frankincense likes me." He hung tightly to the words Rebecca used relating to plants, did as he was asked and helped her put dinner on the plates. As always, Paully arrived early, making faces at Sandy through the screen door and making a game of letting him inside. "Come on, Buddy." He carried a bouquet behind his back, losing it to Sandy, who pulled the herb branches from Paully's hands, comically smelling them and scratching the top of his head with one manically curved finger. "Yarrow, archillea millefolium. It's named after Achilles. He was a great soldier. He took yarrow to war to heal cuts and big gunshot holes."

Paully looked at Rebecca. "True?"

"True." She kissed Paully's cheek. "You have to get out more. Come-on, dinner's ready."

"I'm early."

"Guess not. Come-on, sweetheart." She moved her hips, seductively perhaps, but not anything she could be held accountable for, as she walked toward the table dragging

Paully behind her in his languishing state, holding in emotions in need of freedom.

"Don't say it unless you mean it." A soft chuckle settled his cover rendering what he believed to be a good performance. He had feelings hitting at him from all angles creating a sea of frustration, eagerness and loss.

She threw the cloth into the sink, looked over her shoulder and smiled. "Who says I don't?"

He winked, catching loaded undertones, fueling thoughts foremost on his mind. "Women are trouble."

She turned quickly lighting her face with a satisfaction she wore without resistance. "All women?"

"You're killing me."

"Free pass."

"Is it okay if I wash my hands in the kitchen?"

"Feel free..."

He grinned at Sandy. "I've got the go ahead."

Sandy came from behind pushing him to the sink. "Wash your hands." He wrapped his arms around Paully's legs, holding securely and babbling incessantly. "Yarrow is in the Asteraceae flowering family. Have you heard of chrysanthemums?" He was on his toes getting a look at Paully's face, blinking often exaggerating his expressions. "Call them mums. Mums are in the Asteraceae family. Do you like daisies? Daisies are in the Asteraceae family." He let loose of Paully's leg while Paully reached for a towel, drying his hands as Sandy continued, "Dandelions are in the family. Lily isn't a bully to dandelions."

Paully took Sandy's hand leading him to the table and getting up into his seat. "Let's eat." In a glance he knew he was appreciated, tended to... A feast laid out in careful detail meant more than stuffing stomachs. The center-piece was a hand painted ceramic vase filled with flowers, bright and charming. Large-headed daisies, red carnations and purple monte-casinos, looked over the table with an elegance and showering the room with their heavenly fragrances. The colors matched the cloth napkins, folded like swans, and glasses, sparkling like crystal. The food was summer, in color and greens. Last rays of sunlight came in from the window, glowing over the celebration and Paully was alive inside, with gushy passion. His conversation came easily and he enjoyed Sandy, all the more. "You made salad? Then I'm not eating it." He watched Sandy's face for a grin of recognition.

It didn't arrive. Sandy questioned with his eyes, intellectual lad that he was, with most humor riding high above his head. He furled his brows and braved the mood with a frightful frown.. "You're a bully to salads."

"Okay, you twisted my arm. I'll eat it." He looked toward Rebecca for help, throwing his hands in the air, in question of Sandy's lack of following the fun he believed he was handing him.

"I didn't twist your arm. It's too big." ... Yet another indication that he wasn't able to grasp words except in their most literal and painfully elementary sense, though it brought an often humorous lift from the mundane and often predicted expectation that most people would easily surmise from verbal communication. Even as it could be considered fun with moments of hilarity, at times the best to be experienced was subtle, sympathetic enjoyment. Other times it was a laborious undertaking, and Paully had yet to get on board with Sandy's manner of understanding communication and humor, making it an interesting set.

She set a bowl of grilled garlic and artichokes on the

table. "Yes, he made the salad." She gestured to Sandy to sit near her. "Tell Paully what's in it."

Sandy put a cushion on his chair, raising himself closer to the table-top. "Fresh flowers." He pointed to the large glass bowl. "Nasturtiums, Johnny jump, violas and zinnias." Paully was making eyes at Rebecca. Sandy stopped and stared, frustrated by expressions he didn't understand. He focused on Paully and stood on his chair, raising his voice to over ride the flirty behavior. "Are you listening?" He repeated himself, speaking louder and placing his hands on his hips, the way he'd seen Cara emphasize her status. "Nasturtiums, Johnny jump, violas and zinnias." He laid a heavy weight on zinnias as though verbally underlining the word. "They're flowers. You can eat them, but not Lily." He gave his best angry face. "Do not eat Lily." He put his hand on the table. "She's sitting here and she is not dinner."

Paully behaved himself, but focused on Rebecca, while talking to Sandy. "I already heard that part about Nasturtiums and all that."

Sandy sat on his chair. "That's watercress, arugula, and spinach…" He looked toward Rebecca. "Uh, Mom, what's that plant?"

"Avocado."

Paully took a closer look. "You'll make me healthy whether I want it, or not."

Sandy got onto his knees and patted Paully's shoulder. "Good health is important." He made sure Paully noticed him, moving himself about with his words. "Rebecca Wilkins said that." He made a face at him. "Do you want to be healthy?"

Paully laughed. "I'm out-numbered... And yes, of course

I do." He eyed Rebecca from across the table, "I love you, Mom."

The word love... Sandy jumped to his feet, stood on his chair, shaking his body in a silly dance. "If it's love, marry her. Marry her, marry her, marry her. Lily said marry her."

If anything could silence a room, the word marry could do it. Rattled off recklessly, it could do things to a person's head. None of them good. The room took on a pin drop silence, leaving unintended and unspoken concern, though Sandy, oblivious to his part in the charged stillness, carried on a conversation with Lily. Paully chose deflection, stealing a red zinnia and putting it in his mouth, serving more than one purpose. It would take the attention away from marriage and keep him quiet. He'd thought about marriage, of course he had, but that evening it wasn't on the menu even though if he'd been honest with himself, he would've been up there with Sandy jumping on his chair. All considered, it wasn't the night to shake the earth to its knees.

She cut it short. "Please, sit down, bottom on chair." She threw a look Sandy didn't understand. "Back to dinner."

Sandy kept his eyes in his space, hurrying to put his bottom in the seat. "The less there is to justify a traditional custom, the harder it is to get rid of it." He sat motionless in his chair, his hands in his lap. "Mark Twain wrote that."

Paully awkwardly held tongs between his fingers. "I've never gotten the hang of these." Barely trapped pieces of salad, moved into his bowl, tempting Rebecca to ask how he handled a scalpel, or managed to stitch up a laceration.

Sandy reached into the salad with his hands. "Do it like this."

She stopped him, gently touching his arm. Let's not... We use good manners. Later we'll talk about why..."

"Noble madam, men's evil manners live in brass; their virtues we write in water." Following Paully's lead, he stuffed the zinnia into his mouth. "Shakespeare wrote that."

The meal progressed and common subjects were discussed. Wedding plans were under the table and forgotten. Sandy talked of frankincense and its environment. "A tree will grow in my life." He was alive with over done expressions and outbursts. Each day he was using essential oils, rubbing dabs behind his ears and on the soles of his feet. Frankincense often enhanced his warm bath and in the evenings, he inhaled the sweet grounding scent. Rebecca placed a diffuser in his room and one in the main living area, using essential oils of oregano, basil, lavender, prim-rose, rosemary, bergamot, chamomile, peppermint, eucalyptus, thieves, raven, ginger, tea tree, lemon and others, at one time, or another helping him to achieve a pleasant balance. He knew them well by common and scientific names. He looked at Paully. "Peppermint is a bully to pain." He spelled out in details, his plans to sow, feed and nurture a healthy Boswellia sacra tree in one of the greenhouses, and filled Paully's head with words he'd read and his experiences with the herb. "I'll make a cut in the trunk of my tree," he proclaimed though hardly appeared ready to perform such a violation. His eyes narrowed. He pulled his hands together in self-protective armor and his head dropped to his chest. "I hope that won't hurt." He launched into a quiet moment, promptly regaining composure, "The sap will come. The sap will dry. I will get it and break it. That is my resin." He pushed back his shoulders and puffed his chest, sitting on his pot of gold.

Paully shook his head, hanging onto Sandy's every

syllable with a train wreck kind of absorption. He didn't want to look, but had to... "How do you know this stuff?"

Sandy shrugged. "Books."

Paully wasn't up on volatile oils, therapeutic constituents, or matters related to herbal healing. As a physician assistant, his knowledge was similar to most United States physicians, he practiced western medicine. He worked in a hospital ER saving lives and making healthy decisions for patients who needed answers and emergency treatments. He hadn't studied Traditional Chinese Medicine, or Ayurveda, though his feelings for Rebecca and her interests in alternative healing, opened his mind to possibilities he thought of as apart from his academic learning, but both methods of healing were side by side, waiting for someone to notice. He tapped Rebecca's wrist. "You were doing things with herbs when we were kids, right?" He didn't leave space for an answer. "I thought it was a hobby, but now you've helped my mom with cancer." He was interested, but skeptic. "What do you have for bone pain? She's having a time of it." His eyes were tired. "Prescriptions are knocking her out. She wants to be out of pain, not incapacitated."

"Herbs won't give her the relief she can get from a narcotic, but herbs can help. Everyone's different though, what works well for one, might not work for someone else." She noticed his weariness. "As long as you know that..." She remembered his mother's chocolate chip cookies and picnics in her front yard. "Peppermint kicks pain." She pressed her lips together. "She can try lavender and bergamot. I love bergamot for rubbing into my hips." She took a bite of avocado. "I don't know, my bones hurt in winter. In summer they're fine." She read his eyes, but knowing Sandy wouldn't be in bed for a while. There wouldn't be time to be alone.

"Are those the only ones?"

"No, tree tea is a favorite of a friend of mine." She held his hand from across the table. "I don't know if it's strong enough for her pain, but she can try it." She squeezed his hand. "I'm sorry, sweetheart. Life can be heartless."

"You're a healer." He squeezed her hand, happy just to be able to touch her. Someday all of it would be easy, natural. He wouldn't have to hide his intentions, like a thief.

"Not me, the herbs. If you're in a mood for gratitude, thank the herbs of our earth. They give their healing oils anointing us with their love." Exhaustion, the sister of gravity weighted her shoulders and burdened her mind and beyond that, she'd used the word love, sending it out into the room without thinking. or because she was thinking... "I'm the messenger." She looked into his eyes. "Is everything okay? You have a strange look on your face."

"No, I'm fine. I'm just wondering about the books."

"You know, those old things, papers, typed words, bound and forgotten by a lot of today's population."

"Yeah, I get that, but how he remembers all this stuff... He's four."

"Five, next week."

"Are you having a party?"

"Of course, will you be there?"

"You know it." He pushed his food around on his plate. "But yeah, four, five, no difference. He's a smart kid."

"He is…" She put her fingers under Sandy's chin. "Are you a smart kid."

"Yup."

"He is..."

Sandy had removed himself from the conversation when it was no longer about frankincense. He talked to

Lily, his hand covering his mouth. He didn't listen to group conversation until he heard his name, then politely excused himself and turned to Rebecca. "This is the best time to go to Mount Rainier. Tomorrow is August." He took a deep breath. "Lily Erythronium Montanum said that."

"She's right."

He expected resistance and didn't know how to react when it didn't arrive. He folded his arms. "All the flowers are coming out. Most of the lilies are gone." He frowned. "Lily will show me some, in forest places."

"Right again."

"Can we?"

Rebecca looked at Paully, who returned the gaze, but for a different reason. Sandy brought the attention back to himself. "It's our last chance, Mom."

"We'll get up there." She gave Paully her troubled, how will this all fall together look. He understood, but failed to comment. He didn't have an answer.

Sandy wrapped his arms around himself, saving energy for the big argument. Discontent and opposition made him sleepy. Closing his eyes and dreaming of Mount Rainier comforted him. In his dreams, wild flowers offered their scents and waited for him, high upon the mountain. He pushed back his chair and gave it one last try. "Native Americans boil avalanche lily bulbs." He pouted, pushing out his lower lip. He'd seen someone do that, somewhere and at some time. "I have to go before they eat all of them." Rebecca listened attentively and Paully watched Rebecca, dependent on her cues for his own responses. Sandy continued, "They drank lily milk." He didn't think Rebecca was listening and he tapped her shoulder. "Hello, hello, in there."

Chapter 10

CherylAnne arrived back in South Brook and most of the community knew about it. The forest internet was minus towers, but had a fairly stable wagging of tongues, making it faster than many smart phones. She couldn't get back into her cozy home without someone whispering to another, but as it turned out, her first visitor upon her return wasn't a regular member of the forest community. Thomas had Be Be on his mind. He was there to reel her in, and when he learned Sandy was staying with her, he had a reason to pay her a visit, and actions, having their origin in the formation of a single thought, wedged into Thomas' mind freely romping, alerting mental chambers, creating sympathetic support and pushing his breezy idea into a poorly organized plan, but it was self importance that drove him to South Brook, ready to foster his happiness without taking anyone else's into consideration. He'd traced the pain in his life back to the error of not marrying her. It was a day to right the wrong.

He turned his car east into her driveway, charging like a bull souped up in a can't wait mentality and speeding to her door minus forethought and unknowingly canceling the possibility of success, leaving in its place a vapid, obsessive undertaking not meant to go well. He was rebellious and unbridled, rolling into her domain in his fancy car, but in his mind he was a gentleman on a white steed galloping toward her house to save the fair maiden. He was a prince.

Rebecca stood outside her front door chatting with an employee. The two of them looked up with the spitting of gravel and large cloud of dust. She didn't recognize the car though quickly realized no one in the forest would drive anything beyond a truck, or other appropriate mountain transportation. Her employee stood near her, arms folded with a smile smeared across his face as though drawn with a pencil. He felt her guarded and anxious posturing. She'd suddenly crossed her arms and had gone from a casual stance to one of alertness, her eyes darting, carefully watching Thomas' every move and noting the expression on his face. He saw apprehension in her eyes and an acute change of mood, allowing him insight into her frame of mind, but more than that, he got a clear view of the man in the driveway. He didn't know his name, but he'd seen him there on a couple of occasions. Once again, he looked toward his boss, gauging her reaction and making simple conversation. "Hmm, nice car." She gave him a look of dissatisfaction. He tipped his hat, aware he should move along, but the car held his interest. "Bet the price tags upward of one hundred fifty thousand." She wasn't interested in Thomas' financial success. Money wasn't everything. He and Rebecca made departing nods and he walked to the greenhouses, looking over his shoulder once, or twice, while she eyed Thomas.

He was coming for her, and she waited for the honor of his presence. He didn't disappoint, stepping from his car, dapper and smug with a swagger in a slap in the face condescending fashion he'd perfected, laced with a know-it-all front, enough to poison any kindness he meant to unleash. Truth finds its way through mazes of deception and the brew Thomas was churning was no exception. He sauntered up tearing her heart apart. He may well have been a good man, but he could smell pain from miles away, and he immediately caught the pain in her eyes. It heightened his moment, giving him energy and satisfaction. If he were able, he'd take others' suffering and press it between the pages of a book like an autumn leaf, going back to admire and imprint it in his soul. On that day, he passed her palpable sadness as suffering given to the heart ache brought on by a life without him. He'd prepared himself to win and if it meant sneaking through an open window to regain her good graces, he'd do it.

She remained steady, balancing on her thin legs and ready to run emotionally, physically, or whatever it would take to distance herself. She missed him, but then she didn't... It was a pattern. She put her hand on her chest. Thomas reached for her and held her tightly. He knew what he was doing, controlling, building himself up larger than life and forcing her to feel meek and in need of protection and to finally acknowledge that she was incomplete without him. He'd performed his act too many times, and even though it was effective, it had grown old. Her voice was gentle and quiet, "What do you want?" She saw the evidence of a walking cast inside the leg of his slacks, but knew enough not to mention his failings. It caused her to soften her heart and even want to hold him, but that would've been a mistake.

"I want one of everything." He stretched himself, expanding his size by sheer will. "You won't want for anything."

"Why are you here?"

The two of them stood on the same piece of earth, but in different worlds. He rode in on his high horse and she fended off the intrusion. He saw the crumbling of his game and turned to submission, forced tears and conjecture. "I miss you. It's been so long." He blinked tears into his eyes.

"It hasn't been long enough." She recognized his tricks, yet love remained. Why couldn't he look horrible, with some disgusting malady? Why would they always share an inescapable return to what they once shared? It was the circle that kept them both spinning. When they were apart, she remembered the good. As he stood in front of her, she remembered the bad. He recalled what ever was on his agenda for the hour.

"I love you, Be Be. I've always loved you."

"No." She shook her head. "Don't call me that..."

"You don't mean it." He touched her hair, her face... She backed away... "Be Be..."

"Don't..."

"Come-on, look at me. I'm Tomahawk."

"No."

"Marry me."

"It's too late."

"Be Be..."

She walked to the house. He followed... "I'll make you the happiest woman in the world."

She spoke without turning... "You can do that by leaving."

He raced her to the house, walking faster and despite the limp, he was making headway. She amped her speed and he walked faster, raising his voice. "You're not going to win this."

Sandy met her at the door, beaming behind the screen. "When is Paully coming, Mom?" Her heart sank. Thomas was within range. She wished she could put Sandy's words back into his mouth. Just turn and run, child. Go back into the house and we'll pretend like you were never here.

Thomas stared at him. "Let's go. Time to go home." He snapped his fingers.

Sandy ran to his room, got up on his bed and pulled the covers over his head. Lily joined him and sat beside him. "Are you afraid?"

He spoke from beneath the covers, his voice muffled, "I'm afraid."

"Don't be afraid. The trick is to adapt. Maybe you can get more colorful blossoms, larger leaves, or a tacky adhesive to cling to Rebecca like a vine. That's how flowers do it."

"I'm not a flower."

Rebecca and Thomas were inches apart watching the scenario and catching their breaths. She folded her arms and moved an appropriate distance before she spoke to Thomas.. "Give him a minute, then I'll go in and talk to him." She moved saliva around in her mouth, wanted to spit, but swallowed. "Don't take him, please. He's not ready. He has dreams that he needs to see happen."

"He's a kid. He doesn't know what he wants."

"Listen to what I'm saying." She pushed her hair from her face. "He wants to go to Mount Rainier. I told him I'd take him."

"No."

"It's all he talks about. Don't make me a kidnapper."

He looked into her eyes. "Will you marry me?" He pushed his hands into his pockets.

"I can't..."

"Then no."

"Wait, there's more." She struggled to find the words... "He loves flowers. He reads about them and dreams about them. He wants to go to the mountain to see a wildflower

212

that's become very special to him. Can't you let him do that before he goes back home?"

"He doesn't need to be on a mountain."

"Your dad loved Mount Rainier."

'My dad's dead."

"Do you know how he died?"

His face took on a bewildered expression. He had no idea what she was going for... "He died in his sleep. What's your point?"

She took a deep breath. "He died on Mount Rainier."

"That's a lie."

"He was making his fourth ascent." She felt her heart in her stomach. "On his descent he fell in a crevasse. It was covered in snow. He didn't see it... Didn't know it was there."

"How low can you go? ... Bringing up my dead father."

"No, I don't want to hurt you, but your son has that love for the mountain. It's in his blood. He doesn't even know it yet, but he loves that mountain as much as his grandfather did. He doesn't want to climb it. He wants to see the flowers, the meadows. Please, don't deny him what's his."

"How low can you go, really?'

"It's true."

"How would you know? Why didn't you say anything before?"

"My mom and your mom were best friends. You know that. That's how I know. My mom told me. I didn't tell you because I was a child. I was four years old when your dad died, same as you. I don't think I even knew then. If I did, I wouldn't have understood it anyway and who talks about that kind of stuff at that age?"

"How can I trust you?"

"You, trust me?"

"Don't make it about you. I'm taking my son."

"You'd make up any excuse to take him. It's not because you care. It's because you can't care and you don't want anyone to know that, but we do. We all do."

"Nobody knows anything except what I tell them."

He did take Sandy. He carried him, legs kicking and arms flying, screaming and crying, "You're a pin dot. Your brain is a pin dot." ... But he took him. He put him in the car and made his exit, his tires spinning on the gravel, shaking up clouds of dust, before the car shimmied left and right, regaining balance and making the departure. The engine roar matched the roar in the pit of his stomach. It was win, or be damned, his hostile departure a war dance he'd brought and elevated to present himself in the highest light and he believed he was the highest light. Life on earth lived and breathed for him. If he wasn't near, why would they need to do either?

As Thomas' car raced down the road from Rebecca's home, Paully's truck turned into the driveway. Thomas saw him coming and waited, looking out his windshield and planning his ambush. He stopped alongside Paully's truck and rolled down his window, knowing he had nothing to say, but it wasn't about words, or witty conversation. It was an act of desperation and an illusion of control. "Hey." He despised that blonde lock of hair. If he'd had a machete, he would've whipped it from his side with the gift of surprise and given Paully a trim.

Paully brushed his hair back with his hand unaware that his head was on Thomas' imaginary chopping block, not that it mattered... The sun was at his back and he could see Thomas clearly. "How are you?"

For Thomas, it was a moment to size up the competition,

to find a way to make that initial cut and watch him suffer. "Can't complain. Best day so far."

Pauly rested his arm over the rolled down window. He'd known Thomas forever, kids in the school yard, hunting for worms, eating ice cream by a frozen pond and pulling out their own teeth for a quarter. "Good for you. What's up?"

Thomas heard himself talking, conjuring and delivering with awkward body movements and telling signs of fabrication. "Be Be and I are back on. We're getting hitched." Hitched, it wasn't one of his words, but a word used to distance himself from the lie.

Pauly over-looked Thomas' deceptive body language, laughing when expected and smiling at the correct times though his stomach felt sour and his cheek bones ached. Worse than that, his emotions rode the surface spilling out in a red blush and warming his face, the face of a rosy cheeked child in a man to man competition. The time for a facade was past its prime and he didn't pretend not to care. He reached for the pink peonies tied in a single green ribbon on the seat of his truck handing them to Thomas. "Give these to your mom."

Thomas flicked a twenty dollar bill back at him. "And this for your trouble."

Pauly eyed him with suspicion. "No trouble here." He handed it back. "Give it to your mom."

Thomas rolled his eyes and rubbed his chin. "She doesn't need it. I keep her purse lined. I just bought her a new car." He leaned his head back just a little too far and laughed just a little too loud.

"You bought her one ten months ago." Pauly's mind was at the other end of the driveway where Rebecca was sweet and funny, waiting on him to arrive.

"Yeah," he snickered. "It needed vacuuming." He slipped the bill into Paully's open window where it dropped to the floor. "Have a great day." The little chat was a few minutes meant to put everything and everyone in their place, ending on Thomas' fat dime. It was all he needed to gloat his way down the street. No one walks out on Thomas. Winning was everything.

Paully turned his truck around and followed Thomas to the cross street. Thomas grabbed his sunglasses and put them on, content on his powers of manipulation. He made a fast left toward his mother's house while Paully turned right toward the hospital. In both vehicles, peonies lingered in the air.

Rebecca watched Thomas leave with Sandy in the back seat. She'd given him the child's seat, but he'd thrown it out the door, hitting the gravel and landing upside down like a turtle in its shell. She walked into her empty home where Sandy had become part of the woodwork and a circle of light, she couldn't replace. It would be a mistake to leave her thoughts there though Sandy wasn't her child and she had no rights in his regard. She had no say in anything in his life, but she loved him. She would call him later, after Thomas calmed himself.

She moved about the kitchen putting a quick lunch together for herself and Paully, who would arrive in minutes. She considered canceling the hike, but needed the time on the trail to contrast the stress. Sandy could join them another time.

She dipped a spoon into a bowl and raised it to her lips, an herbal Infused raspberry syrup sweet upon her tongue. It was Sandy's favorite. She seared tofu burgers, plopped them on aioli frosted sour dough buns and piled on crumbled blue cheese, arugula, pouring raspberry syrup over the top and wrapping them in colorful paper and tied bows. She set them into her backpack, added two bottles of water, an orange juice, zipped the pack and set it by the door.

She checked her watch and felt a hollowness in her chest. He wasn't coming. She looked out the window and sat at the table thinking of the things that could've gone wrong. Paully was always on time. What happened? Was he sick, injured...? He would've phoned. Could he have changed his mind? She slumped in her chair, her head hanging as though her muscles had given up as well... She remembered the lasagna and turned off the oven, moved the food from her pack to the refrigerator, took apart the table settings and turned out the light.

Chapter 11

Sandy remained quiet in the back of Thomas' car. He held Lily and soothed himself in the softness of her voice and comfort of her tone. When they reached the house, Thomas opened the car door as though opening the gates of hell. His anger was caught between his shoulder blades and backed-up in his gut, tying his intestines into knots and bloating his abdomen. He could feel his digestion system close-down like a bank on Sunday. Ire flowed through his veins and showed on his face. Sandy saw no choice, but to get out of the car and march toward the house, his dad pulling up the rear to cue to his every move. He walked the sidewalk, not bothering to count cement squares. He didn't count steps to the porch, or painted floor boards before the threshold. Once inside, he made hasty strides to his room, entering without comment and closing the door. It would've been a good day to have a lock.

CherylAnne heard the commotion, meaning to run to them in a welcoming embrace, but there were no open arms reaching for her. Thomas said nothing and Sandy stomped toward his room, his heart broken. He had no sense of self suffering because he didn't recognize his suffering. To him, it was written into the scene. He would ride it out, until he couldn't... She wrapped herself in her apron, arms flying about then disappeared into her kitchen and going into her default. Always, at first inclination of an uprising, she went into her act. She put graham crackers on a baking sheet, topped them with chunks of dark chocolate, a marshmallow and placed the sheet in the oven, oblivious to the circus clowns performing in her house that day. Whatever the two of them had going would be dismissed by her baking, and she let it flow. The heavy smell of macaroni and cheese hung in the air, her idea of balance in the house. She licked chocolate from her hand. "I have something to make you happy." She pointed toward the oven.

He could smell the chocolate. "I'm not eight years old." Clown one was moving in on her, juggling frenetic irons in the fire, but unable to make out the faces in the crowd. Friend, or foe, he didn't know... "Damn it Mom, you can't cook out the crap heap called life."

"I can try." She jumped, acting as though she was startled by his words, or ambushed by truth, but in all honesty, she couldn't make sense of the idea that food wasn't everything. She placed her hand on her troubled face. "Oh my, profanity in my home." She put her hands over her ears. "God is listening."

"Damn isn't profanity." He followed her with his eyes, thinking of her as an archaic chunk of wood, not a thinking, progressive member of society. He ran his eyes over her thick frame and bungled hair, swept into no specific style. He caught the bulge of her abdomen and chunkiness of her arms, his eyes traveling down to her swollen fingers. "What's that?"

She gushed, her emotions a bowl of creamy pudding. "It's a ring."

"Where did you get it?" He snarled, but kept it cleaner

than he would've, if she hadn't been vulnerable in her sack like dress. "Gum machine?"

She paused with a self conscious sheen, spotted his frustration and came up on her toes, bopping like a teen, face aglow and bringing her heels together as though there really was no place like home. "I'm getting married."

"What? Stop it." He looked every bit the tyrant and his over shined shoes and sharp jacket only made him look less genuine. "Those aren't words I want to hear."

"I'm happy."

"Oh, you're happy…" That's the last thing he wanted, for her to be happy. Happiness was for him. Everyone else was expected to take a number and take a seat. "My life is falling apart and you're happy. Where's my happiness? When am I gonna find some of that sugar?"

She shrugged, offering a smile that promised nothing and showed up more like pity. She scanned his features and made an artificial search for the answers. "I can't assure you happiness, but I can guarantee you a long walk searching for it, if you don't fix yourself first." She glowed like a candle in the dark, radiating love and happiness, the kind of thing everyone can see a mile away and the same thing that often sends them running in the opposite direction, but she wasn't willing to step from her safe spot. She'd operated in the same fashion for years, waited too long and since she'd found what she didn't know she wanted, she wasn't going back. He was an adult. He could fend for himself. All the logic in the universe piled upon itself and packed into a giant box, wrapped in pretty paper, tied in a glorious ribbon and presented to her would not convince her to open those divine gates in an effort to squeeze in an ailing other. It was over and in the past. To talk with her, meant speaking with

Jaimie. When he wasn't there, he was, they'd become one. She smiled with that old annoying love light shinning in her eyes. "I'm happy. Is that a crime?"

It wasn't that he didn't want her to be happy. No, that's exactly what it was, so yes, in his mind, it was a crime. He was in purgatory and there was no way he was hanging there alone. "I want you the way you were, unhappy like everyone else." He knew as well as anyone, that sharing space with a bouncing happy soul, was a recipe for homicide and although he wasn't a killer, at that instant she was someone he didn't want returning his stare.

She pulled open the drapes, bringing a rush of sunlight and illuminating old worn furniture. He covered his eyes. "I've tried to do the right…"

She interrupted him, just when he'd finally come up with something interesting.

"You haven't tried…"

"You don't know." He pushed his hands into his pockets. "I asked Rebecca to marry me. She said, no. Can you believe it?"

She ran her hand through her hair, letting her hand rest on the top of her head. "Can I believe it?" She made sounds of discontent. "Yes, I can believe it. What I wouldn't believe is if she said yes."

He looked at her, looked away and looked back. "Cruel."

"No, cruel is marrying another woman when you were engaged to Rebecca."

The last thing he wanted to hear was the truth about himself without a filter and shadowed by his thoughtlessness. His shoulders slumped. He had no trouble donning a forlorn demeanor and absentmindedly shuffling his feet. If he was authentic in his presentation, it might've been passable as something a little more than pathetic, but she wasn't buying what he had to sell. "I was…"

"You were what?"

"I was going to make it right." He moistened his lips and nodded as if agreeing with himself. "I made a mistake."

"I'll say…"

"It's so easy for you to sit back and watch my life crumble."

She swallowed hard. "No, honey, it isn't… It's heartbreaking, but you made your own choice. You can't decide the consequences. You can't predict what people will do, or how badly you've bruised them."

"If she loved me…"

"If you loved her…"

"I do…"

"You don't…" She ran a dusting-cloth over the hard wood and places she could reach. "I'll have Cara get those areas when she's here. I don't know what I'd do without her." To CherylAnne, housework had always been grounding. It made life simple and manageable, but with Jaimie, housework became something of a chore because she'd rather have spent time with him than the vacuum cleaner. "All that is water under the bridge. Rebecca loves Paully. Everyone knows that." She paused, leaving the cloth idle. "Well, everyone but her."

"He's not good enough for her."

"He's a doctor."

"He's not a doctor. He's a physician assistant."

"Same thing."

"Not in the eyes of the law."

"Well, Rebecca's a doctor."

"She's a farmer."

"She has a Ph.D in botany."

"She's a glorified farmer with a piece of paper." He felt the boiling of his blood.

"Accept it."

"Never. What does he have that I don't?"

She moved the cloth along the mantle moving knick-knacks and photographs. "A fresh start, clean slate…?"

"Be Be and I have history. We were lovers. That's a forever connection."

"The connection is forever, but it's the only thing left. She's gone. You broke her heart. It's over."

"I can get her back."

"Go home to your wife."

Wife, the word echoed through the room. It set off something in his head that spun him like a top. He kissed his mother's cheek, grabbed his coat and went for the door. "I did something horrible." He stuttered and moved in circles. "I don't know what the hell I've done and don't know if I can fix it." Then without warning he turned, his face wearing a mangled look of frustration and anger as something horrific just came to mind and he was bent on releasing it. "Wait a minute, you think you're better than me? Let's talk about my dad."

"Not now."

"You lied to me."

"What?'

"You said he died in his sleep."

"He probably went to sleep at some point."

"Don't put lies on top of lies?"

"He fell."

"Where?"

"Mount Rainier."

"I want the truth."

"He fell in a crevasse."

"Is his body in the cemetery, the cemetery you've been dragging me to all these years?"

She became quiet, her voice almost undetectable. "No."

"All those hundreds of trips to the cemetery meant nothing? You pulled me out of school, took me out early from baseball practice to visit a tuft of artificial grass?"

"They couldn't get to him. He'd fallen deeper."

"You made me out to be a fool. Everybody knew. Everyone except me, his own son. I was out there every day praying to an empty tomb, like a Halloween joke."

"I was protecting you."

"You were protecting yourself. Thanks for nothing."

She watched him walk away, saw the limp and was reminded that they'd been down that road before. They'd been down every road. How convenient he'd made a quick recovery, but the limp, she didn't believe that would go away until his false beliefs had gone away, but what did she know? She made the sign of the cross and began to pray, stopped and wondered what she had to pray about. God could take a break. She had this... She wanted to show she could take responsibility and do it kindly and humanely. There'd been a shift. Days ago, she would've hog-tied him, taken his pain and left him with nothing to wrestle. That day, she handed it back to him. She basked in what she'd deliberately dipped her toes within. In one way, or another, she was home. She'd taken a lengthy trip, ending back where she started, enjoying life and living on love, hope and honesty. It had hurdles, but hurdles gave life texture. She tried to protect him. It was true. She still wanted to protect him, but she couldn't even protect herself.

By the time she thought of Sandy, an hour passed... It's

always a challenge to yield to a clock when one's head is in the clouds, and the clouds had her bound like an infant in a swaddling blanket. With her son running away from her, she rode directly into her default, food. Of course, she did.... Candied ham, french fries, pumpkin pie, those were the things that would break her fall, the things that mattered and made sense. It was the way she was conditioned to act. Food was more than nutrition. It was peace, love, relaxation, kindness, hope, gratitude and oh, so soothing... She set a plate on the counter and piled it with kindness, taking it with her to Sandy's room. She rapped a happy tap and asked to enter. He didn't reply. Of course he'd fallen to sleep. She'd figured as much, tiptoeing inside, ready to remove his shoes, bundle him and put him beneath blankets, but he wasn't there. The rocking chair was vacant and cold without his touch The room fell into a guilty sleep with a detectable change of pressure and an eerie, gloomy, just before it rains embodiment, without his bright spirit. She could feel the emptiness and began to shiver. Goosebumps were a layer she hadn't expected and her head filled with everything that made little sense, with the ray of light from the window accentuating the dismal thoughts running through her mind. He was gone.

She couldn't bear another minute, but checked his closet and under his bed. He liked hide and seek. She examined the areas, encouraged by the plastic smile on her face, but it wasn't a family weekend. No one was throwing horse shoes, or hitting a croquet ball through a hoop. Common sense would've had her searching the yard through briars and over-grown foliage, the places everyone knew were the best spots to take cover, but she wasn't there yet, instead she rushed to his bedroom window, looked out, and saw nothing. She called his name, opening closets and cupboards, making it an honest hunt by letting him run through her mind tracing back through her hours spent with him and bringing to mind his favorite places. He enjoyed crawling inside cabinets and folding himself into small spaces where he could sit confined for hours. She opened every door, curtain and drawer until it became a relentless flurry of doors opening and closing like a flapper door on a fan. It would take too long to sit and cry, which meant she'd have to pull herself together and run out the front door, moving swiftly around the yard and calling his name. She did that, first in a calm outward posturing, more of denial than of choice, and moving into an all-out frantic begging for his appearance. Her throat was sore and tears made their way into her mouth. She fought the urge to lie down and die, simply to wish herself dead, but she was aware that death by desire was much harder than one would suppose.

Chapter 12

Thomas had carried Sandy to his car, leaving Rebecca shellshocked in the driveway. At CherylAnne's house, Sandy could hear his dad and Grandma in the kitchen though it meant little to him. He wanted nothing to do with either one of them, thinking his grandma had everything to do with his father swooping him up and dragging him away from Rebecca. Resentful and forlorn, he paced in his room, biting his finger and touching stacks of books as he moved by them. Lily rode on his right shoulder, her delicate white petals brushing his ear. She waited for him to speak and when he didn't, she encouraged him. "It's difficult for you being taken from Rebecca." He covered his ears and Lily bowed her head in grief before garnering the courage to speak again. "Contained plants aren't as strong as those living life in the wild." She beamed, seeing him remove his hands from his ears. "Contained plants, those cultivated by humans, rely on someone to bring water, nutrient rich soil, food, even light." She looked over at his bedroom window. "The light coming from outside the window is a comfort and a necessity, but many potted plants are left in unsuitable conditions." She paused out of politeness, allowing him to process the information. "Plants in nature have to fend for themselves. No one brings them water, food, or sunlight.

They get what they need from the sun and soil and they survive within the well played ecosystem. The better a plant can adapt to their environment, the greater the chance they can grow and make it through the cycles of life." She was quiet, watching the pine tree outside the window. "Plants with good strong roots are more able to avoid being turned upside down by fierce winds. Plants with long extensive root systems have an easier time fetching water and nutrients. Plants with tangled massive, trunk like roots can strangle out competing plants for space to thrive." She smiled at him. "You're a contained plant." She looked around the room. "This block you live in is your container, but you're lucky because you can get out of your container. You can be free."

He placed his hands over his face and his breathing slowed. He was silent though a dynamic energy flowed from inside him. He jumped up, went to his closet and got his coat. He touched Lily's stem. "My backpack and hiking boots are at Mom's and my house."

Lily met his words with a look of confusion. "Are you seeding?"

"Yes." He threw on his jacket, looked around and took two notebooks and three books from his desk. "I'm going home." It wasn't enough to merely declare it. He had to get his feet moving and be on his way without getting caught. He lifted Lily to his shoulder and opened his bedroom door, peering from the slight opening. He heard his father and grandma in the kitchen and made his quick exit. Once out the front door, he crossed the street and climbed the embankment to the trail. "I know it's this way." He walked north, aware he was on Companion Trail, but recognizing he'd never been south of Rebecca's house. "My ten essentials are at Mom's and my house."

Lily listened intently adding her own variety of wisdom. "Adaptation is vital. A plant must do exactly what is necessary to prolong its life. Desert plants learn to store water inside their leaves and stems and rainforest plants sometimes piggyback to survive. Plants in pastures put their roots far down in the earth so the hungry animals can't take their lives. On mountains plants stay small and close to the ground to stay warm. What are you going to do to adapt?" You don't have ten essentials, but you have a two strong stems to move you really fast. Let's hurry."

He walked slowly at first then quickened his pace. Lily remained on his shoulder, taking in the scenery and sensing his mood. "It's not too far."

"I know not all that may be coming, but be what it will, I'll go to it laughing." He scratched his head and tugged at his collar. "Herman Melville wrote that." He gave his greatest rendition of exaggerated laughter. "Moby Dick."

Lily held onto his shirt, thinking she would fly off any moment. "Is Moby Dick a flower?

"You don't know about whales, but you might if you were a sea weed." He walked with eyes darting about the sides of the trail, identifying plants and counting clouds above his head. "I spy a black bear." He watched the large bear from his spot on the trail, calling out to the large mammal. "Don't look me in the eyes. I might take that as a challenge to dominate me." He walked on down the trail, looking over at the bear now and then and continuing his one sided conversation. "Don't surprise me. I might growl like this." He set his books on the ground and held his hands up like claws, growling loudly. "Don't feed me. I might come to your house and eat all your food." He continued his stroll until the bear was out of sight, finding he missed the company and wanted the bear to return, but his legs had given what they could and he let them have their way. He dropped to the dirt and sat in the center of the path, not interested in surveying his surroundings, or getting a reading on the weather. He merely sat where he was planted and read one of his books while Lily, watched him from her spot on his shoulder. He read a few pages in one book then a few in the other, before looking both directions and stretching out on his back. "That cloud is a saffron plant." He didn't point it out, only expected Lily to find it on her own. "The big cloud is the boss of the other one." He felt an insect on his arm, made a rapid scan and found a lady bug, starring it down and declaring, "You were here first." He got up shook out his legs and strolled down the trail, until discovering ripened black berries along the way.

Lily was content riding on his shoulder and listening to his musings. "Should we hurry to get to Rebecca's before dark?" It was more a plea than a question. She had her concerns about his abilities on the trail and was encouraging him to move along without as many rest stops. "I only give off oxygen in sunlight. At night I must prepare my dinner with all the nutrients I've taken in while sunlight is abundant."

"Yup, it's photosynthesis. You have enough time." He pulled berries from the branches. "... It was the season of light. It was the season of darkness." He ate the six berries staining his fingers. "Charles Dickens wrote that." He wiped his hands on his shorts. "A Tale of Two Cities."

She acknowledged the fact she was unable to push him down the trail any faster than his legs wanted to travel and with that she relinquished any hope of a success in that area. "A sip of rainwater would be nice."

"Where waters do agree, it is quite wonderful the relief

they give." He stood still for a moment scanning the area for his bear companion. "Jane Austen wrote that." He snapped back to life and walked until his legs were tired, once again taking a break by sitting in the center of the trail, though on that particular pause, a low hum came in seemingly ready to bring him a promise of deep relaxation and a rest from his constant stimulation. He opened both of his books and read both, a line here and a line there with the understanding that no book was complete without competition. One assisted the other, leading with thoughts conveyed by one author, while the other debated those same thoughts with ideas of his own. He enjoyed finding meaning in the blending of sentences from both writings, desiring smoothness and compliance uplifted from chaos. The funny little buzzing sound had him waving his arms about in a casual manner, pushing away the annoyance. His world turned silent except for the steady hum adding texture to his hours, and a peacefulness he thought might last as long as he thought it necessary, but chaos was about to address him with thoughts of its own. The low humming rolled into physical form in the shape of a curious group of bees, intent on focusing their attention on the delicate pleasure of his soft supple skin. He jumped with the initial piercing sting and again on the second and third, internalizing the pain, keeping his body still and drifting down onto the path, his face in the dirt. Swelling began with a throbbing heart beat type of thunder calling him to consideration, but he preferred to remain where he'd positioned himself. His face and hands were thick with a redness and puffy clumsiness that did him no favors. He closed his eyes and let sleep take him, the path of least resistance.

Lily's mouth fell to an open state she couldn't control.

She stared and discounted the harm a bee might be capable of putting forth. She knew them as useful for purposes in her life where they were needed. "I think they thought of you as a flower." She remained on his shoulder. "That can't be wrong."

Chapter 13

On the drive to the hospital, Paully thought of Rebecca. She was always on his mind, but with things the way they were, his thoughts weren't as bright as they'd been. He had to sort things and find a way to erase her from his life, or live in sorrow. He tried to leave it behind, be a guy, find someone new, but she was in his heart. Everything went walking through his head as he attempted to hunt for red flags and nuances he'd obviously missed. He could feel her lips on his cheek and her hand in his hand. What went wrong? He thought of their last time together and brought Thomas to mind, the rescue, the competition and the failure. He gave himself a mental punch, knocking himself for even giving Thomas air time inside his head as if that was the straw that dropped the camel. He recalled the smell of her skin, hearing Thomas' voice like a bugle from the bowels of hell and shaking his head in disgust. Thomas was always there intruding, stepping on toes and explaining the truth with lies. Paully thought back through the conversation he had with Rebecca asking her about her feelings for Thomas. "What about you and Thomas?"

"He doesn't understand me, you know. I'm a free spirit. Let me be free and I'll be by your side forever." She turned her head to the heavens like an angel. "Box me in and I'll kick my way out and never return."

He remembered her voice and his desire for more. "You're smart as a whip, Beck."

She did that little thing with her lips as though she was ready to speak, but didn't... She smiled. "Yeah, well..." She put her arm around him. He remembered his surprise and the feeling that warmed him. He felt secure. She laughed. "I need the sun on my face and the wind on my back." She giggled like a child. "I can take the wind in my face at times."

He put his arm around her. "I know you can."

Where was all of that now? What changed? He parked his truck in a space near the ER. He'd asked for the day off, but he knew the shift was short handed and he'd be welcomed and put to work. There was not much chance he'd have time to think of Rebecca, or himself. Patients in an emergency room were going through problems far worse than his own, which was always a push to place things in perspective. Life has its manner of forcing everyone of us to form more truthful viewpoints and to open our eyes and take a look around.. That was the truth, his truth and with it, he met with patients, wrote prescriptions and moved on in his calm, methodic style, treating patients presenting with head colds, ear infections, flu symptoms and other non life threatening conditions until the call came through of a young child minutes out, coming in by ambulance with anaphylaxis as a result of multiple bee stings. It was what emergency rooms were made of, emergencies, and he knew what to do... He found Sandy, thin and pale beneath a light hospital blanket. His team of nurses, lab personnel and others had started an IV, drawn blood and readied an injection. Epinephrine had been given at the scene though one injection wasn't always enough to stop the symptoms. Paully secured the limp blood pressure cuff, loose on Sandy's small arm. "Sandy, can you see me, buddy?"

Sandy's eyes were swollen shut. "I can see." His eyebrows pushed upward and his facial muscles pulled in the opposite direction, but his eyelids stayed as they were. "I swallowed a mountain." His voice was not more than a squeak, but Paully understood.

"Listen, buddy, You've got a room full of help. I promise you, you'll be fine and before you know it, up on Mount Rainier." He held his emotions, observing him for signs his little friend understood and as he watched him a white avalanche lily came in and sat on Sandy's pillow. Paully blinked to focus and make sense of her arrival and she was gone, but in the seconds he saw her he thought he detected a weariness, or deterioration. In the past, when Sandy spoke of her, she was portrayed as embodying great energy and strength. She wasn't projecting those traits in the emergency room though he passed it off as sadness over Sandy's situation. Seeing her at all, whether she was strong, or weak ranked much higher than her condition and eyeing things that weren't real had to be discarded. He focused on Sandy while the space around him became a frenzy of lab coats and authoritative voices. Directions were given, monitors connected and quickly moving gloved hands tore open IV kits and prepared Epinephrine injections. The smell of heparin hung in the air, just as it did that night on the trail with Sandy's father, then moved on with the noise of a busy room, leaving Sandy alone amid a beeping monitor and hum of air conditioning.

Intermittently, a nurse came into his room, checking vitals and asking questions, but as his condition was stabilized, the visit were less frequent. He felt his pillow for his friend. "Lily, where are you?" He felt her beside him and the comfort of her kindness. "You will always stay with me." He slept, one arm around her tiny long stem, dreaming and walking through the Mount Rainier wilderness before waking to hear Paully walking into his room and taking a seat on his bedside. "How are you feeling?"

Sandy laid his head back on his pillow, his arms behind his head. "I'm fine, but I can't play the piano."

"Since you've been here?"

"Yup."

"Could you play it before?"

"Yup."

Paully played along... "Why do you think that is...? He'd been given a heads up from the nurse.

Sandy giggled. "Because there's no piano here."

Paully tickled him. "You got me."

"Yup, Brenda Johnson, RN said that."

"You'll be fine." He patted Sandy's knee. "Maybe you shouldn't look in the mirror just yet. There's still a lot of swelling. It may take a week before it all settles, but you'll be on that mountain." He smiled. "You think about that, nothing else." Paully thought of Rebecca, how she must be worried and heart sick. He wanted to hold her hand, whisper words of sympathy, support and give her his shoulder to rest her sorrow. He wanted to give her news that Sandy would be fine. Things between he and Rebecca had changed too quickly, leaving him no place to prop his feet and find his foundation. He smiled at Sandy and gazed through him for just a second and again noticed the white flower with long white petals sitting on the pillow. Lily's sad eyes, held his then she was gone. He cleared his throat, patted Sandy's head and got back to his rounds, anxious over sighting things that weren't there to see.

CherylAnne arrived at the hospital after the hubbub. She had Rebecca on the phone before she got to Sandy's room. "Better not come up tonight. Thomas and Elizabeth are coming. They'll be here in an hour.

Rebecca wiped away tears. "Okay."

I can tell you when they leave."

"That's alright. They'll probably spend the night. I'd expect that."

"Okay, sweetie. I'll call you in the morning. I'm staying over."

"Is he in a room?"

"No, the ER. He'll go home tomorrow. They'll watch him tonight."

The disconnect caught Rebecca's breathe like a freezing winter breeze. She felt isolated and alone without details and feeling a part of the family she imagined gathered in the hospital waiting room. She wanted to be the one okayed to go back to Sandy's room for a short visit and designated to receive his doctors prognosis. She felt as though she was loitering in her own home, walking around looking for something to do, anything that would take her mind off the one thing that nothing could distract her from pondering. The sky became dark and the black night made its appearance. She picked up a book, but set it in its place. She didn't eat, or go on with her routine. As the hour became late, she couldn't sleep. She rubbed lavender into her temples and frankincense behind her ears, steeped chamomile and catnip, carried her peace lily to her room, chanted, counted, inhaled and exhaled her way to deep breathing, but sleep couldn't find her.

In Puyallup, CherylAnne laid awake on a twin bed wheeled into Sandy's room. Her eyes were wide, staring at a white ceiling while electronic monitors alerted her to the purpose for her visit. It wasn't about her comfort, or her growing annoyance at a beeping box she was ready to roll from the room at a high speed. It was about her grandson and she knew that. She felt guilt and insignificance, but avoided the web of self absorption choosing to focus on flittering thoughts. She wondered how many wishes fit on a penny and how many pennies would fill a wishing well. She thought of Thomas, somewhere in Seattle and Paully, up all night in the ER. Everyone was licking their wounds.

The following morning, Rebecca stood beyond her back porch, her feet bare in the tall grass and her hands lifted upward feeling for rain. She moved rain barrels and brought a quilt in from the line. She poured hot water over tea bags of California poppy and dandelion leaves, putting her feet up and anticipating CherylAnne's call.

CherylAnne stood outside Sandy's hospital room wearing a hard look of concern. She tapped her fingers across the keyboard and had Rebecca on the phone. "Come out. Thomas and Elizabeth didn't show up."

Rebecca ignored her tea while miles away, CherylAnne looked through ER visitors, doctors and nurses as though she could see out their other sides. She waited in the hall numb with anxiety and stone cold with lack of movement and communication. The only things that moved around her were the hands of the clock on the wall. She thought of Thomas and Elizabeth, admonishing them for not making an appearance, but putting more blame on Elizabeth and all the things she hadn't done for her child. She could hear Rebecca's soft voice, but couldn't match it. "Maybe Elizabeth isn't here because she had to get her lips plumped." A technician stared at her from across the hall. She bit her thumb nail and lowered her voice.

Rebecca snickered, "Not nice."

"I'm entitled."

Two hours later, Rebecca pulled her Jeep into a parking spot at the hospital and took a tiny amber bottle of frankincense from her glove compartment dropping it into her purse. She set the shopping bag from the passenger seat onto her lap, peeked inside and item by item removed price tags. She took six red dahlias from her bag gently arranging them and tying them together with a red string around their stems and before she opened her car door, she looked about the lot hoping to see Paully's truck. Her heart beat rapidly, eyes searching and checking as far as she could see. It wasn't there and with that distressing information, she walked toward the hospital entrance alone, very alone.

Not far from the door, she stopped in her tracks and made an instantaneous, yet thorough examination of Paully's truck from several cars away. The parking job was shoddy, crooked, owning more than one space, tires muddy, but he was there. He was inside the building. Her head flooded with emotion, frantic with a rush of thoughts she couldn't weed and no place to hide. Instead of Sandy, she was thinking about her hair, her shoes, lipstick and no sleep. How she must look with red eyes and weariness. She looked down at her shopping bag, centered herself, walked to the hospital and met CherylAnne who was waiting for her in front of the hospital pulling at her dress, trying to stretch the wrinkles from the fabric. She patted her hair, combing it with her fingers. "I didn't bring a brush, or jammies." The two held each other with fear, sadness, guilt and frustration seeping from their pores and engaging them in a sisterhood, a symbiotic psychological dance.

Rebecca carefully set the dahlias in CherylAnne's hands as though the flowers were made of glass and it was some kind of cult like ceremony willing Sandy back from illness.

CherylAnne pressed her nose into the large blossoms, bringing the heavenly scent in through her nostrils. "Oh my, could you be more of a love? You brighten an old woman's heart." She quickly covered her mouth with her hand and giggled, a child's playground display of frivolity. "Oh, if Jaimie could hear me now. I mean, I'm a young woman." She allowed her arm to drop, the flowers tight in her hand.

Rebecca didn't get her meaning and didn't care. She had other things on her mind and CherylAnne knew it. CherylAnne had other things on her mind as well and was taken with Rebecca, her eyes deep into hers, seeing a loyal and open heart and gentle soul. Love poured from her heart filling Rebecca with appreciation she wanted for herself. Once again, she raised the flowers to her nose. "Mmmm, fresh from your garden."

"Of course." Rebecca watched her for a moment. "... And yes, you're not old, so stop saying it." She stared at the diamond on CherylAnne's finger. "What is that?"

"I met someone."

Rebecca wrinkled her nose. "I talked to you a day ago. You met someone and got engaged since then?" She pursed her lips and let her head fall to her side, her hair hanging in her face. "I've heard of fast women."

CherylAnne spun herself around, stopped herself and looked down the hall. "There he is. They're bringing him out in a chair." She walked rapidly toward Sandy, and motioning toward Rebecca. "Come on. I'll tell you about it later."

Rebecca lagged, but followed, cautious of her presence in a family moment where she didn't feel she belonged. She looked over her shoulder for Thomas, or Elizabeth. One of them would be a cringe, but both of them, a nightmare. They were no where in sight which initially gave her relief, then suffering. They should've been there. They should've been the first ones there.

The nurse wheeled the chair close to where CherylAnne and Rebecca stood. They watched Sandy's face change as he recognized his grandma. He sunk in his chair, lowered his chin and raised his eyes, catching both ladies in his sight and squirming in embarrassment. He was not fond of becoming the center of attention.

CherylAnne scrutinized him, going over him with a fine tooth comb. "He's puffy. His face is swollen." She glanced at Rebecca. "They call that edema. It's a medical term." She threw a knowing look at Rebecca. "I know that because Paully is a physician assistant."

Rebecca nodded though shook her head in disbelief after CherylAnne had looked away. She thought of Paully, Thomas and Elizabeth. Her head was clogged and the cranks had slowed. She reached into her shopping bag and handed a small, colorful cylinder to Sandy, thought twice and hugged him. "Maybe I'm doing things out of order." She was speaking to herself. "First the hug then the gift." She knew she was talking too much. She leaned forward, her hands on her thighs. "It's a kaleidoscope."

Sandy sat with his hands in his lap. He stared at her.

"Look through it. Put it up to your eye."

Slowly, he raised the cylinder to his eye. "Flowers inside."

"Spin the end." She moved the end piece with her fingers. "Like this..."

"Can I keep it?'

She nodded.

"Thank you, Mom."

CherylAnne eyed Rebecca, "Mom?'

Rebecca rolled her eyes. She handed an electronic notebook to Sandy. CherylAnne smiled with a suspicious bent. "Santa's bag."

Rebecca did her best to ignore her, focusing on Sandy. "You can type the names of herbs and flowers, you find. You can take pictures too, to remember their faces."

CherylAnne made sounds of discomfort, speaking under her breath. "As if his memory needs a boost." She touched Rebecca's shoulder. "I thought you didn't want him on the Internet. ... All that ionized radiation stuff and all that."

Rebecca sighed, "He wont be on the Internet. He can use this without a hook-up. It's just to help him with his research. He doesn't write well yet, but he can type."

"Uh huh, that's how it starts."

The nurse left them with instructions. They chatted, going over after care and symptoms that could result in a return to the emergency room. CherylAnne took over behind the chair and wheeled Sandy to the car. He nervously patted around the extra space in his chair, checking his shoulders and feeling his arms and legs. "Lily... I forgot her."

CherylAnne ran back for her, putting the brakes on at the hospital doors and walking inside the lobby. She turned, eying Rebecca through the glass. She waited, tapping her foot and counting down seconds for what she believed to be a significant amount of time spent searching for the flower. She gave it a couple minutes more to be sure, then returned, pretending to hand Lily to Sandy, waiting patiently in the sunlight.

He glared, "Where is she?"

"She's here. See...?"

But he didn't see... His eyes narrowed and his face filled with anger "Lily is not here."

CherylAnne shrugged while Rebecca crouched near him. "Tell me where you left her. I'll go back and get her."

He tapped his index finger on top of his head. It was bent at the knuckle, a hook helping him do his best thinking. "She's in my room, where the sun crosses the shade."

Rebecca eyed him with suspicion. "I'll find her." How would she find her? She held her head high assuming a posture of confidence. "I'll find her where the sun crosses the shade." It seemed a losing battle.

CherylAnne yelled the room number. She followed Rebecca with her eyes, expecting her to turn around and to acknowledge her though Rebecca did no such thing. CherylAnne mumbled, making herself feel better. "She didn't hear me. It's always the same." Not being heard was a bitter pill, but easier to get down than being disregarded by a friend and it was true that she herself had failed getting Lily the first time. She didn't expect Rebecca to fare any better.

Rebecca went back into the hospital and entered the room. She walked on hollowed ground, moving in small steps in keeping with her uncertainty and apprehension. Her eyes grazed the surfaces of the room where she treaded with caution, squinting out the bright sunlight coming in through the window.

The cleaning woman leaned over a bucket, ringing out her mop with gloved hands. A ringer was permanently fastened to one side of the wash bucket, but it set unused.

Rebecca shivered at the thought of billions of germs covering the woman's gloves. She stared at her, unwilling to advise her though the woman felt Rebecca's objection and looked up at her, dropping the mop into the bucket, wringing it out once more in the same fashion and carrying on with her duties a sunlight shot a bright ray across the room in the shape of a triangle laid out on the floor, the tip crossing the shade. Of course it did... Rebecca rubbed her eyes and opened and closed them repeatedly while Lily sat inside the triangle, sunlight on her face and her long green stem in the shade.

She bent down and picked-up the flower, her eyes open wide and her body free of movement. The heaviness of the flower, stalled her. It had substance, weight, the obvious bulk setting off an alarm sounded inside her head. She discovered no sense in any of it, the talking flower, the weight, yet for the sake of her own sanity, she would try to move on with her mission as though it was normal, something everyone did on a daily... She was thinking herself through her situation, mentally calling out her steps. "I'm carrying a talking flower." She shook her head, in disbelief. "I'm carrying a flower who talks." In an instant she saw the ludicrous nature of her actions, deciding it best and most certainly polite to introduce herself, before picking up a stranger and carrying her off without words. She swallowed with ceremony and looked at Lily. "My name is Rebecca. Thank you for being here."

The cleaning woman peered up at her, leaned on her mop and wrinkled her brow. "You're welcome, but this is my job. I have to be here." She pushed the mop across the floor, stopped and looked over at Rebecca. "Nice to meet you, Rebecca."

She nodded and hurried through the door, walking as

fast as her flats would carry her without flying off her feet. She hoped not to call attention to herself and had barely squeezed by the emergency room desk before Paully stepped from an opening. He walked with a colleague, perusing a chart in his hands and offering an account of labs, radiology, or what ever was on the inner pages. She hadn't a clue. She couldn't hear him, but she smiled when he smiled at her. He continued on his way, but looked directly into her eyes for a moment that ended too quickly. "Came back for Lily? I thought someone would..."

"You knew?" She was intrigued and curious, wondering how he could see Lily, if he did see her though her chest collapsed into a heap of sadness looking into his eyes. She wanted to run to him, kiss him and hold his hand, though the importance of the flower was not lost on her. Had she lost Paully? She bunched her brows and bit at her lip, moving excessively like a nervous witness on the stand.

He said a few final words to the doctor and excused himself before walking closer to her. "I saw her sitting there."

It was worse seeing him up close and not feeling she could nudge him, or hold his hand. He wasn't hers. She looked around for a spot to set the flower and then back at him. It was silly to carrying something no one could see. Her arms were out there in a carrying position as though holding on to something, but nothing was there. "I guess I look weird."

He tapped his fingers on the chart. "You look beautiful, but for someone else."

"You didn't show up for lunch and the hike."

"I thought it best. He lowered his eyes. "I wish you happiness."

She held back tears and watched him walk away.

"Beautiful for someone else?" Her heart raced and her mind fragmented her thoughts and slowed the sequence. She needed to know everything was okay, that he would fly into her driveway in his big red truck and flip the world back onto its feet. Every word he had ever uttered and every action he'd ever taken had free rein in her mind throwing her emotions into a whirlwind of illogical thinking. She needed to wrap him in her arms, but at the same time, head out the door and not look back. She walked to the parking lot, her heart bumping in her chest. CherylAnne's car door was open and Sandy's legs were swung over the side in a constant wiggle. Hives covered his skinny legs and jolted her memory. She wasn't there to repair her relationship with Paully. She cringed, noticing red dots on his neck and swelling in his face and limbs. CherylAnne leaned on the hood of the car reading her Bible. Where could Rebecca look and not find sorrow?

Sandy spotted Rebecca. "You found her." He reached for Lily. "I'm a satisfied boy, not on a mountain."

She threw him a look saying she really didn't need any of that right then, but he didn't read her look and she didn't expect him to... He danced Lily on his knee.

CherylAnne eyed Rebecca with a blooming curiosity. "I don't get it." She closed her Bible. "How did you make it seem like she's real?"

Rebecca open her mouth, but said nothing. She waited a few minutes. "Can you see her?"

"See who?'

"Lily."

"Can you?"

She was careful. Whatever happened inside, wouldn't be introduced into the conversation. "No, no, I can't... I meant like Sandy sees her." Behind the ladies, Sandy fawned over Lily's white petals, smiling and chatting with her. Rebecca turned to listen and kept her eyes on the twosome. She looked at CherylAnne. "I think he needs to visit the mountain."

CherylAnne closed her eyes and her shoulders slumped. "Here we go again. I think if we just let it go, it will go."

"Did anything you wanted as a child just go?" Her body tightened and balls of muscle hardened in her back. "Or did someone make you think it wasn't important?"

"Rebecca, Rebecca."

"What about the Jack-in-the-Box you wanted when you were five?"

CherylAnne laughed. "... Bought it for myself when I was fifty nine."

Rebecca let her head fall to the side. The warmth in her eyes told the story. "You just now made me love you all the more." She took a look at Sandy then back at CherylAnne. "Get him on the mountain." She touched her hand. "Let's not make him wait until he's fifty nine."

Chapter 14

There's no place like home and nature is our home, whether it be lying tummy down head in hands, gazing into an artificial pond, holding sheers and shaping shrubs, lacing up and owning the trails, blazing the wild, or cultivating herbs on a city porch, the outdoors is the best life has to offer.

Mount Ranier, a glaciated peak, at 14,411 feet, holds court in the state of Washington, settled comfortably, in the South Cascade Mountains. The picturesque snow covered volcano can be seen from Canada, to the north, Oregon, to the south, Idaho, to the east and the Olympic peninsula, to the west. The Cascade mountain range extends seven hundred miles, from British Columbia through Washington, Oregon and Northern California. Mount Rainier is the tallest mountain in Washington and the Cascade range. It's placed twenty-one on the world's most prominent peaks and ranked seventh on North America's most isolated peaks. It comes in at seventeen on the United States highest peaks.

Mount Rainier, in its summer splendor is a dazzling display of deep green forests, mind quieting reverence and colorful meadows filled with wildflowers, bees and butterflies, though the soft warm breeze of the lazy days of summer can change in an instant and without warning, to weather that challenges even the most skilled outdoors men and women with blizzards so intense, one's hand can not be found, held inches from one's face. It can just as easily switch back to a pristine summer day gracing those who dare to tame the tempest.

Every inch of rainfall, drop of sunshine, spec of soil, slab of rock, deadly cold and uplifting heat, is home to sixty five mammal species, fourteen amphibian species, fourteen native fish species, over eight hundred and ninety vascular species, and more than two hundred sixty non-vascular plant species and fungi. The mountain is ninety seven percent wilderness, all of it captivating, but for Sandy, it's the abundance of wildflowers, the beautiful darlings of the meadows, that kept him up nights enthusiastically turning the pages of any book he could find on the subject.

The outstanding wildflowers with their flair for enchanting visitors, arrive some where between June through August, depending on the snow melt. Visitors flock to the meadows, taken mind, body and soul by breathtaking displays of color, every visitor enchanted under nature's spell. Sandy, too, was bewitched, caught by the beauty and inspired by an unspoken promise of freedom and adventure, yet he'd only seen the meadows from the pages of his books.

He sat in his room, bare tootsies rosy pink and wiggly, on the ends of two tiny feet, his legs crossed at the ankles, like a grown-up. On this day, he'd flipped the last page he'd pushed under his view point, before dinner was on the table. He pressed his hand against his forehead, as though pushing his brain back into his head, that magnificent computer in his noggin, exploding with mountain trivia and wildflower facts, enough to pop an encyclopedia, at its spine.

He raised his body from his chair, set those little feet on the floor and pitter-pattered to the kitchen, tugging at

Rebecca's shirt sleeve and looking up into her face. His eyes, weary with strain and red with hours spent. Through those sleepy eyes, she became a painful image. He whined and moved aimlessly in a lemon sour dance, his feet projecting irritation and fatigue. "When are we going to Mount Rainier?" He threw himself to the floor. "If I wait another minute, I'll die."

She ran the cool water over the greens, moving as though she didn't notice the shivering tickle across her shoulders and the tingle of stimulated nerves about her forehead. The fruitful month of August had caught itself between them, not knowing the collateral damage it had done by stepping in before Rebecca was ready to make Sandy's dream come true. She would've been quicker to the gate if Grandmother wasn't dragging her feet and fighting her every step of the way, never-the-less numbers on the calendar were flipping daily and still, no decision had been made. She bent down and ran her fingers through his hair, his scalp sticky with sweat. Strands of hair were wet and clinging to his temples. He closed his eyes. "My name is Nobody." He opened his eyes. "Homer said that."

She worked his frail shoulders, palpating, kneading and smoothing out his muscles. He was lean and bony, an aspect she took it on as her own misdeed, feeling guilty and running her tongue over her lips, in her own way, spreading her lack of satisfaction over minutes she didn't own. Whatever had taken place before she'd met him, didn't bear her name, but she'd picked out the problem, which made it hers. His vulnerability weighed on her as well. "It's been a long wait. I'm sorry about that."

He looked at the floor. She was behind him and couldn't see his face, but she could feel his disappointment. It filled the room, hanging like large clumps of fog and cooling the temperature. She inhaled it bringing it inside her lungs and feeling it burn into her core. It haunted, drove her and sabotaged her belief in the things that made her real. "I think we can talk your grandma and your dad into giving permission."

He blinked his eyes as though his eyelids were in a hopeless fight against gravity. He held his body in a standard, submissive posture, yet folded his arms, in a behavior leaning toward rebellion. In any case, he contradicted all of it and rapidly came to life, as if renewed and nothing had taken place. He eased into a domestic mode where his hunger was solo, on his mind. "What will I eat for dinner?" He patted his tummy, climbed up onto a chair and looked out the window. He didn't mention the mountain.

She put finishing touches on the salad, snipping nasturtiums and adding them to the bowl of arugula. Sandy jumped off the chair. "Yup, I'll wait longer, then I'll go by myself." She made no sounds. There was nothing to say.

He raced to the door and peered through the screen. "Paully's here. Paully's here."

Her heart was heavy in her chest. A lump lodged in her throat. "Are you sure?" She leaned over the sink to see out the window.

Paully moved from his truck, as though suspended in time. Locks of blonde hair fell into his eyes in a slow dreamy motion in Rebecca's mind, but it was far less a dream come true to Paully, who found his hair in eyes a bother and would've gotten a cut, but the night shift at the hospital had him sleeping most days when hair salons were alive. On that day, as he walked from his truck to her door, she saw someone bigger than life. When had he progressed from an ordinary man, to perfection? What day? What hour? When had he become a man who had her hurrying to her bathroom, to wipe tears from her eyes? She looked into her mirror and ran to the freezer, taking an ice cube and holding it under her eyes, one then the other and encouraging herself, "He's Paully, just Paully, my friend. There's nothing to see here."

She rummaged her closet for a blouse, something special, pretty, romantic, alluring... She'd never dressed for him, or made herself attractive for him, but that was when he was Paully. Now he was Paully with hearts. She slipped into a silk blouse, she'd been given as a gift long ago, at the time, too fancy, too feminine, but at that moment, it was what she needed. She pulled the tie from her hair, played with her loosened strands, while watching herself in the mirror. From the kitchen, muffled voices rang out in an odd rhythm. He was inside her home. He'd been there hundreds of times, for a good many years, but that day, his presence pushed her to a state of anxiety. She sat on the edge of her bed and allowed tears to fall down her cheeks, wallowed, straightened and walked to the kitchen, telling herself, he's just Paully.

He reached for her hand. "Hey."

She tried nonchalance, but dismissed it. "Hi."

"I've missed you." He looked like he did...

She hid behind a smile. "You probably miss the woods. The city must be exhausting."

He took her hand, "I've missed you."

His words cut, wounded and left her undone. "I've missed you too."

"I haven't been around."

"It's okay."

"It's not." He shook his head. "I want to explain."

"You don't have to..."

He pulled her hands together, in his and kissed them. "Don't let me off easy. I walked away."

"Don't---"

"Just listen." He looked around for Sandy.

"He's in his room."

He melted, losing composure he'd mustered. His stomach churned and his knees weakened. "Oh, my God, may I please just hug you. I've missed you so much." He held her. His eyes closed and stress left him. He let his words drift into her ears. "I heard you and Thomas were back together."

She shook her head, side to side, pulling away from him.

"I couldn't deal with it." He fell silent. "I've never felt such loss."

She watched him. "I'm not back with him."

"I know that."

She rubbed her nose. "Who told you I was...?"

He scratched his chin and rubbed his forehead. "The only thing that matters is it isn't true." He brought her closer. "Let it go."

The second embrace should've ended in a kiss, though Sandy was at her side pulling on her belt loop. "Can we eat?' Children, tiny creatures, building the world to their vision. She felt Sandy as an inconvenience and immediately corrected her focus, miraculously turning off the crush and losing the fantasy eyes. She was mom and mom had her look, her bearing, her movements and manner of conversation. The posture of mom had no place up close to the mystery of romance. She threw together dinner basics, rushing through the steps. The sooner Paully was across from her at the table, the more efficiently her life would fall into order.

Sandy set his fork on his plate and wiped his mouth. "I

want to go to Mount Rainier." A passive anger covered his face.

Paully looked from him to Rebecca. "He hasn't...?"

She bit the side of her finger. "He hasn't yet. It's... You know.... He has parents."

Paully nodded. "Thomas isn't giving an inch...?"

"Well..."

Sandy press his hands over his face. "I'm not the kid that didn't go to Mount Rainier." He put his head on the table.

Paully rubbed Sandy's shoulders, something he'd seen Rebecca do. He knew her heart and was aware that she was feeling the burden. "It's hard, Beck, but make it happen." Why wouldn't she? What was the stall?

Sandy came between them that evening, both emotionally and physically. He talked and talked of the mountain and sat between the two of them, stood between them, keeping words from being said and feelings from being shared, yet intimacy in the air made itself known by the magic that comes from two souls finding one another at just the right moment.

When the evening came to an end, Rebecca walked Paully to the door and glanced around for Sandy. "Do you think Lily is real?"

He laughed, "Do you?"

"I asked you first."

He shook his head. "Everything is real to someone."

"That's your answer?"

He put his hands on her shoulders and slid them down her arms. "This is my answer." He lowered his voice. "Get him on the mountain." He smiled. "Just get him on the mountain. It's where he belongs."

Chapter 15

Morning sunlight from the open window kissed her face, asking her to place her feet on the floor beside her bed and hear the sounds of birds and the gently wind in the trees nature had prepared for her. Getting her out of bed was one thing, but moving out into the day was like carrying on while dragging a little red wagon. The night had been cruel, keeping her mind on alert and disguising itself as a long lost friend going over memories she didn't want to recall. She'd had little sleep, but guided Sandy through his meal, got him into the car and drove to CherylAnne's home, rapped on the door, heard the greeting and stepped inside to a warm hug and the smell of cinnamon and maple sugar. CherylAnne patted Sandy on the head questioning him about the books he'd been reading. He'd had a better nights sleep than Rebecca and of course, was willing to talk about books "Books are always good company if you have the right sort." He held his head high. "Louisa May Alcott wrote that."

CherylAnne grinned and spoke in an animated manner. "You read Little Women?"

He tossed his hands in the air." Who hasn't...?"

"You get in the kitchen and grab yourself a cinnamon roll, fresh from the oven."

"Gluten-free?"

CherylAnne eyed Rebecca. "What's this gluten-free business?"

He wrapped his arms around himself. "Gluten irritates my stomach. I don't need the inflammation."

CherylAnne extolled the virtues of gluten, but he held his hand up to stop her. "I've heard it all. You can't convince me." He put his arms around Rebecca's leg. "Mom and I like to be healthy. We're going to Mount Rainier." He leaned his head against her leg.

CherylAnne eyed Rebecca and Rebecca held her eyes. No words were needed though Rebecca expected them. CherylAnne had misgivings about the mountain and she meant to school Rebecca, but instead she pressed her hand down the front of her dress and blinked a bit more than usual and placed her soft hands on Rebecca's face. "Sweetie, you getting enough sleep?" She pinched her brows into a look of confusion. "Or should I say, Mom, are you getting enough sleep."

Rebecca stared directly into CherylAnne's eyes. "No, not enough."

"Worried about something?"

Rebecca thought of Paully. "No, I'm fine.

"Bad night?"

"Up too late."

CherylAnne played with the ends of Rebecca's hair, tenderly threading them through her fingers and pulling them over Rebecca's shoulder's. "Make yourself at home. Lie on the couch, or my bed. I'll help Sandy get his things together." She started for his room and looked back over her shoulder. "He's here to get his things, isn't he, or is he staying here?"

Rebecca shrugged. "He's getting things." She stepped into the living room looking around as though it was her first visit. She found the small home to be exactly as she remembered it, almost too similar to the days long ago when she shared the couch with Thomas, reading over each other's essays and writing I love you on each other's hands. She felt a sickness in the pit of her stomach, setting her hand there and groaning away the meaning of those remembrances. Her weariness would help her collapse and dissolve the things better left behind her. She found her place on the couch, stretching her legs in comfort.

CherylAnne walked back into the room, slowed her steps and smiled a smile that told a story of her need to be the caregiver, the one with the warm water bottle and bowl of chicken noodle soup. She pulled a blanket from the closet and covered the daughter she wished was hers with the care one might employ handling a priceless painting, or a newborn, crinkled and wrinkled with skin used for the very first time. She leaned to kiss her forehead and exhale her warm breath on Rebecca's face. "Have you heard Elizabeth's pregnant?"

Rebecca opened her eyes. "Does she know who the father is?" Both ladies giggled.

CherylAnne patted the blanket into place. "Catty..." It was meant as a disclaimer and she enjoyed it as much as anyone who knew Elizabeth would...

"I'm aware..." She wanted to know what Thomas thought, but didn't ask...

She stood, straightening her apron, turned, but eyed Rebecca from the corner of her eye, stating what's better left unsaid, "Thomas isn't happy."

"Why would he be...?" Rebecca checked CherylAnne's expression. "Sorry, I didn't mean it." ... But she did mean it, thinking back to when Thomas was hers. Cobwebs cloaked most of the memories, but they were accessible. She inhaled a cheap few minutes, recalling the past, meadow walks, cloudy day swims, mud puddles... All of the memories she vowed to let go... She loved him. She would always love him, but secrets were worthless, if not held... No one needed to know.

CherylAnne turned out the lamp and pulled the drapes to a close. She removed Rebecca's shoes and stayed a moment to look at her, beautiful as she was in CherylAnne's eyes, a gift to her and once a gift to her son. Why did life have to change things, disturbing peace and bringing heartache? She was the daughter who was supposed to be hers. The daughter of her dreams. Why couldn't she have that? What happened to a happy ending?

In his room, Sandy piled books. He looked about the space and meticulously lined some of his books across the floor end to end in a path not unlike the yellow brick road. CherylAnne stood in the doorway, eyebrows furled, her mouth a straight line, tight and rigid. She folded her arms and watched him. He didn't see her, which to her, meant she didn't see him. She decided to walk away, but she stayed invisible in the doorway watching his activity and noticing his movements were short and quick, sufficient to accomplish what needed accomplishing. He had an eye for what he required causing him to painfully calculate, placing books by measurement, numerics, or confidential, careful consideration, but however his book placements were rendered, he was on his belly going over each book with his hand and his eyes in faultless delivery. He stared at each placement long after setting it into is groove and he grieved by mentally adding, or subtracting minuscule amounts of space making sure the final landing spot was fine. There were more adjustments and considerations, but through it, he was satisfied, sitting back on his heels and admiring his work.

in a world where life bumps against us with a hostile scream, a routine of lines, patterns, or repetitious dialogue smoothes the unknown into a palatable delight holding the plot steady to the needs of those spinning out of control at every slight change in schedule. The world is often a maze laced with bewildering expressions, confusing innuendo and haunting eyeballs looking into one's soul. It's those things that can overload a mind leaving one unable to filter and cope. Playing the scenes on replay, rocking in place, pacing and perhaps laying out books in even rows slows the world until patterns can be recognized. Understanding situations of laughter and grief curb a need for isolated hand flapping and various other degrees of compulsion and obsession. Turn down the heat by eliminating the unknown and watch the world bloom in beauty and freedom for each of us. It was as it was though all of it was lost on CherylAnne. She saw the motion, but lacked the ability and desire to get inside the engine and see the reality, the workings and how things work.

She moved on to her kitchen, her strongbox. Sandy, in his zone and Rebecca in her slumber filled an otherwise empty house with a soulful element she couldn't quite explain. It was like the smell of pot roast, or a toy box so full that dolly arms and Tonka trucks hung over the sides. She set about her tasks, shuffling in fuzzy slippers and moving both quickly and at a snails pace, just not at the same time. She couldn't decide if she was in a hurry, or lazing along seeing the sights.

Her large and unsightly ankles carried her, matching big wrists, large hands and oversized ears. They were a fix for a heavy workload a petite woman could not have carried off. She was not conventionally pretty, but she knew her value. She had limbs, not in themselves attractive, but looked upon in physical structure, may have been quite handsome as much as a brick, ideal in shape and set comfortably into the wall of a building. She was the framework, a favorable formation in a master plan. More importantly, she didn't undo herself by misunderstanding her place, nor did she pick herself apart flaw by flaw. She knew who she was, what she was and where she was. On that basis, she was exemplary.

That's not to say at times she couldn't be squirmy and crawling about under feelings of gloom, but when those tidal pools of despair came along, and they did, she recovered rapidly. She often lamented life's eloquent packaging of highs and lows, but found it wasn't those indisputable instances that took one to the mines of depression, it was the act of indulging, the constant following of a poor thread which inevitably expanded the initial pain and created a life of its own. "Nip it in the bud", words she held close, served her. Only now, when she felt bombarded by the insidious plans to get her grandson to Mount Rainier, she stood unable to grapple, or compromise. However, she did note that she was becoming soggy around the edges and fear of losing the battle was displayed on her face. The plausible doom headed for her and tugged at the corners of her mouth, inching them downward and shifting her brows to a meeting place at the center and while she wandered her kitchen musing and second guessing herself, reality came knocking in the form of a pip at the front door which had her hollering, "It's open."

Jaimie sheepishly entered, narrowing his eyes to better focus, in the dimly lit room. CherylAnne put a finger to her mouth, shushing him and throwing her arm out to draw his attention to the sound sleeper on the sofa. He mirrored her, his finger to his lips, nodding and tip toeing as though the patter of his steps would wake the dead. He pointed, "Who...?"

"Rebecca."

His eyes widened. He acknowledged her and recognized the name. "Oh, yes."

She explained, "... Tired, long night."

"I see." He kissed her. "So happy to see you." He checked out the house, glancing around himself. "It's fun to see you in your environment." He dropped his suitcase by the door and his coat over a chair. "So, so happy to be with you." She gushed through similar incites as they peeked in on Sandy and headed for the kitchen.

She spread spicy mustard over homemade bread, her hands moving rhythmically, keeping time to a cadence known only to her. He nodded in appreciation, the scent of dill opening his senses. She squeezed thick garlic mayonnaise and with the precision of an architect, placed homemade pickles, her body gently moving side to side, her words falling from her lips in time with thinly sliced roast falling into excellently executed piles, juices dripping over lettuce laid out like a carpet. Bits of toasted artichoke dotted the final layer. She peppered and salted without a pause in her cheerful chatter and plopped crusted bread on top. She turned and smiled at her audience of one, and set it before him. He was under her spell.

She sat herself down, holding the side of table for support, set her elbows onto the table top and with a good degree of anticipation and excitement and dreamingly watched him take his first bite. It was a day at the carnival, her eyes fixed, careful to catch the moment and the flavors, bitters, sweetness and heat as it hit him like an explosion driving the enjoyment on his face. As she expected, it set his taste buds soaring. It was her finest moment, her piece of heaven. He moaned respectively. "Unbelievable. Mmmm," He licked his lips and closed his eyes. "A little bit of heaven."

It was everything she wanted to hear and she savored the moment allowing his words of praise to play repeatedly inside her head while she poured fresh perked coffee into his cup, being attentive and as the minutes wore on, refreshing it now and then. He rewarded her with the manner in which he judiciously appraised her offerings. He wiped his mouth, dabbing at the corners. "Is he going to Mount Rainier, or are you still putting the kibosh on that one?"

She lowered her eyes. "I don't want to talk about that."

"But you should..." He folded his hands on the table. "You're sitting in the middle of August. He's not going up there in the dead of winter." He raised his eye brows and waited for her reply being fully aware he was stepping on some big toes and at any minute she could rise up and throw him out without a goodbye, but to him, loving another meant integrity must be foremost and certain. He was willing to stand up and be counted.

She took her time. He was right, but that didn't mean she had to agree with him. She wrestled with her feelings wondering how much of herself and her ideals had to go because she'd become deeply passionate about another individual. She loved him, but loving someone didn't mean bending to their every whim. Did it...? Certainly disagreements were permitted and in some cases stubbornness most assuredly would be acceptable. Wasn't it...?

He made a point to be gentle and neutral in his

presentation. "I understand your apprehension, but by George that little boy is not going to die on that mountain leaning down looking at wildflowers." He hit his hand on the table to emphasize his position.

The sound of his hand on the table was mild and drew her attention rather than alarming her. She nodded though inside she had not budged an inch and showed it by avoiding his eyes. "Things happen."

"Things do happen, but not much happens to a child looking at wildflowers." He threw his hands in the air. "Okay, bee sting... I'll give you that, but I guarantee you there are no crevasses in the wildflower meadows." He sighed, his chest raising and dropping. "I don't mean to offend you. I realize your husband died in a tragic accident, but I'm telling you, you can't stop living and most of all you must not stop your grandson from living his own life."

She rested her face in her hands. "Maybe I should think about it."

He shook his head. "Thinking about it will do nothing but dig a deeper hole."

Tears welled in her eyes. "What do I do?"

He held her eyes. "Let him go."

Rebecca awakened to the soft voices filtering in from the kitchen. There was a moment when she wondered where she was, but she recovered quickly, pulled herself together, combed her hair with her fingers and removed sleep from her eyes. She scanned the room. ... Not a mirror on the walls. She walked to the bathroom and splashed water in her face, patted dry and found CherylAnne and Jaimie in the kitchen, deep in conversation. "Good morning, early risers. Am I interrupting...?"

Jaimie raised his head. "How are you doing there, sleeping beauty?"

She smiled, "You're Jaimie."

He stood and offered his hand and his chair. "I am..."

"I knew it," She motioned toward CherylAnne. "Look at her face. She looks like an eight year old with a crush."

CherylAnne rolled her eyes, her round cheeks sporting a crimson blush. She fanned her face with her hand. "There're worse things."

He laughed, "Like what?"

Rebecca laughed, "She could be pregnant."

An explosion of laughter broke the tension. CherylAnne turned to Jaimie. "Elizabeth is pregnant."

He scratched his head and rubbed under his once. "Now, Thomas has someone else to think about." He ran his finger over the side of his mouth. "He can let Sandy go up the mountain."

Traces of sunlight reflected off the toaster and the metal mixing bowl setting on the counter, but the minuscule glow of light wasn't enough to balance the dark quiet that had come over the kitchen. He folded his arms and leaned back in his chair. "Come on, you two, it's suddenly so cold in here, I need a sweater." He crossed his legs and clasped his hands behind his neck. "Let's crack this thing open, discuss it and put the kid on the mountain."

Chapter 16

August brought blistering heat, extra watering and an abundance of bottled water. Flower heads were vivid and large. Trees were competing for a water source. Blue sky was overhead minus clouds and sounds of wildlife was as clear as a wind chime dancing in a breeze. The smell of raw meat sloshed in marinade searing on a grill rode bouts of wind, turning up under the noses of neighbors and children waded in lakes, ponds and rivers.

Rebecca worked long days and spent most evenings soaking in the tub and reading. Sandy did the same. Everyday they hiked a trail in the vicinity. He could load his pack, navigate by compass and build a shelter of leaves, sticks, branches, anything available on the forest floor. He had a 2.6 ounce stove and he knew how to use it. He was ready for the mountain.

When the call rang through, she was settling in for the night. She stepped into her slippers, slipped into her robe and walked to the kitchen, pressing the phone to her ear. CherylAnne's voice was as clear as a bell. "Go ahead, take him up the mountain."

Rebecca's eyes blinked rapidly. There was a sickness forming in the pit of her stomach, a green nauseous mess coming up her esophagus and into her mouth. It was bitter and burned, yet she held in her mouth for an instant, then swallowed... She couldn't say nothing. The words wouldn't come.

"Are you there?

"Is it true?"

"Better hurry before I change my mind."

One day rolled into another. ... Still no mountain. Sandy continued to read about wildflowers. and Rebecca found happiness in having him around... Their relationship became as natural as if he was her biological child. Things were good, as they should've been, They could relax, and they did, then the sky took on a darkness at least in Rebecca's mind, and ironically Thomas pulled his car into the driveway, stopping in front of her home. He primped before getting out of his car, arriving at the door and being asked inside. She hadn't meant to invite him into her house, but It happened fast and chaotic. Perhaps too fast to give her an opportunity to unleash the red flags, though never the less, on that day a dark spot marred the the surface of the sun.

He was there, polished and larger than life, his large hands with manicured nails fiddling with the buttons on his dress jacket. Her heart raced and her brow carried beads of perspiration. HIs smile was impish and wide, his teeth straight and white. He tipped his head in a romantic gesture, eyes politely filled with adoration. It was a show, a circus act and she bought it. She bought it for a second, but what could've been her undoing, was thwarted in four words she whispered without the weight of significance. "What are you doing here?" Her head wanted her to ignore him, her legs begged her to walk away, but something warm inside her heart stayed to listen to his story.

"To see you."

She watched him as he spoke, glancing at his lips. It was dangerous and she knew it. She took a step back and extended her hand. "If you're here to lie, tell me a good story. Amuse me. Don't waste my time."

He scoffed. "I'm not shaking your hand." He moved in before she could resist and he kissed her like he owned her. "Like coming home, and damn it, you're sounding like me. I taught you well."

Unthinking, she wiped off his kiss with the back of her hand.

"What's that? You don't like that anymore, little touch me not?"

"Reflex."

"I can teach you something about reflexes." He looked at her with eyes reflecting superficial love pretending to be real with smiles, entwined hands, and romantic plans laid out on the table, but that was the past. There was none of that, that day.

They walked to the house and she let him inside, but just to the kitchen. It was maybe twenty minutes before Paully clomped up the steps and peered in through the screen door. She noticed him and Thomas followed her eyes. He was close to the door, so unlocked the screen door and put out his hand. It was a man thing. She watched the two, her two men sharply dressed, yet scrappy with testosterone leaking from their pores. The room reeked of competition and silent barbs meant to unhinge and annihilate. It was like boxers in the ring. She couldn't watch. Instead, she turned her attention to her clematis in the corner, pulling and discarding discolored leaves, leaving the boys to chew the fat. Her flower plant had more pizzaz than the two strutting peacocks.

Paully watched her from the corner of his eye, while Thomas watched him, watch her. In turn, Thomas had his eye on her, while Paully scrutinized Thomas' every move. The two chatted about work, weather and the Seattle Mariners though both of them knew the topic of conversation was Rebecca.

Paully pushed his hands deep into his pockets. "So, is Sandy going up the mountain, or hanging around down here like a deadbeat?"

She stopped what she was doing. Thomas glared at her, but spoke to Paully. "Doesn't matter much now. I have a replacement."

Her jaw dropped. Paully cocked his head and wrinkled his forehead. "Replacement."

Thomas lifted his chin, looking down over his own nose. "Beth's pregnant." He had a smirk ready for show as though it had been in the wings in waiting... "Oh, yeah, she's carrying the prize." He rocked back on his heels. "Last one was a dud, but this one..."

She raised her voice. "He's is in his room."

Thomas blew it off. "He can't hear. He's in there filling his head with garbage."

She held her ire and walked toward him, lowering her voice. "He's reading about flowers."

Thomas laughed, a nervous laugh, pompous and pretentious. "Like I said, garbage." He shook his head in disgust. "I wanted an attorney. I got a gardener."

Paully might've thought to laugh in politeness and a show of brotherhood, a man kind of thing, but Rebecca's eyes were boring holes through his head, besides, he loved Sandy. He said nothing.

Thomas looked back and forth between the two of them. "I see I'm alone here. Lighten-up. Come-on..."

She grabbed the broom from the closet and swept the area around the Clematis, stopped, and leaned on the broom handle. "You know, Thomas, it would be good for you to sweep the floor."

He threw his head back and laughed. "You think I should sweep the floor?"

"Not my floor, any floor."

"You want me to sweep a floor in some undetermined location?"

She returned to her sweeping. "I think it would be good for you. It would bring you back to your roots."

"You think my roots are in the janitorial profession?" He rolled his tongue around in his mouth, made sounds of discontent and shook his head with an air of disbelief.

"No." She set the broom in the closet and turned to give him a second chance. "I think you would benefit from a little manual labor."

Whatever she was saying fell on deaf ears. Thomas roared with laughter, a boisterous release ripping through the kitchen. He pointed at Paully encouraging him to join him, but Paully was on an endless journey trying to date Rebecca. He knew it wouldn't be wise.

She spoke in a slow manner, carefully enunciating every word. "It would be good for you to push a broom, chop wood, rake leaves, anything to connect." She watched his face. "It would free your mind and reduce your stress."

"Are you out of your mind?"

"I'm not out of my mind." She caught her breath, took a second to think of what she was saying and to who she was saying it. "You sit in front of a computer screen allowing it to rewire your brain." She gave him a tiny window to reply. "But yeah, I get it. You don't want to sweep the floor. Then go outside and breathe the air, smell the trees and listen to the birds. Go jump in a mud puddle. We used to do that."

"We used to do a lot of things." He winked. "Why can't I do some of those other extra curricular things?"

She rolled her eyes. "Don't make this something it's not. It would be good for you to get up on the mountain. It would clear your head and make you appreciate what you have."

His jaw tightened. "I see where you're going with this. It's all about the kid getting to Mount Rainier." He shook his head. "You're just going in the side door." She folded her arms. His eyes narrowed. "You think you're slick, but I have to tell you. Take him up the mountain, flush him down the toilet. I don't care."

She stood speechless, not daring to move, watching as he walked to the door, nodded at Paully and was gone. She heard the car engine, spits of gravel and the sound of silence. A tinge of embarrassment held her. She didn't look a Paully. How did it look to him, carrying on the way she had, but he recognized the awkwardness before she, and grinned, wrapping his arms around her. "It's all about Mount Rainier."

She smiled. "People keep saying that." She didn't think Thomas meant what he said. She expected him to change his mind. There was no reason to think he would let her take his son up on Mount Rainier without a bigger fight. He had to win and she knew it, at the very least, expected it, but that's what it was... When life is good, every door is unlocked, every face has a smile, noise is music and obstacles are merely texture. Chaos highlights the delightful by comparison., only she didn't need a highlighter. For her, chaos was a step behind and inching up to keep pace.

Chapter 17

Sandy hopped through the front room, zipping in and out the screen door, running his hands along every surface and carrying on an intense dialogue with Lily. He found Rebecca in the yard, removing the heads from sunflower plants and ran his fingers over the harvest of seeds. "Oh yeah, the seeds. At first I thought you were killing them." He moved rapidly, jumping in and out of the rays of sunlight. "Lily is happy." He ran in circles and spinning." Lily is happy. Lily is happy. Lily is happy."

She set the flower tops on a baking sheet and covered them with a net. She touched Sandy's shoulders. "Lily is happy?"

"Yup.' He settled as she manipulated his small muscles.

"Let's save energy for the mountain. You're bouncing around here like a bunny. You'll be tired to go..."

"To the mountain?"

"Yes."

He looked up at her. "I better sit down. Lily is tired."

"I bet she is..."

"When am I going?"

"Soon." Thomas popped into her head in the same way he entered her home, unwelcome. Time alters, shifts and creates irreparable cracks, but eventually everything must go. She placed her reading glasses on her head like a hair band and moved around the house sprucing up here and there and beginning searching for her glasses, an indication she had too much on her mind. A meaningless glance in the mirror as she walked down the hall garnered a giggle and her glasses were in position for a fine mornings reading. It had become the routine.

Sandy set the timer and ran into his room, grabbed a book from his towering stacks, admired his lines of books trailing across his floor and glanced at Lily, before sitting to read. "Did you bring a book?"

Lily stretched out on Sandy's bed, her head on his pillow, her snow white petals fanned out around her. "I'll watch you read."

He propped his feet and leaned back in his chair. "Can you read?'

Lily smiled, a dreamy glow coming from her soul. "No, flowers don't read books. We are sensitive to the world around us. We learn from our environment."

He set his book in his lap. "I like you."

She pushed the anther from her face. "I like you too."

"Will you stay with me forever?"

Lily's green leaves were relaxed at her sides. "We'll say goodbye on the mountain. It's time for me to set seed."

Sandy straightened, "I don't want you to go."

"I'm a flower. There're phases a flower goes through. This is life. I must seed for a new generation."

"I won't see you anymore."

"You'll see me every year in the spring flowers. We're all connected."

"I will be sad."

"You will be happy. You'll see... When you hike the mountain, it will change you. You will be home."

"It's your home."

"It's your home too."

He closed his book. "I hate the mountain. I won't go." He folded his arms.

"You will go. I can't get back to the mountain without you."

He smiled. "Then I won't take you."

"I must seed. If I stay here, I'll die without sending seeds for your future. Every spring new flowers come up from beneath the snow and fill the meadows with bright white petals, just like mine. Without wildflowers, the mountain would be barren. As I told you, the soil would flush away with rain and snow melts. Native animals would lose their food sources and move away. The birds would leave. The trees would die."

"Maybe I'll go..." He looked at her. "Maybe I won't..."

She pushed the back of her head into the pillow and sighed. "You'll go. Mount Rainier holds your destiny."

He grunted, jumped up, stuck out his tongue, raced from his room, ending up at Rebecca's bedroom door, where he barged in before receiving an invitation. "Is destiny permanent? Can I change it? Is it real? Is it fake? Is it a fairytale?"

She lowered her glasses on the bridge of her nose. Her brows lifted... She put her hand up. "Okay, slow down. Let's make sense of this."

He paced with uniform steps and an endless stare. "Destiny can't tell me what to do."

She eyed him. "Not everyone believes in destiny."

He rubbed his ears. "You're talking quietly like an ant." He squinted and frowned.

"An ant?" It was like everything else, let it go... "Maybe

you're not a person who believes in destiny." She waited for him to catch-up.

"I'm a person who doesn't believe in destiny." He dropped his arms and the pacing stopped. He rushed from her room. The timer blared. He ran back into her room. "Stop reading. We have our hike."

She looked up. "Has it been fifteen minutes? Time went so fast."

"The timer went off. The noise said it." Her fifteen minutes to herself was at its end. It was time to head to Mount Rainier. All of the preparation and training, the morning and evening hikes, along with a myriad of daily routines took them into the big day, the day they would climb the mountain. Rebecca carried the ice chest to her Jeep. Sandy carried one item at a time, finally excusing himself and watching her from a section of tree trunk he was using as a stool where he remained silent except when she was near taking gear to the car and going back to the house for more. His legs were swinging and his fingers were tapping. To hear him tell it, he didn't have all day. Each time she passed, it was, "I have a cut." "My leg hurts." "My back hurts."

She stopped, set the coats on a chair and looked down at him. "Are you telling me you don't want to go? Is that what this is all about?"

He sat like a statue, and she studied him, her eyes irritated slits. "Wait here. I have something for you."

She entered the house as Paully pulled into the driveway, getting out and standing near Sandy, ready to greet her as she returned to the yard. She winked at Paully, carried a small box and directed her attention toward Sandy. "I know you like bears." She put the box in his hands. "You'll like this."

274

She glanced at Paully and smiled. He came in closer, put his arm around her and kissed her cheek.

Sandy lifted the vest from the box, dropped it in his lap and kept his eyes on the gravel. "It's not a bear."

"It's a Bear Hug vest. It's like getting a hug from a bear. You wear it under your shirt and you can think of bears all day."

"I'd rather be a bear." He let it crash to the ground.

"Let's try it." She lifted his tee-shirt over his head, wrapped the vest around him and secured the velcro. "We cinch it up for a hug."

Sandy patty his tummy. Paully looked at Rebecca and shrugged. "What's this all about?"

She slipped Sandy's tee-shirt over his head and put her hands on his shoulders, turning him around. "Walk. See how it feels." She leaned toward Paully. "It's a pressure vest. It's snug, gripping him like a hug and giving him a sense of security." She watched Sandy awkwardly walking about the yard. "It helps him to know where he ends and the world begins. It'll keep him focused and settled when things are too much for him."

Paully put his arm around her. "I need a Bear Hug vest." He grinned.

"I'll buy one for you."

He kissed her cheek. "You see, this is what I love about you."

"Because I bought him a vest?"

"No, because you thought to buy him a vest." He sighed and his heart melted into hers. "Beck, you're killing me. You know how much I love you." He was turning into jelly and didn't mind it, but loving someone so much that it hurt was ceasing to be anything like a reward.

"Thank you."

"Thank you? You can't say thank you when someone tells you they love you."

Her smile gave him nothing to go on. "Everything in its time." She called to Sandy, turning her back on Paully and moving apart form him, trying to make sense of things, to define and label them. At the same time she wanted to turn and catch Paully's eyes on her, but she didn't dare. Sandy came running and Rebecca allowed him to fall into her arms though she wanted Paully in her arms. She took that extra look at Paully and smiled. He returned the smile. She hadn't lost him. The puppy was still on his leash, or she was on his. She remembered love and the misery, but let the feelings pass, and followed Sandy around the yard. "Come, come, let's go." Sandy ran into the house to get his books while Paully carried the last fews items to the Jeep. She went over things in her mind. She'd fed the dogs. She'd turned off the oven, but what she hadn't accounted for was the visitor speeding toward her house and the sound of gravel flying in the driveway bringing that guy from her past a few feet from her. She tensed her body, drawing in her arms and ready with a firm expression. Paully looked up. "Cue the villain."

Her smile was faint and fleeting. She knew she would stand her ground in wait for the crunch. Paully whispered, gesturing toward Thomas, who was coming their way in his shiny slacks and jacket. "Dressed for the occasion as usual."

Thomas continued sauntering across the small stretch between them, making it seem like hours. His noticeable limp was nothing up against the perfection of his features, his swagger. He was always worth the wait. He could bring it and he would, casually unbuttoning his suit jacket and making the best of what he had, though he saw the tightness in her body and lack of happiness in her eyes. "What? Where's the funeral?"

She ignored the sarcasm. "Why are you here?"

He stood like royalty, chin too high, smug, and posed. "If I didn't know better I'd think you didn't want me here."

"I don't..."

"What's going on?"

"We're leaving for the mountain."

"Not with my son."

She took in a large amount of air and released it shaking her head. "You said he could go."

"And you believed me?" He walked closer, a gleam in his eyes. "Be Be, you know I didn't say he could go." He made it seductive, intimate, calculating...

"Thomas..."

"Call me Tomahawk."

"Don't do this." She marched into the house, picked up Sandy and carried him to her vehicle, strapping him in his car seat and locking the doors. She walked back up to Thomas. "I'm leaving. Do what you want."

He called after her. "Kidnapping. Don't go there, Be be."

She turned, "You wouldn't dare."

"Try me." He felt the walls come down between them leaving him to think of what his thoughtlessness might pour upon him though his need for control stiffened the muscles in his face and beckoned him to stay true to the fight and honor the cause, however misguided it might be.

She got into her Jeep. Paully hurried over, trying to seem casual. She opened the window. He shook his head as though there wasn't much to say. "I'm sorry, baby."

She put her head on the steering wheel, a place of contentment, miles away from the confusion, but a mere foot, or two from the fire. She had her moment of discomfort, regained composure and looked at him. He appeared different in the unintended ring of anger, separated from the core of the fight, but embroiled just the same. She wished things were normal. "Come to the mountain with us."

"I have to work." It was the wrong answer. "I want to, but really, I have to work." He was stifled by responsibility, unable to run that last mile. He wanted to be there for her.

She nodded. "Okay, I'll tell you about it tomorrow." She had reason to pout, but didn't... "I wish you could be there."

He kissed her forehead. "Be safe." He stared at the empty driveway once her car had become smaller in the distance. Thomas was where she left him in the middle of the gravel area in front of the house. He looked out of place in the forest opening, a plant nursery environment, dogs barking, birds chirping, dust blowing from the recent roar down the driveway and there in the midst, a debonair man in a three piece suit. He was a stranger on a familiar piece of land, a place he'd been to hundreds of times. The irony wasn't lost on Paully. He glanced at Thomas then back again and walked toward him.

Thomas met him halfway. "No one crosses me." The smile on his face appeared superficial and dark giving Paully the impression the pleasantness would be missing from what ever was to follow. He cracked his neck with a sharp turn of his head, adjusting his shoulders and widening his stance. Paully made little movement. He watched and waited. If he had to fight for Rebecca, that might be what he'd do, but it wasn't who he was, or who he wanted to become. The two men stood in silence. The sound of the sprinklers, green house workers and wheel barrows trudging over bumpy ground gave an eerie cast to the stand off. Paully understood nothing physical would take place, but he allowed Thomas time to act as though it would... Thomas needed a war zone. Paully needed to find Rebecca on the mountain.

Thomas lightly chuckled as though it was all in fun, no one hurt, just part of the game. He played it off, taking in his surroundings, the daily goings-on in Rebecca's world. It was a place he craved, but through his actions, had little chance of possessing. Garden hoses were pulled across cement foundations spilling water into containers, squirrels made twists and turns and blue jays kept watch on high branches. Sunflowers had been harvested and blackberries had been picked, all without his blessing and void of his manipulation and control. It unsettled him, causing him to move his thoughts closer and more profoundly into her sunflowers and blackberries which brought memories of Rebecca's toasted seeds and berry pie. He recalled his and her berry stained fingers, so many years ago. They meant to pick berries for pie, but ate the berries as they picked them, feeding each other and staining their tongues. "I reign supreme."

"Always?" Paully was left in the yard with his long time friend and foe, yet alone with his thoughts. He had a front row seat witnessing Thomas surveying the damage, gathering up his defense and his ultimate denial, then leaving everything behind without a hint of remorse. It was unsettling.

Thomas laughed a resentful laugh, matching with a spiteful sneer and tightened his jaw. He slapped Paully's shoulder and walked off toward his car, hurling his final blow without turning back. "I've got this one."

Paully held his disappointment inside, feeling the tension build. He called after him. "Is this really what you want? It's Rebecca. What's wrong with you?"

There was nothing. Thomas got into his car minus as much as a snicker. Paully checked the front door of the house and sat on the front porch with his head in his hands. He had a chance to settle, to go over what had happened and what the hours would bring. Birds hid in brambles and the dogs rested in the shade of their fenced yard. Thomas was on his way to his mother's home while Rebecca headed toward the mountain. Paully thought of everything and nothing, finally mustering the motivation to get behind the wheel and drive to Puyallup.

Chapter 18

Sandy sat in the back, boxed into his car seat. His legs were flying and his hands touched windows, seat cushions, where ever he could reach. "I'm a kid going to Mount Rainier. I'm a boy going to Mount Rainier." He kicked the back of the seat and slowed, turning his head and looking out the window, dreaming of the mountain. "How can I study from below, that which is above?" He sat quietly watching the world go by... "Aristophanes wrote that." He closed his eyes. "The Clouds".

She waited until he came back to his movements and handed him a book tied with a red ribbon. His legs once again found the back of the seat though he kept his hands to himself. He held the book before his eyes and read the title. "Intelligent Plants." He giggled.

The rear-view mirror gave her a view of his face. "Is it funny?'

"Lily laughed."

"I see."

"Human beings know plants are smart, but they choose not to believe it." He scratched his itchy arms and pulled at his sleeves. "Lily Erythronium Montanum said that." He talked about plants and trees, herbs and flowers and moved with animation and enthusiasm. He talked to himself, or chatted with Lily. Rebecca couldn't tell the difference, with him playing both sides of the conversation. He asked and answered questions with a rhythmic hypnotic melody that nearly put her to sleep, but she held to her responsibilities as the driver, and treasured her time with him.

The vehicle moved through Eatonville, Elbe and Ashford and came to a stop behind the line of traffic outside the park gate. He straightened in his seat and stared at designated logs standing tall and strapped to horizontal timber meant to signify the park entrance. He read the white lettering on the wooden sign hanging from the logs. "Mount Rainier National Park." Beyond it were the payment booths where time seemed to stop and a half hour passed slowly like a punishing wait for Santa, without the sugar plums and new bicycles. Finally they arrived at the booths and Sandy spotted the rangers and their hats. He couldn't speak. He was captivated, watching every detail and memorizing buildings, faces and words.

Rebecca handed her card to the ranger and received a map of the park. She drove away from the booth area and handed the map to Sandy. He jumped with excitement, smelled it and tossed it into the front seat. "It smells like yuck. I'll be sick." He looked around the back seat for his mask. "Did you bring it? I have to have it, or I'll die."

She pulled to the side of the road, got out, stuffed the map into a plastic bag and pushed the bag into an empty space in the rear cargo area. She lifted him out of his seat and stood him outside the Jeep, beside her. "Breathe in fresh air."

He grumbled and took measly breaths, keeping a watch on her. "They're bullies to allergies."

She spoke to herself under her breath. "I'm a bully to allergies. Who isn't...?"

"They tried to kill me. Call 911."

'No one tried to kill you. "Let's take off your shoes and rub a little lemon grass on your feet."

He hurried to remove his shoes and to enjoy the smoothness of the oil and its fresh lemon scent moving over the sensitive parts of his feet. "Someone did try to kill me." He stuck out his feet for her to massage.

'You're a kind, intelligent, wonderful boy. I don't think anyone would try to harm you." She massaged the oils into the soles of his feet, kissed his forehead and got him back into his seat, found her place behind the wheel and followed the winding road up the mountain. They passed Longmire and Kautz Creek. They saw the glacier river to the right and waterfalls on the left, but when the first glimpse of the mountain came into view, He missed it. Rebecca consoled him. "It's okay, they'll be other occasions. You'll see it. Can you feel the elevation?"

He recovered quickly, grinning and swinging his legs. "We're going up." He stared out the windows and invited Lily to join him, putting his nose to the window opening and inhaling the icy touch in the air. "I will live in a refrigerator and I will like it."

She wrinkled her nose. "Only if you couldn't smell the condiments and leftovers." She wondered if she'd have to lock her refrigerator. "Refrigerators are unsafe. There's no latch inside to get you out."

"Then I'll live in a flower garden."

She shook her head, but conceded. "It would be better."

Except for the car engine, there was a stillness reaching far into the earth, brushing against living roots and whispering healing and regeneration. He held his hand out the window and leaned his head out, his hair blowing back away from his face. "It smells like raw air, not cooked yet." He brought his hand inside, wiggling, checking his fingers and sticking them in his mouth. "I don't need my mask."

She pointed out highlights. "Look, there's a waterfall and a deer."

"I see it."

She spoke with an urgency. "Over here, this side. Look, look, look, you're missing it." She gave up. "You have to look in the direction I'm pointing. You can't look all over the place."

He turned his head to the left and right. "I see it."

She shook her head in frustration. "It's gone. We passed it. You can't see it now." She glanced about wondering if he'd seen another deer. "I don't see anything here. Do you?"

He sat quietly. "If you see a deer, tell me."

"I will..." She pointed to another waterfall. "See the waterfall? Right there, look..." The car had already gone by it. She flipped her hands in the air. There was nothing she could do... "You didn't see it."

"I think I did..."

"But you didn't... You weren't even looking in the right direction."

"I don't need a mask."

"But maybe you need glasses."

"I don't need a mask. I don't need a mask. I don't need a mask."

"True, you don't need a mask." She thought it through... "Maybe bring it just in case..."

Perfect stands of Douglas fir, western hemlock and western red cedar decorated both sides of the road at higher elevations giving way to roadside Sitka valerian, bistort, arnica, lupine and indian paintbrush. "It's about fifteen minutes to Paradise." She looked over her shoulder, taking in Sandy's full form, his squirming, grimacing and everything else he had to offer. "It's quiet there."

"Yup, and no angry eyebrows." He moved his hand in the air outside the window.

"Who has angry eyebrows?'

"Thomas."

She pushed her hair from her eyes. "I'm sorry you know that."

"Yup."

They came up on Narada Falls where she pulled into a parking spot and turned off the engine. She stretched her neck, turning it from side to side and leaning back on the head rest. "Do you want to get out for a few minutes?" She opened the door and stretched her legs. "It's beautiful here. The waterfall is 188 feet tall and crashes down into a pool, like a pond. Do you want to see it?"

"Is this it?"

"If you mean Paradise, no, not yet."

"Then no." He ran his hand along the car seat. "Lily doesn't want to..."

She got back into the car and continued to Paradise. "When I'm on Mount Rainier, I don't think about anything except the mountain." She focused on her driving. "I don't want you to worry about your dad."

Few minutes passed before he saw the parking lot filled with cars. He was moving in his seat and hardly able to contain his excitement, whispering to Lily, then to Rebecca, "We're here. This is it. Lily said this is it." He was bouncing in his seat. "This is it. I can tell. This is it. Is it, it?" He watched everything from his window as Rebecca sought out a place to park. Visitors walked up the sidewalk, sat on benches, or relaxed at picnic tables. Lines formed at restrooms and the snack bar. People wandered and snapped photographs. Hiking trails surrounding the center were heavy with visitors, hiking with a companion, solo, or in groups. The large Jackson Visitor Center was a storehouse of information provided by rangers and volunteers, the main building amongst the Paradise Inn, climbing center and tall A-frame government structures. It was a friendly face, within the wild. When the car settled into a spot in the lower lot, Rebecca was out first, walking around to Sandy and releasing him from his protective seat.

They took off their shoes, replacing them with hiking boots and put their packs on their backs, ready to head toward the center, the base for heading up the mountain. Sandy walked up the sidewalk with Lily comfortably on his shoulder. He giggled, flapping and rejoicing over the abundance of native flowers bordering the walkway and pointing to each, yelling out the names. Arriving at the center, they went inside, looked around the great building, walked through the upstairs displays and talked to rangers at the front desk, before Rebecca felt ready to head up the mountain.

Once outside, Sandy gestured toward stone steps near the center. "The most luxuriant of all the alpine gardens I ever beheld in all my mountain top wanderings." He paced looking at the words spelled out on the steps. "John Muir said that." He repeated it, flapping his hands like bird wings. "John Muir said it and I read it. John Muir said it and I read it."

She stood behind him, her hands on his shoulders. "Look up. That's why we're here."

His eyes widened and his mouth fell open. He was motionless. The mountain, there it was, the largest thing he'd ever seen. It had emotion, fever, energy, majesty and excellence. It didn't command attention. It didn't have to... It owned the blue sky and white clouds, the blue tint of the glaciers and eerie fast moving fog, often coming in like a moist, textured, dark blanket. It explained life in a way that nothing else could... It was meditation, conversation, beauty and immortality though the paved trails of Paradise brought a human factor. People passed through terrain ascended and descended, feeling pavement beneath their boots. The paved trails gave a false security and vanished farther out the trail giving credence to the fact that the mountain area was indeed the wilderness. Those who dared took their life into their own hands, or left it to fate and will of the gods. The mountain sought no friends, nor enemies. It stood alone. Keeping eyes open and entering the environment aware of the dangers sorted the skilled from the pack.

He looked up at her and she patted his shoulders. "Up there, see... That's the Nisqually glacier." He remained silent. "We came through the Nisqually entrance." She waited for a reply, but it didn't arrive. "Do you want to hike now?" She adjusted his backpack on his shoulders and tightened the strap around his waist. "Are you ready?"

He stared at the snowy mountain. "I want to live here."

She guided him along the path. "I do too, but it's a national Park."

He followed the paved trail, reading every sign. "Myrtle Falls. I want to go there."

"Myrtle Falls, it is. It'll get us toward the meadows." She took his hand. He pulled away. The altitude pressed on his chest. Breathing wasn't as easy as it had been. She watched him. "It's only 5,400 feet, but I feel it."

"I'm as strong as a table. I don't need a mask."

"Do you need your inhaler?"

He ignored her. "I want to live here."

"You'd have to be a bear." She smiled. "Or some other native wildlife."

He didn't look her way. "Could I be a lily?"

She pushed up her sunglasses up on the bridge of her nose. "I don't know..." She shook her head, noticing the tiny wildflowers along the path. "That spots probably taken..."

He watched his feet as he walked, shuffling and showing signs of discontent. She mosied up the trail. It became clear the tides had changed. He set his backpack on the path way and sat, knees pulled to his chest and head set on his knees. Park visitors avoided the obstacle, relieved the child wasn't their own, and continuing on their way enjoying the views and watching for wildlife.

She sat beside him. pulling her knees up and putting her face on her knees. Sandy bopped her on the head. "Wake-up."

She lifted her head. "Not nice." She rubbed the area on her head. "Can we get going?"

"I want to live here."

She lifted her pack onto her back, but left Sandy where he sat. "I can't make that decision. Again, this is a national park."

"Lily lives here."

"She's a flower."

A pair of dusty hiking boots stopped where he sat. Sandy's eyes followed upward, green pants, shirt with badge, green baseball cap, National Park Service insignia, volunteer. She bent down and carefully examined him. He saw the name tag. She got down on one knee and removed her sunglasses. "My name's Patty. I'm a meadow rover. What's your name?" She glanced at Rebecca and smiled.

"I want to live here."

Patty giggled, saw he wasn't joining her and changed her game. "I love Mount Rainier too. I want to live here, but you know what I did?" She had his attention. "I became a volunteer." She lifted her cap from her head and placed it on his. "You look great."

"It's big."

"It is, but you know what? You can be a Junior Ranger." She put her hand over her heart. "Explore, Learn and Protect." She continued, talking with her hands flying. "You get a badge like a real ranger." She motioned toward Rebecca. "Mom can get a Mount Rainier ranger vest for you online."

"Are you a Junior ranger?'

"I'm a meadow rover." She twisted, displaying her right shoulder. "See, it says meadow rover."

He got to his feet and stood near her. "I'm a meadow rover."

She caught Rebecca's eye. "You have to be a little older, but your mother can sign-up and take the training then you'll hike with her. You'll be a family of meadow rovers."

He puffed his chest. "I'm a junior ranger meadow rover. I will not bully flowers." He made his salute, hand stiffened above his right brow. "I live on Mount Rainier."

Patty raised her eyebrows and shrugged. "Whoops, didn't expect it to go that way." She was talking to Rebecca. "Yeah, go online. There's a lot of Mount Rainier stuff. There's a gift shop upstairs in the Center too." They said their goodbyes.

Rebecca and Sandy started up the trail. They moved

faster with Sandy's new enthusiasm dragging him up like a cable. Rebecca drew his attention to marmots and orange butterflies. "We can get you a junior ranger workbook at the center." Soon their pace slowed with the elevation. "We'll come up again and you can find all the plants and animals then turn it in and take the oath."

He tucked his chin into his chest. He was shy, preparing for his moment. He closed his eyes and raised his chin toward the sky. "I will always protect the flowers. That is my oath." He raised his right fist, rapidly deflated then stepped back onto the trail and in a few short steps onto the foot bridge over Myrtle Falls. He stomped back and forth pounding his feet. "I'm thunder." He scrutinized his every step, the bend of his shoes as his heel left the surface and the rise of his toes, pressing back onto the wood. "I make clouds cry."

"She took his hand, pulling him close and feeling under his shirt. "You're still wearing your hug?"

"Yup."

"Let's see what else we can do."

"Do you have more ideas?"

"I have a couple."

He wrinkled his brows. "That's not much for your age."

Of course, he was right. A couple of ideas wouldn't be much of a stash, given her days on earth, but there he was chipping away at the world with his literal sensibilities. It would've been nice if he got her, though quite routinely, things are more perfect than we think. It's fine to leave words where they lay and find something else to pursue "Let's rub a little sandalwood and chamomile into your wrists."

"Yup, sandalwood Santalum album, sandalwood Santalum album, sandalwood Santalum album, chamomile

Anthemis nobilis, chamomile Anthemis nobilis, chamomile Anthemis nobilis"

Wildflowers dressed the meadows in striking hues of blue lupines, magenta paint brush, fireweed and mountain asters. Sandy placed his hands on his cheeks. The extraordinary array of beauty reflected in his eyes. "This is where flowers touch the sky." As far as the eye could see were flowers and a never ending field of the best nature could provide. Nisqually Glacier shivered in the background, almost close enough to touch and causing beholders to stop and question their human existence. It was a massive frozen swirl of thick ice, a warning to the faint at heart and a seductive orange carrot to adventurers and those who easily yielded to nature's potent adrenaline drip.

Sandy stared at the meadows. "Genetian, western anemone, broadleaf arnica, subalpine daisy, American bistort, lousewort and pearly everlasting." It was a who's who of the plant world and an invitation to groups of visitors who ignored the posted signs and walked off the path and into the meadows, moving deeper into the field. Sandy pointed them out, his arm wildly waving and his legs in frantic motion. "The murderers."

Rebecca whispered calming words, guiding him from where visitors exited the trail though he wiggled from her grip. "Murderers, flower bullies."

A meadow rover raised her voice, asking visitors to return to the trail. The majority of the meadow invaders snapped their selfies and returned to the trail like scolded children while Sandy clapped his hands in approval lengthening his stature with shoulders drawn back and head high and cringing while strays brought up the rear unintentionally crushing flowers under the weight of their shoes. Sandy glared, "Flower bullies." He slipped his hand into the meadow rover's hand.

She looked down at the small hand connected to hers, owing it to her work on the mountain and hearts she was able to touch. She gently released her grip, exchanging the warmth of her flesh for a 'Don't be a meadow stomper' pin, she placed in his hand. "We need you on the team." Rebecca bowed her head in agreement.

The meadow rover crouched engaging him. "The meadows are fragile. Staying on the trails is a must." She understood the excitement in his eyes. "But you know that." She glanced at Rebecca. "He might like MeadoWatch. You can look into that too." She eyed visitors coming down the path and reminding them to stay on the trails and reached into her pack for a MeadoWatch pamphlet and coming with nothing. "I don't have the information with me, but you can find it online." She patted his head. "Protect the wildflowers." She looked at him closely. "You know it takes about fifteen people to walk on the same area and break down wildflowers creating a path that we like to call a social path. A social path is not an official park trail, but once it's there park visitors think its a trail and continue to use it until the flowers die. People like you can save the flowers. You get yourself a meadow rover patch and start saving the flowers, okay?"

"Yup."

She straightened, "Be safe hiking." She moved farther down the path and turned, waving to him. "Thank you for helping me."

He watched her closely, making certain she'd moved on and was no longer taking up space. He raised his fist in the air. "I'm a meadow rover. I rule the world."

Rebecca looked around, but no one was near. "You're taking this seriously."

He lifted his hands over his head. "I'm a meadow rover. I protect wild flowers. I arrest stompers and put them in my jail."

"Alright, meadow rover, let's get up this mountain and save wildflowers."

Rebecca and Sandy got back to the climb, Sandy, seeking out the perfect spot and anticipating a tap on the arm when the patch of field was perfect. Lily rode on his shoulder prepared to join the flowers while he walked head down, his hands in his pockets, making it difficult to keep his balance. Soon, Lily tapped his arm. He stopped, dropped his pack and followed her to the edge of the trail.

Skyline trail was a winding mountain path bordered by a miraculous spray of red, purple, white, blue and yellow wildflowers, enough for the largest centerpiece in the world. The fabulous wildflowers, so late in the season were on their way to their last performance. He scanned the area expecting to see avalanche lilies in the midst, but saw none. He felt a darkness coming over him and he wrapped himself in his arms. "I don't see your family and I don't see your friends."

Lily moved into the meadow, snow white petals dropping as she eased between stems of green and tall western anenomes. "We're early bloomers. We're out with the snow melt as it runs down the mountain." She positioned herself among lupine and mountain aster joining the flowers gently swaying in the breeze. "We arrive early. We leave early." The last petal dropped from her side. "Good bye, Sandy." Her voice was weak. "Protect the flowers."

He squinted, wrinkling his forehead and maddening his

brows. He had no way to gauge emotions pouring into his head and making his stomach churn. He decided to do nothing, but wait until it was over then curl up and die. He watched in horror as the beauty of his friend was vanishing before him. He extended his arms as if to bring her back, but was locked in his place on the trail, confused and saddened.

Lily changed from a white goddess to a plain brown capsule. Her snowy white petals had lost their brilliance easing into mottled, unfussy sepia settled upward creating a capsule much like a brown cocoon forever evolving as he watched through his tears. She became a common soil hue as though one with the earth moving through her changes with grace and necessity in keeping with the rules and time restraints of nature. For Sandy, tIme stopped. The sky became gray and clouds filled with rain water. The capsule enlarged and with magical precision opened its top releasing a heavenly spectacle of seeds floating along air currents as miniature travelers guarding their destination and moving in tranquility. The sensational array glimmered charming the heavens and earth genetically programmed for their mission and when the moment was right, Rebecca rushed to his side wrapping her arms around him, intrigued by the miracle and sorrowful seeing the pain in his eyes. His small body shook with emotion as each tiny seed disappeared into the distance.

He leaned into the security of her embrace. "Can we go?"

She held him closer. "It's okay to cry. It's okay to feel emotions."

He met her head on... "You see these angry eye brows?" A frown changed his face. "She's a stupid flower. I'm glad she's gone. She's a bully to everyone on earth and I hate her."

She held him, tears rolling down his cheeks. He tightened

his fists. "I don't like her, can't you hear me? She's a pin dot." His nose dripped and the sound of his pain echoed across the white capped mountain. She leaned her head on his, her tears dampening his hair. His body quivered and confused him. He distrusted his own flesh and the blood running through his veins. She cried for his suffering and innocence, mourning for all who had found love and let it slip through their heart. There wasn't enough time in a life span to correct all ones errors which was certainly a failure in production, a mess up causing pain to pass through a multitude of lives before calling it a day. She was spent wondering of life, death and the passage of moments that cease in a societal understanding of time, yet if granted permission, stay forever in the heart and mind.

From behind, a strong embrace broke through her sadness nudging at her soul and encircling her and Sandy. She craned her neck and met Paully's eyes. Sandy jumped into his arms pressing his face against his chest. She leaned into Paully's side, but Sandy pushed her away. He kicked her and growled in pain. Paully settled Sandy with a light touch to his legs and a squeeze that softened him, then pulled Rebecca near, kissing her cheek and tasting salt and perspiration.

Sandy raised his head touching Paully's face "Why are you here?"

"That's not nice." He messed up Sandy's hair. "You two are family."

"Did you kill your family?"

No, of course not..."

"Don't you have a family?"

Paully patted Sandy's back side. "Nope, You're it."

"Will you ever have to go away?"

"Well, someday I'll die..."

Rebecca gasped...

Paully caught her eye, "I mean, diet..." He shrugged. It didn't seem that important.

She looked up at him, burdened with life's daunting reality and her perception of such, saddening her eyes. She was a dusty angel with tears running streaks down her cheeks. "I'm glad you're here." She choked through the words, nasal fluids altering her voice and sopping her lips and wiped her mouth with her sleeve.

He tightened his arms around her, lost to the meaning of the moment, the flowers, Lily, seeds... "What, baby? What?"

She spoke through her mangled emotions. "Lily's gone."

He looked at Sandy. Sandy pointed, squeaks coming from inside himself.

Rebecca corrected the direction of his pointing finger. "Over that way." Not that it mattered...

Paully looked into her eyes. "I love you."

She sobbed, "I know..."

He brought his face to hers. "No, I love you." He reloaded his hold on her, got down on one knee and lifted a small velvet covered box from his pocket. "I've loved you all my life. There's no one else I want to spend my life adoring." He hoped she felt the same, or it would be his undoing. "Will you marry me?"

Sandy scooted close to her and tugged on her sleeve. "Say yes, it's your destiny."

She touched his arm. "You don't believe in destiny."

He folded his arms and stepped on her foot. "To everything there is a season, and a time to every purpose under the heaven. I think God said that." He crunched her other foot. "You're a bully to love." She held Paully's eyes, while Sandy squeezed in between them. "Ecclesiastes 3:1, King James Version, Bible."

She couldn't take her eyes from Paully's gaze. Her life ran through her mind. Everything she'd experienced was meant to bring her to the moment she was living, an instant when all fell into place blessing her for keeping to the path and side stepping those times of waning faith. She shook her head in disbelief cleverly caught within passion. "Yes, I will marry you." A new generation of tears dampened her face. The best moment in her life was equally awkward. "Now get up, everyone's looking at us. It's embarrassing." Park visitors applauded and Sandy joined them. A small crowd had formed leaving her mortified and Paully unabashed. He fought back tears. "Prepare to be further embarrassed." He kissed her lips. "I've been waiting a life time."

Together, they began their ascent into their future and their descent toward Jackson Visitor Center. Rebecca secured herself into forever with eternal belief in timelessness hovering over her new intimacy and settled in under the weight of Paully's arm over her shoulders, kicking foibles of uncertainty far from her grasp and looking up at him unable to believe that anything about the day was genuine. It seemed too good to be true. "Do you think Lily is real?"

He chuckled, thinking it would go on forever. "This again?"

"You saw her at the hospital."

He scanned the meadows absorbing the colors and the aromatic scent of wildflowers. "She's a pooka"

She watched the ground under her feet. "Hobgoblin?"

"No, good magic."

"She's a flower."

"I know."

She was attentive to her foot placement and intermittently looking over her shoulder at Sandy. "But you did see her at the hospital?"

"I did..."

"You still think she's a pooka?"

"I do..."

"Okay.

He pulled her close. "Okay?"

"Yeah, that means I can marry you."

"Because I saw something that wasn't there?"

"Because you allowed yourself to see into someone else's world without judgement."

"That makes me marrying material?"

"Yeah."

"Do you know you're weird?"

"Always."

Notes

MeadoWatch - University of Washington - Department of Biology
Box 351800, Seattle, WA <u>98195-1800</u>
<u>mwatch@uw.edu</u>

Meadow Rover -
E-mail: <u>MORA_Meadow_Rovers@nps.gov</u>
Phone: Kevin Bacher, <u>360-569-6567</u>.
55210 238th Ave. E., Ashford, WA, 98304

References

Aristotle, (Greek philosopher, lived from 384 B.C.-322 B.C.)

Louisa May Alcott, *Little Women*, (Roberts Brothers 1868)

Aristophanes, *The Clouds*, (423 BC)

Jane Austen, *Emma*, (1815)

Jane Austen, *Pride and Prejudice*, (T. Egerton, Whitehall, 1813)

Charlotte Bronte, *Jane Eyre,* (Smith, Elder & Co., 1847)

Marcus Tullius Cicero, (Roman poet, lived from 106 B.C. -43 B.C.)

Charles Dickens, *A Christmas Carol,* (Chapman & Hall (CRC Press, 1843)

Charles Dickens, *A Tale of Two Cities*, (Chapman & Hall (CRC Press) 1859)

Charles Dickens, *Great Expectations,* (Chapman & Hall (CRC Press) 1860-1861)

Charles Dickens, *Oliver Twist* (Serial: Bentley's Miscellany, Book: Richard Bentley, 1837-1839)

George Eliot, *Silas Marner* (William Blackwood and Sons, 1861

Homer, *The Odyssey,* (Believed to have been composed bear end of 8th century B.C)

James Joyce, *Ulysses,* (Sylvia Beach, 1922)

King James Version, Bible, (Ecclesiastes 3: 1)

Hugo Kugiya, *Mount Rainier, Three Hikers, Killer Storm,* (Los Angeles Times, 12 June 2008)

Titus Lucretius, *On the Nature of Things,* (First century)

Edward Bulwer *Lytton, Richelieu or the conspiracy,* (Act 1 scene 2, 1839)

Herman Melville, *Moby Dick,* (New York, Harper and Brothers, 1851)

John Muir, *Wanderings, An Ascent of Mount Rainier,* (1888)

John William Polidori, *The Vampyre and Other Tales of the Macabre,* (The New Monthly Magazine, 1819)

Ann Radcliffe, *The Romance of the Forest,* (T Hookham & Carpenter, 1791)

William Shakespeare, *Henry VIII,* (Act IV, scene 2, 1613)

William Shakespeare *Measure For Measure*, act 5 scene 1, *Measure for Measure*, act 5, scene 1, (1603 or 1604)

Harriet Beecher Stowe, *Uncle Tom's Cabin*, (John P. Jewett and Company 1852)

Suetonius, *The Twelve Caesars*, (AD 121)

Mark Twain, *Following the Equator,* (1897)

Mark Twain, *Tom Sawyer*, (American Publishing Company 1876)

Oscar Wilde, *The Critic as Artist*, (1891)

Printed in the United States
By Bookmasters